P9-CQT-196

An Ordinary Woman

ALSO BY DONNA HILL

Rhythms

Anthologies

Della's House of Style

Welcome to Leo's

Sister, Sister

Going to the Chapel

Rosie's Curl and Weave

ST. MARTIN'S PRESS
NEW YORK

An Ordinary Woman

DONNA HILL

For information, address St. Martin's Press, 175 Fifth Avenue, New York, N.Y. 10010.

Book design by Gretchen Achilles

ISBN 0-312-28191-9

How do we begin to covet? Do we seek out things to covet?
We begin by coveting what we see every day.
—*from* THE SILENCE OF THE LAMBS

ACKNOWLEDGMENTS

I want to take this opportunity to thank my agent, Pattie Steele-Perkins, for making this project possible for me. To my editor, Monique Patterson, who helped me shape my story, and to Eliani Torres, a truly great copy editor.

Robert, so much love and thanks to you, you continue to make me believe I can fly. Thanks to my children, Nichole, Dawne, and Matthew, and my grandson, Mahlik, for always loving me and allowing me to love you all back.

Mom, I love you, and thanks for being there—always. Thanks to my sister, Lisa, and my brother, David, for always being in my corner—my personal cheering squad!

To my sisterfriends, Antoinette, Val, Gwynne, Linda, LaToya, Francis, and Jessica, for being real in good times and bad, and for listening to all my stories, even when you didn't feel like it.

Thank you so much to my readers old and new who have supported me these past twelve years. I hope that I can continue to entertain you for many years to come.

Most of all, to God, who continues to bless and amaze me with the doors that He opens, the paths that He sets, and the choices that He offers me each and every day.

ASHA

You'll find out soon enough. So I may as well say it now. I slept with my best friend's husband. There is no explanation. Not a real one, anyway, not one that people will accept, especially the people who know me. I don't understand what happened. It just did . . . over time, I suppose. I've been going over every detail in my head from the first time I met Ross Davis right up until the moment Lisa found out what went on between us. If I ever wanted to die, it was at that moment. But I didn't die. I had to face what we'd done. What I'd done. I had to look my best friend in the face and try to explain.

They have names for people like me: tramp, whore, home wrecker, mistress, the other woman. But in my mind, in my heart, I'm none of those. I'm just like you, like your sister, your aunt, or your mom . . . an ordinary woman. I'm sure Lisa and maybe even Ross would have a different story to tell, but I want to tell my side. I want to try to explain. Just hear me out. . . .

The Wedding

ASHA

It's the first Sunday in June. The tiny room behind the chapel is filled with the elegant beauty of calla lilies. Their petals are like silk, their stems held together by delicate threads of green ribbon. Light from the high-noon sun floats through the stained-glass windows, casting a kaleidoscope of radiant color that washes the white satin-and-lace gown in a rainbow of brilliance. The oval mirror reflects the beauty of the bride.

Everything is perfect. As it should be. Lisa Holden and Ross Davis are made for each other. Everyone says so. Everyone.

"Asha, I'm scared," Lisa says out of the blue. "Happy and scared out of my mind."

I step up behind Lisa to fasten the pearl buttons of her dress, and my heart aches in a way that I don't quite understand. For so long we have been friends. Friends since grade school. Real friends, not the kind who come and go, but friends who dream together, laugh and cry together. We even dreamed this day. Nothing has ever come between us, not even our differences. Until now. This moment. The realization saddens me so deeply I feel its weight in the pit of my belly, a hollowness in the center of my chest that I'm not sure will ever be filled. At least not in the same way.

Change is not easy. I know that, understand it. I understand what Lisa and I have will evolve and become something else—new, different—maybe even better.

I'm happy for her. Really I am.

Lisa turns toward me, and oddly, I'm not surprised to see the shimmer of tears that make her light brown eyes sparkle, catching the sun. After all, today is a big day, a joyous day, perfect for tears. Besides, Lisa is good at crying. She cries at comedies. She's quirky like that.

"I understand happy. But scared—of what? Tripping over that six-foot train, forgetting those two simple words, 'I do'? What, hon?" I laugh, hoping to ease the tense expression from her face.

With a tissue I quickly dab at the corners of her eyes before her perfect makeup job is ruined. I search her face for a hint of what is troubling her. A part of me knows, and I wonder if she sees the secret I try to hide behind my lowered lids.

The swish of her gown as she sits suddenly reminds me of a small boat casting off from the shore, buoyed by the gentle embrace of the waves that carry it out to unknown destinations. I can almost see her drift away until she takes my hand and pulls herself back—if only for a moment.

Lisa holds my hands between hers as if it's I who need comfort. Maybe I do. She sniffs loudly and releases a giggle. She does that when she's nervous.

"I love Ross," she confesses as she's done hundreds of times. "I know I do. Love him like I've never loved another man in my life besides my father."

"But? . . ."

She pulls in a short breath of air and exhales her response on a puff of peppermint-tinted sweetness. "It's just that I've never been a wife before."

I want to laugh—maybe from relief that it wasn't something worse—but I know how serious she is, and it would only cause another crying jag.

"It's a lot of responsibility," she continues. "I don't want to fail Ross. And for the first time in my life, I feel so incapable."

"You?" Surprise at her admission lifts my voice a notch. "You're the most capable person I know, Lisa. You're the one the family turns to in a crisis—and me, too, for that matter. You're the one who stuck it out in school and got a full professorship before you hit thirty-five. You breeze through life and never let anything deter you from your goals. Lisa—"

"This is different, Asha," she says in that precise, enunciating-every-word-way she has when she is upset. "This is not something I can figure out, create a lesson plan for, study in school, or write a few letters to straighten out some corporate error. This is my life—meshing it with someone else's, my dreams and my hopes. There is no right way to do it, no plan." Her pencil-thin brows draw into a tight line across her otherwise smooth forehead.

"But isn't that part of the joy, the excitement?" Reluctance to explore new horizons is a trait in people that has always been difficult for me to understand. Especially in my dearest friend. After all our years together, one would have thought that some of my zest for life would rub off on her.

"I'm not like you, Asha. I can't walk into a strange room and make it mine. I can't get on a plane and land in some out-of-the-way place and know just what to do. And I'm scared. Scared that I'm going to screw this up." She blinks back a fresh set of tears and looks directly at me. "I'm afraid of losing you as my friend."

The memories float between us, unanchored, within the shimmering pools of her eyes. And I wonder: How does she know it is *that* possible loss that is the demon I've been wrestling with since she announced she was getting married? How does she know that her big, glorious day keeps my ever-ready smile from being fully in place? That I feel my anchor being lifted and I'm being cast forever adrift? But of course Lisa would know. Nothing is secret between us. Not even thoughts unspoken.

I look into her eyes and try to convince her and myself with the words I've practiced in my head over and over. "You'll never lose me as a friend, Lisa. Never. So forget that, okay? You and Ross are going to have a great life together." I smile and squeeze her hands between mine. "And I get to play auntie to that house full of raunchy kids you're gonna have."

"Really? Do you really believe that, Asha?"

She sounds so much like a child, I think. A child needing reassurance. Yet I know, too, that the imploring wide-eyed look is an Oscar-winning camouflage for the steely resolve that rests beneath. I'm sure it's the magnet that drew Ross to Lisa: his need to nurture and protect, and her ability to project the illusion of helplessness. A perfect pair. They give each other what they need. And as her best friend, it's my job to convince her, make her believe something even I'm uncertain of.

"Yes, I believe it from the bottom of my heart." I smile reassuringly. "And I know you do, too."

Lisa glances away from my half-truth, quickly searching for an explanation that would make it whole, then turns back to me with the answer on her lips. "Wedding day jitters?"

"Big time."

We both laugh—hard and long—relief, sadness, joy, and pain erupting in wave after wave of almost giddy exaltation. A release, a balm—a veneer. By degrees, the merriment, the moment of reprieve subsides.

"Come on." My voice is still shaky. "Let me touch up your makeup and get this veil on you. Don't want to keep that man of yours waiting."

Lisa leans toward me and kisses my cheek. "I love you, Asha."

"Love you, too, girl. You're going to have a wonderful life with Ross. Believe that—in your heart."

"I know." She giggles again. "I know."

The church is packed with family and old friends, the air ripe with the scent of fresh flowers mixed with perfumes, colognes, and oils. The magnificent altar ahead is braced by rows of white tapers, the yellow flames dancing with the joy of the moment.

The sound of the organ pumps through my veins, giving purpose to my step, a holy quality to the gathering.

I make my way down the aisle, just as we practiced in rehearsal, smiling at the sea of faces that instantly blurs into a myriad of colors. Taking my place on the opposite side of the aisle, I face Lisa's brother, Clifton, the best man, and smile encouragingly at Ross. I wonder if he and Clifton had a similar man-to-man talk behind their closed door.

Something tells me no. Ross Davis is anything but unsure. He loves Lisa the way women dream of being loved—totally, without question, unequivocally. There are no doubts in Ross's mind. No uncertainty. And if there were, he would never voice them. That much I've learned about Ross in the brief year that he's been in Lisa's life—that we've all been friends—the times I've observed them together. I wonder if Lisa realizes this about her husband-to-be? Or has she been swept up in the romance of it all? Ross, her handsome knight who came along at just the right time to soothe her old heartaches. Hmmm. But aside from that, it's easy to see why Lisa is attracted to Ross Davis. Though he's not magazine-cover material, he's attractive in a solid way—from the ruggedness of his milk-chocolate brown face to the solidness of his body. Ross's very presence in a room gives one a sense of security, of being protected—much like Lisa's father does. I think those are the things that draw Lisa so tightly to Ross, beyond the sincerity in his brown eyes or the way he can make his mouth stretch into a tight line when upset, or fill with warmth when he smiles. Yeah, anyone can see why Lisa would want a man like Ross Davis. Or at least I could.

All eyes turn toward the back of the church as the white-jacketed ushers open the heavy wood doors.

There stands Lisa, framed in a moment of absolute perfection. Behind her, the sun blazes, seeming to surround her in an ethereal glow. The congregation gasps in a collective voice of awe as the organist begins the strains of a wedding march.

For all of Lisa's earlier protestations and moments of doubt, she has lived for this moment—as most women do. And she takes it, making it totally hers, from the demure turn of her head, the almost catlike gait down the carpeted aisle, to the way she lightly pats her father's hand as he escorts her to meet her soon-to-be husband.

As I watch her, all I can think about at this very moment is the day we first met. Not how important right now is, not how it must be momentous for her, but how important that other time was for *me*. A time that brought us to this place—together.

It was the summer of 1976. I was almost twelve. Funny how that date sticks in my mind. But I suppose it would. It was two years after my father left us. My mother moved us onto Putnam Avenue—in the Bedford-Stuyvesant section of Brooklyn—said she wanted to start over, which was fine with me.

I was sitting on the stoop, fooling around with a beat-up camera I'd found in the basement, when I looked up and noticed a girl staring at me from across the street. I tried to ignore her, but it was as if I could feel her gaze on me, burning through the top of my skull, hotter than the sun.

I stood up, my red shorts high above my knobby knees, and I put my hands on my nonexistent hips. "What you starin' at?" I shouted.

She just turned her head and ignored me, acted as if she didn't hear a word I'd shouted. But I knew she had. Slowly, like in one of those scary movies, she turned to stare me down again.

"Nothing," she'd said.

Nothing! Well, what was I, a fig-a-ment of her imagination? I snatched the beat-up camera from the stone steps, marched right down them and across the street without looking, I was so mad.

I gave her one of my meanest looks—from the other side of her gate—just in case she had a dog and said, "Whatchu say?"

She did that thing again with her head, turned it *just so*—far enough away that she looked like she wasn't looking, and just enough that she could catch me from the corner of her eye.

"I said—*n-o-t-h-i-n-g*," she uttered from the side of her mouth, and that's when I noticed the slight drawl in her voice.

She propped her fists beneath her chin and kept staring at whatever she was staring at—like I wasn't there. But I was there, and I wasn't gonna be ignored. I had enough of that at home, enough of being treated like I didn't matter, like an afterthought.

"You don't know who you talkin' to."

"I'm speaking to you," she said in that tone only grown-ups used, like they knew something you didn't.

"You betta not be," I tossed back, working really hard to maintain my edge. Whoever this girl was, she wasn't scared of me. "If you wanna get along around here, you betta ack right," I warned.

"I'm not going to be here long," she said in that proper tone again. Finally she turned and looked at me, and her eyes were all shiny like she was about to bawl. Her bottom lip trembled. "I don't want to be here." A single tear ran down her cheek. "I want to go home."

All of a sudden I felt really bad for her, kinda sad, in a way. Up close she didn't look so prim and proper, all stuck-up and tough. She reminded me of an Indian, the kind we learned about in history class, with her high cheekbones, slanted eyes, and long black hair parted down the middle and braided just past her shoulders. Looked the way the Indians must have looked when they saw their villages burned to the ground and their land taken away from them.

I stepped a little closer, not wanting to be so mean anymore. "Where's home?" I asked.

She sniffed. "North Carolina."

I'd heard of it. Somewhere down South. I imagined kids running around without shoes, on dirt roads with fat bugs and wild animals always chasing them, and couldn't understand why anyone would want to live there. And I thought I remembered hearing the adults talk about how white folks didn't like us too much down there, anyway.

I frowned. "Why would you wanna go back there?"

She sniffed again, harder this time, and wiped her eyes with the back of her hand. "All of my friends live there. My family. My school. Everything," she said, sounding as if she was really ready to start wailing.

"Can't you make no friends here?" I looked up and down the black-tarred street and concrete sidewalks, at the kids running, hollering, and playing. Then I turned and stared at her, trying to understand what her problem was.

"I-I can't," she muttered and turned away again—*just so*.

Now I was really confused. Maybe folks from down South had some strange rules about making friends that wasn't in our history books.

"Why?" I asked.

Two more really fat tears plopped onto her cheeks and then ran down to the corners of her mouth.

"I don't know how."

I started to laugh, but then I realized she was serious. "You kiddin', right?" I asked just to be sure.

She shook her head and started crying for real.

Well, I'll be damned, I thought—something my mother always said when she was taken by surprise. *This is a dilemma*—another one of my mother's favorite lines.

"You want us to be friends?" I asked, not knowing what else to do. All her crying was making my stomach feel funny.

She shrugged her thin shoulders, then said, "You want to?"

I shrugged my shoulders back at her. "I guess."

"You go first, then," she said, wiping her eyes with the back of her hand, then her nose with the hem of her shirt.

"Whaddaya mean, go first?"

She straightened her shoulders. "You tell me your name first—then I'll tell you mine."

Well I'll be damned, I thought for the second time in less than five minutes. Even then she'd honed her powers of passive manipulation. "Asha," I said sticking out my chin. I put my hand on my hip and leaned back on my legs, the way only bow-legged people can do, my grandmother used to say.

"Lisa Holden," she said, as if it should mean something to me.

"Hi." I peered around her. "You got a dog?"

She giggled, and it reminded me of a hiccup. "No. Don't like dogs. They make me sneeze, and cats." She screwed up her face.

"Me, too," I said, feeling a sudden kinship.

I took a step inside the gate—now that I knew it was safe—then another until I was right in front of her. I noticed that her eyes were a light brown. I'd never seen eyes like that on somebody so dark before.

"My brother is always begging for a dog," she offered, before scooting over on the step.

I sat beside her.

"Do you have sisters and brothers?" she asked, sniffing back the left-over tears.

I shook my head. "Wish I did sometimes, though," I confessed.

"It's no big deal. You're better off without them," she said in that grown-up voice again. "The older ones tell you what to do all the time, and the younger ones always want you to play with them when you don't feel like it."

I laughed. She didn't.

"I have an older brother and sister, Clifton and Sandra, and a younger sister, Tina."

We sat quietly for a few minutes.

"I'll be your sister . . . if you want," she said.

I turned to look at her. No one had ever offered that to me before: not Tracey, or Stephanie, or Glenda, or any of my friends.

"Asha!"

"That's my mom. Gotta go." I stood and immediately headed for the gate. My mother didn't like it when I didn't come right away. "See ya."

"What's that?" she asked, stopping me in my tracks.

I turned toward her. "My camera."

"Sisters!" she said.

I raised the camera and clicked. The flash popped, and Lisa smiled.

Just as she's smiling now. The hot white light from the photographer's bulb dances behind my lids, momentarily blinding me as that first day on the stoop fades into the background. The words of the minister drift toward me as in a dream.

". . . *Do you, Lisa Holden, take Ross Davis to be your lawfully wedded husband?* . . ."

The words, words that I've heard so often in movies and on television, take on new meaning today. They settle deep inside me, stir something within me. For the first time, I think I truly understand the power of these centuries-old words. This standing before God and man and pledging your love and fidelity—and how much love it must take to want to give that much of yourself away to another human being. I wonder if I ever will. Ever could.

I know Lisa can. It's the type of person she is—total in all that she does. Ross, too. I guess they will be just fine together. I guess. Even though there are probably things about each of them that the other may never fully know.

Looking at Lisa now accepting Ross's ring makes all of this inescapably real, final. And behind all Lisa's tears and smiles I wonder if she truly understands that—understands that the dress rehearsal is over. Elvis has left the building. This is the real thing.

LISA

". . . *With this ring, I thee wed . . .*"

Ross takes my left hand into his. For a moment he hesitates, and my heart thunders in my chest. Slowly a smile spreads across his mouth as he slides the platinum band along the length of my finger. Relief and a thrill like none I've ever experienced flow through me. The light from the candles and the rays of sun streaking in through the stained-glass windows dance along the band, almost as if it's been kissed by heaven itself.

Look how it sparkles. Platinum is much more precious than gold. That's what the jeweler told me. Up until then I always thought it looked like silver. But if he said so, it must be true. After all, it is his job. Asha agreed.

I look into Ross's eyes, and I know that he is finally mine.

Married. Me. After the last two fiascoes, I never thought I'd marry anyone. Two broken engagements. They say things happen in threes. I was determined to break my unlucky streak and make this wedding a reality, whatever it took. I don't think I could have lived with the shame of yet another failed engagement.

I turn to Asha and take Ross's ring from her hand.

I was certain I would wind up an old maid. I have the perfect occupation for the stereotype: a teacher. An old maid teacher—wouldn't that have simply been lovely? Asha constantly assured me that would never happen. She told me that Steven and Carl were just assholes—*her words*—and didn't know what they were letting go. She said I was a good woman and that some lucky man would be happy to have me in his life.

I don't know if I want to be considered a "good woman." "Good woman" has a boring sound to it, the kind of woman who has sex only in the missionary position.

"Lisa, repeat after me. . . ."

I slip the ring onto Ross's finger. "With this ring, I thee wed."

Ross says I'm a good woman, too. I wonder what he sees when he thinks of *good*. I know I try to make certain that our sex life is varied and lively. I know how important that is to a relationship. It seems to me that proves I'm more than just a good woman. I work at being everything Ross needs, everything he wants. I'm willing to do whatever it takes to make this marriage work. I won't allow Ross to become my unlucky number three.

". . . If there is anyone who knows some reason why this couple should not be joined in holy matrimony, speak now or forever hold your peace. . . ."

This is the part where everyone holds their breath, praying that some ugly scandal from the past doesn't jump up and simply ruin months of planning and preparation. I should be so lucky to cause that kind of an uproar. Fortunately for me, my past is pretty mundane. Asha, on the other hand, might have to bring oxygen while she holds her breath and her parade of past suitors—who never seem to be able to get over her—form a procession to the altar.

I glance toward Asha, who looks as radiant as a new bride herself. Her honey-brown complexion is flawless as usual, and the champagne-colored satin gown fits her curves like a glove. She flashes me a smile and her trademark wicked wink. I almost laugh. Everyone loves Asha. She has that uncanny ability to draw people to her. If it hadn't been for her, I don't know how I would have gotten through school—through life, for that matter. She was always there. Right at my side, every step of the way.

My entire family has front-row seats. Mom looks fabulous and ten years younger in the salmon-toned suit we selected. It took weeks, but I finally convinced her she would look incredible in it, and she does. If only she would stop crying. She's going to ruin her makeup. And Dad looks as if he's going to burst the buttons on his shirt, his chest is so puffed up with pride. My younger sister, Tina, is grinning from ear to ear, but big sis, Sandra, looks as if she'd rather be anyplace other than here. I know my sisters are a little upset that I didn't choose either of them to be my maid of honor. But this is *my* day. I made sure to oversee everything: from flower arrangements to the guest lists, from the food to where Ross and I would honeymoon. I had no intention of leaving anything to chance, opening the door for things to fall through the cracks. Nothing could go wrong. Not this time. And what better person to see that it didn't but me? I let Ross know what he needed to know. Men have such cavalier attitudes toward the intricacies of planning a wedding, and they've got no clue how important it is for the bride. There was no point to my involving Ross, which would only muddy the works. I wanted everything to be perfect. And what could be more perfect than having Asha, my dearest friend in the world, stand at my side on my day?

Besides, Tina is five months pregnant. Nothing fits her properly. Sandra is divorced, for heaven's sake. *Maids*. I don't think so. I'll have to find a way to make it up to both of them. I hate for them to be upset with me.

"Ross and Lisa, would you please kneel?"

Asha comes to my side to adjust my gown and gives me a quick squeeze around my waist.

Asha says I worry too much about other people and what they think. That I shouldn't let other people's behavior and attitudes affect me, but it does. I can't help it. I want things to be peaceful and have everyone happy. Happy the way I am with Ross. And I am happy, really I am.

Everything is exactly the way I wanted it, the way Asha and I talked about since we were teenagers. Well . . . the way I always talked about it. Asha listened mostly. She never said much. I was always the one who talked about weddings and husbands and kids. I suppose it was because I want what my parents have. *A perfect marriage*.

Asha didn't feel the same way, not really, and still doesn't. She says, *"Marriage is fine for you, girl, not me. I'm not the marrying kind."*

I don't believe that. She says it's not what she wants, but I know Asha like the palm of my hand. She wants this whole marriage thing as much as I do. The way most women do. She simply has doubts sometimes because of how her father walked out on her and her mother. It scarred her in some ways—ways that she won't talk about, not even to me. That bothers me at times, the part of her that she keeps tucked away all to herself. Friends shouldn't keep things from each other. Sometimes Asha does, and that upsets me and has, ever since we were kids.

Like the time she dragged me to that basketball game in the middle of the school week. I didn't want to go. I had a test to study for, but I went anyway because I knew it would make Asha happy.

I think it was about 1979 or '80. . . .

"You'll breeze through that trig test," Asha had said as we trudged the six blocks from home to the school against a bitter November wind. "You don't have to study. You got *skilz*." She laughed that infectious laugh, and I had to smile. She always made me smile.

"The reason I breeze through tests is *because* I study. I want to get into a good college," I said, stepping over a muddied pile of snow.

"So, you think I don't?" she teased. "But I want to have a good time while I'm getting there." She hunched her shoulders against the cold. "And what better place to check out the fellas than at a basketball game? They'll be all hot and sweaty, muscles ripplin'." She rolled her eyes heavenward as if she'd just eaten chocolate, then turned to me and winked.

I simply shook my head. Asha was crazy that way.

She hooked her arm through mine as we approached the gym door. I could hear the screams and yells from the other side and knew that it would smell truly funky before long. I never could understand what the fascination was about watching long-legged, skinny boys run up and down chasing a ball. Male sports, in general, are hard for me to understand. For the most part, they're brutal. My preference has always been brains over brawn. But I couldn't convince Asha of that. I didn't understand the point of being with someone—even if he was cute—if all he could ever talk about was one kind of ball or the other.

We finally squeezed around the bottleneck of girls who hung around the team's bench and found some seats after Asha said hello to practically everyone there. I always wondered if there was anyone in our entire school that Asha didn't know. Sometimes I wished that I could be more like her. But only sometimes.

"This is going to be great, Lisa," Asha said with her usual exuberance. "Thanks for coming with me."

"No problem."

I looked around the packed gymnasium. Everyone seemed thrilled to be there. So excited about the game, seeing friends, being loud, having fun. Everyone except me.

Did I look as uncomfortable and out of place as I felt? Being with Asha usually camouflaged me from the rest of the world. She was my big maple tree, with her long arms and wild Afro. She was the umbrella that shielded me. She absorbed the sun. Always.

I glanced at her from the corner of my eye. Already she was in rapt conversation with some girls from the rival school. Oh, yes, Asha knew them, too. Why had I come again?

Then suddenly, as if she read my mind, she turned to me and draped her arm around my shoulder. "Denise, Pat, this is my ace, Lisa Holden. Lisa . . . Denise and Pat. They go to Stuyvesant High School."

"Really? Good school," I said, giving them my best smile, and realized that I sounded just like my mother. I cringed, searched for something hip to say.

Denise, the heavyset one, shrugged her right shoulder. "It's awright." She turned her attention back toward the court.

"Your man playin', too?" Pat asked.

She had a little girl face, the color of tea with milk and a headful of tiny cornrows. I wondered how long it must have taken to braid all that hair.

"Who, me?" I asked when I finally realized she was staring at me, waiting for an answer.

"Yeah. Your guy out there?"

I shook my head. "Uh, is yours?"

"Naw. He hurt his ankle. Got benched. But *hers* is." She grinned and nudged Asha in the side until she started laughing.

I stared at Asha, and frowned in confusion. This Pat or whatever her name was obviously had Asha mixed up with someone else. Asha didn't have "a man" or "a guy." First of all, her mother wouldn't allow it until Asha turned sixteen, and second, she would have told me if she did. I know she would. That's not a secret you keep from your best friend.

But I didn't want to press the point, not in front of a bunch of strangers. I'd ask her about it in private. I decided to let it go for the time being.

Later I wish I had let it go. I wish I hadn't decided to go to the ladies' room when I saw Asha slip away, only to see her squeezed up in a corner in the dimly lit hallway with this guy—I forget his name—kissing him like her life depended on it.

I stopped cold, halfway down the corridor. It wasn't so much the entwined shadows that stopped me, but the awakening moans of a teenaged boy, blooming into manhood, and the teasing laughter of a budding young woman.

Young, eager hands slid up Asha's blouse, while hers caressed the curve of his back, their lips locked in a passionate kiss. The scene stunned me so intensely that I couldn't move, speak, or breathe. Was this her guy, that everyone knew about except me—her best friend? Was this a side of Asha that she kept hidden from me—*her best friend?*

The echo of a locker door being slammed shut startled us all. I quickly darted back the way I'd come, the bathroom totally forgotten.

I couldn't focus on the game. I couldn't understand how Asha could sit next to me and not tell me, not say a word—to her best friend. I tried to see if she looked different somehow, changed in some way. She didn't. And for some reason that I didn't quite understand, that realization scared me most of all.

I asked her about him on the way home. I felt so stupid having to ask. Stupid and angry. Those two girls, those strangers knew, but I didn't.

She looked at me like I was crazy. "Now you know good and well, I wouldn't be caught dead in some corner with some guy," she insisted, looking straight ahead. "Don't you think if I was liking some guy I would tell you?"

I shrugged. "I suppose."

"You know how many couples were out there tonight," she stated in that flip way she has sometimes. "You probably *thought* it was me. Anyway, if you saw something like that, I know you wouldn't wait till now to speak on it. Knowing you, you would have walked right up to me, tapped me on the shoulder, and asked me what the hell did I think I was doing. Right?"

I laughed, starting to feel a little better, wanting to feel better. Maybe I *was* mistaken. The hallway had been pretty dim. "You're right."

"You know I am."

She hooked her arm through mine and tilted her head so that the top of hers rested on mine. "You're the best," she said in a quiet, almost melancholy tone.

And I knew in that instant that it was her way of saying thank you. *Thank you for believing the lie. Thank you for not making me confess.*

It wasn't until years later, stretched out on my sofa, and after three glasses of wine that she told me about him and that the night was not a figment of my imagination. She'd been too ashamed at the time to tell me. Didn't want to be diminished in my eyes.

During many of our late-night phone calls or when Asha would sleep over, I would always bad-mouth those "fast girls," the girls with the extra-short skirts and boys all over them. Over many a shared Holden-family dinner, my mom and dad would emphasize the importance of being *ladies* at all times.

"Lisa, between you and your parents," she said between sips of white wine, "I was scared silly and a little embarrassed to let on how my body was really feeling. I couldn't talk to my mother, that's for sure. I don't know if I could have handled it coming from you and your folks—your mom especially—looking at me differently, treating me differently."

I told her there was a part of me that always knew, a part of her that had confessed. "There are just some things you can't keep from friends, real friends, the ones who know and love you, Asha," I said. "You know I love you. I would have understood anything."

"I know, girl, I know. I love you, too. To friendship," she said, and raised her glass.

"To friendship." I touched my glass to hers and smiled. That's what friendship was all about—*trust and honesty*—no matter what.

Now, as I stand here on the threshold of a new kind of life, what I'm most uncertain of is not marriage itself, but what marriage will do to *me*—to my independence—to Asha and the friendship we've built over the years, the trust, the loyalty, the secrets we've shared, even the ones we were ashamed of. The late-night chats, after-work drinks, heartache, tears—all of it—the things you share with your best friend. Now *Ross* must be my best friend, my everyday companion, my first confidant. Now I must give those things to him—my husband. I've *never* had that kind of relationship with a man, that kind of giving, that kind of openness, and it's scary. Like walking into a poorly lit room. You can make out the shape of things but can't really tell what they are.

Sure, Ross and I talk. Of course we do. But it's not the same. We talk about plans, work, basic things we have in common, and our love for each other. Standing here now, I realize for the first time, that Ross and I don't share *secrets*, the inner workings of ourselves. But we will. That's what married couples do—share and discover each other. There is so much I really don't know about Ross. It's going to take time to develop the kind of intimate relationship with him that I have with Asha. I'm just being a silly, jittery bride. I've known Asha for nearly twenty years and Ross barely one. We have the rest of our lives to nurture our relationship.

Asha assured me back there in the chapel room that nothing would change between us. If anything, things would be even better. I want to believe that. And I suppose a part of me does believe her the way I always have. Yet, another part of me realizes that in order to give my marriage the time and care that it needs, my garden of friendship may go untended. I know Asha will understand.

ROSS

Cliff gives me the thumbs-up sign, and I turn toward Mr. Holden. Slowly he nods his head in approval. Lisa grips my hand as we face the minister.

My bride. *My* woman. *My* Lisa. She looks like an angel from heaven, perfect in every way. Standing here in front of all these people, saying these words is like a dream. But this is all for real. Forever. To be truthful, it scares me, and not much of anything scares me. I'm not saying that marriage scares me. I know I can handle it. It's this whole love thing, you know. I've never had it before, not real love. Well, maybe once, a long time ago, back in college with Michelle. What I'm talking about is the other kind, the kind that fills your everyday life, that responsible love. The kind you have for your family, or sports, or your buddies on the basketball team. Not what I'm feeling, the kind that makes me feel weak and strong at the same time, makes me want to take this forever step. I didn't believe I could feel like this.

Sure, I'm thirty-five years old and there have been women in my life. Some relationships were better than others, but nothing like this. Lisa is different. When I look at her as I am now, something softens inside of me, the rough edges smooth out.

I mean, I had my mom as a role model, and she was one helluva woman. I know why my dad loved her the way he did. Nothing was too good for *his* Ruby.

But I'd heard the stories, too, from the guys sitting around on Friday nights nursing their drinks and their wounded hearts. They would talk about how sweet the woman was in the beginning, how they would treat them like kings. Then *bam!* Like my old man used to always say, *"If it looks too good to be true, it probably is—with the exception of your mother."*

Women don't realize this, but we hurt, too. We hurt in ways we will never talk about to each other and especially not to a woman. Hurt changes us. I've known hurt. It changes how we think about ourselves, and our view of the world. Men aren't so hard and unfeeling as women make us out to be. The problem is most of us have been wounded—bad—by a woman. Often the very first woman to cause us pain is our mother. She hurts us when she showers the love and hugs on our sisters, but not us because they don't want us to be soft. Or when she belittles our fathers and blames her own and the world's woes on the defects of men. Or when she sends us out into the world unprepared on how to love, how to express ourselves completely, expecting us to unravel these mysteries on our own. When she won't allow us to express emotion because she's been told that's not what men do—then blames us all when we grow up indifferent, distant, and untrusting.

But a good woman can change all that. A good woman has more power than she'll ever know, more power than the average man will ever allow into his life.

Lisa is a *good woman.*

A woman like my mom—solid and loving with just the right amount of femininity to make me feel every bit a man. Lisa respects me. She never puts me down. She respects my opinions. And respect is half the battle. I want this to work. And it will.

To be truthful, since grad school, I never really had the time or the inclination to work on building a committed relationship. Most of my time has been spent on taking care of Mom when Dad passed, then my sister,

Karen, after Mom died. In between, there is my architectural career, with occasional dates thrown in every now and then. The career and work came first. Hey, I'm not complaining; that's what men do, take care of their families. That's what's important. I learned that from my father, and I watched him live it right to the very end.

I wish they could be here to see this. They would be so proud, and I know they would love Lisa. Karen thinks she can walk on water. It'll be good for Karen to have a woman to talk to. I know it was hard for her getting through her teens without a mother. Well . . . that's all behind us now.

Lisa's cousin Vanessa steps up to the microphone next to the pianist. Vanessa looks just like a gospel singer, big, kinda busty, and a voice to rock the house. Lisa picked out the song, "When I'm with You." I see Lisa's smile beneath her veil as she watches her cousin. She turns to me, and I'd swear I see tears in her eyes. I hope they're tears of happiness. Never could figure out why women cry when they're happy.

It's so strange that Lisa and I hadn't met sooner. Cliff and I have been friends for about five years, but my path and Lisa's didn't seem to cross. I met Cliff when I came to work at Morgan and Holloway, the architectural firm, where I'm a senior designer. I'm not sure why Cliff and I connected—if it was the love of the job or the fact that we were the only two black men in a company of more than 75 staffers. That part doesn't matter to me. I know who I am. I feel comfortable straddling both worlds. My folks made sure that I was prepared, from the private schools to the mixed neighborhood I grew up in on Long Island. I've spent plenty of time at Cliff's folks house for one cookout or the other and visited him at his own apartment more times than I can count and I'd always *"just missed her."* Frankly speaking, I'd written her off anyway after hearing that she was either engaged or just breaking off an engagement on more than one occasion. I would never say it to Cliff, but his little sis sounded like the kind of woman we discussed over tap beer on a Friday night after work. Not the kind of woman I was interested in meeting, anyway. Cliff, on the other hand, is a great guy, somebody I can relate to, talk to. Cliff is a pretty heavy dude, has an opinion about everything.

I remember one Sunday afternoon we were hanging out at his apartment watching a football game. Lynn, his wife, was in the kitchen whipping up one of her fancy snacks that she knew we loved.

Cliff took a long swallow of his beer. "You ever think about settling down, man?" he asked me.

"Naw. Don't have the time or the inclination. I have enough on my plate with making sure my sister Karen is taken care of and my career stays on track."

"That's not enough, man, believe me," he said, leaning back and putting his size thirteens up on the ottoman. "One of these days you're going to realize that you want more than work and a woman every now and then. You're going to want forever."

"Forever! Please." I shook my head. I saw what losing my dad did to my mother, how it ate away at her spirit day by day, what losing Michelle did to me. I never wanted to feel that kind of pain, that kind of loss, and I wouldn't have to if I didn't allow anyone to get that close—again.

"It'll happen when the right woman comes along. Mark my words."

"Is that what happened to you with Lynn?"

"Yep. I felt the same way you did. Catch me if you can." He laughed. "And then one day, there she was and I knew I was caught. Forever." He pointed the beer bottle in my direction. "It'll happen when you least expect it."

"Yeah, Cliff, whatever you say. Just drink your beer and watch the game."

I didn't know how right he was, until the day I met Lisa barely three months later when she'd stopped by the office to meet Cliff after work. Morgan and Holloway, our office, is a pretty big outfit. The building used to be an old warehouse. So each floor is enormous, with enough of those giant windows to give a washer a real fit. But great for the natural light. All the designers have plenty of space to work, and a fair amount of privacy. The owners put in a winding staircase that runs right up the center of the building. I get a pretty good view of the comings and goings of the staff and guests from my vantage point by the staircase. I know this sounds corny, but from the moment I saw Lisa coming up those stairs with Cliff, I felt something—

knew that she was different. Don't ask me how, I just knew. She was tiny in comparison to Cliff's bulk and reminded me of a black Pocahontas.

"So, you're, uh, Lisa," I said after a brief introduction from Cliff, and felt ridiculous for stating the obvious. Out of the corner of my eye, I saw him chuckle and subtly ease away to the desk of one of our coworkers.

She extended her right hand to me and tucked her straight, dark hair behind her ear with her left. "I'm so glad to finally meet you," she said. "I've been hearing about you for years."

"Yeah, uh, same here." And all the things I'd heard and believed went right out of those big picture windows. "Do you live nearby?"

"Still living in Brooklyn. And you?"

"Out on the Island. Hempstead."

"Really? I hear it's lovely in some places. I've never been."

"Maybe when you have some free time I can take you on a tour."

She smiled, and I felt my insides take a dip. "Maybe."

"Hey, this guy isn't bothering you, is he, Sis?" Cliff interjected, stepping into the conversation and slipping his arm protectively around Lisa's waist.

"No. We were getting to know each other—after all this time." She looked straight at me. "Ross was being the perfect gentleman."

"You busy after work, Ross?" Cliff asked.

"Not really. Why?"

"We were planning on stopping by the folks' house to see how they're doing. I know they'd love to see you."

"I think it's a great idea," Lisa added, flashing that smile again. "If you're not busy."

"Sounds like a plan."

"Great, we'll meet you in the parking lot." He pulled Lisa a bit closer and then ushered her away. "Come on, let me give you the grand tour."

She glanced at me over her shoulder, and I knew I was hooked.

After that first meeting, we spent most of our free time together, either on the phone for hour-long conversations late into the night, or meeting after work for dinner or a movie. I have to be honest, though, I was still a bit skeptical of Lisa in the beginning. She was too good to be true, and my father's warning rang in my head once more. But she got to me, bit by bit, easing past the barriers. It was the little things at first. Maybe slipping a note in my jacket pocket or sending flowers to the office, e-mails telling me she was thinking about me or fixing dinner when she knew I was too beat to take her out. She never complained about the long hours I kept or the work I often brought home at night. Before I knew what hit me, Lisa Holden had me thinking about forever.

So here we are, barely a year after we met, ready to take the biggest step in our lives. Sometimes I think about how quickly everything happened between us. We met, fell in love, and before I knew what was happening, I'm walking down the aisle. Don't get me wrong, I'm not saying that I'm not ready for this or that it was rushed—but sometimes I just wonder if we should have waited a little longer, gotten to know each other better. But it's what Lisa wanted, and I want her to be happy. Seeing her smile is one of my greatest pleasures. She said to me one night after making love. "I love you, Ross, with all my heart, and you love me. That's what's important, not how long we've known each other." I didn't want to risk losing her, losing a chance at happiness, so I took the plunge—took a chance on forever. I didn't want her to think that I was like all the other guys: sleep with you a few times, profess my love, and then cut out. I'm not that kind of man. I'm going to work at this marriage. I've seen too many of them fall apart, those of aunts, cousins, friends, even big stars with money. Sure, maybe the love was there in the beginning and the sex was great, but it takes more than that. It takes work. Every day. And looking at her now—all beautiful—I know I made the right decision.

Vanessa belts out the last notes of the song, and the congregation breaks into applause. Lisa giggles.

"*. . . You may now kiss your bride. . . .*"

Damn, my heart is beating so fast I can hardly breathe, and Asha is taking her sweet time lifting Lisa's veil, prolonging the moment, making me sweat. Asha is always one for the dramatic, from her grand entrances into a room to her wild tales of her European photo jaunts, from her avant-garde style to her provocative statements just to see if she can get a rise out of someone. Asha is an interesting woman who seems to pride herself on taking the world by storm—a woman who doesn't need anyone but herself.

She and Lisa are like night and day, and I often wonder what is the glue that binds them together and what her relationship will be with Lisa now that *I am* fully in it. How is Asha gonna handle that; how will Lisa? Because now Lisa and I have to work on *us*. We have to concentrate on *our* marriage. It's gonna take more than love. *We* have to come first in each other's lives now. And that's going to take time.

Come on, Asha. Lift the veil. Let me see—

—God . . . She's beautiful. And her lips . . . just as sweet as the first time I kissed her in front of Junior's restaurant. "I'm going to make this work, baby. I swear I am," I tell her before taking her in my arms. "I'm going to do everything in my power to make this work," I whisper against her mouth, before tasting her for the first time as my wife. I have to. We have to, and we will.

"*. . . I present to you Mr. and Mrs. Ross Davis. . . .*"

After the Vows

ONE

Picture Perfect

ASHA

The great lawn behind the chapel is overflowing with wedding guests. At least two hundred. There are just enough trees to offer shade, but they're spaced far enough apart to give the attendees moving space. The umbrellas over the circular tables are all a soft pink color, reminding me of budding baby roses. Men in every size and shape are decked out in tuxedos and dark suits, and the women glide by in their designer gowns, jewelry glittering at necks and slender wrists. The band Lisa hired is doing a great job of keeping couples dancing, playing everything from seventies ballads and disco to millennium hip-hop. Even the old folks are out there shaking their thing. I ease my way between a shimmying couple. There have to be a least two dozen white-jacketed waiters and waitresses scurrying around refilling champagne flutes and passing out hors d'oeuvres. I must admit, Lisa's done one helluva job with this shindig.

"Asha!"

I turn, and Vincent points the camera in my direction. The flashbulb goes off, and I start to move out of range.

"One more, babe," he coaxes.

"Just one. I thought you didn't like doing weddings," I taunt, planting a hand on my hip.

"Anything for you, babe," he tosses back, then points and shoots.

Smile pretty for the pictures, Asha. I repeat it like a mantra to keep my mind off of my aching feet. Walking out here on the dirt and grass doesn't make it easier. Lisa insisted on an outdoor reception. Of course, I agreed. But I should have stuck to my guns on this shoe thing. Mind over matter. *Smile, Asha, smile.*

"Can I refill that for you, miss?" a handsome Jamaican-accented waiter asks.

"Thanks." I hand him my glass, which he quickly replaces with another before hurrying off to the next customer.

Everywhere I turn, flashbulbs are popping, blinding me with white light, and the heat from the afternoon sun has sweat dribbling between my breasts and down my spine. Even my forehead is probably glistening with it.

It's odd being on this side of the lens, the object of curiosity, *my* moment in time forever frozen. I'm used to setting up the shot, framing the subject and capturing that precise moment. If I'd had my way, I would have hired myself as the wedding photographer, chucked these shoes and this dress for some flats and jeans, and slung my equipment over my shoulder. But Lisa wouldn't hear of it. This is her day, after all, and she wanted me at her side. Of course, I did the next best thing. I got my business partner, Vincent, to take the pictures. He hates doing weddings, but he conceded as a favor to me and to that animal that prowls within both of us—the challenge of seizing a raw moment—that instant that no one else sees but you. Next to me, Vincent is the best photographer I know. He has that same edge, that eye for seeing life in frames, each phase a snapshot—quick and gone—here and now. Many of my photographs are in book collections and have appeared in gallery exhibits across the country.

I love what I do. I love the nuances of it, the power I have to make my subjects appear the way I see them, reveal hidden truths behind the eyes, the false curve of a smile, the challenging angle of a chin. I can show the world what is invisible to the naked eye, I can make truth manifest—or not. I thrill at the elusiveness of it, the rush of the immediate that must be snared at that very instant or be lost forever. It is all an extension of who I am, I believe—living for the moment, the perfect opportunity, the perfect shot.

"Shrimp, miss?"

I turn toward the sound of the clipped island voice. The waitress is very young—model material. My first thought is to capture her lithe body clothed in black and white, set against the elegance of diamonds and pearls. "Thank you." I watch her walk away and wish I were nineteen again. Taking a long, cooling sip of champagne and a nibble of the broiled shrimp, I think that I should get her number and possibly have her come in for a session. But the truth is I have more work than I can handle. Vincent and I are always in demand.

The images I capture are more often than not harsh and graphic backgrounds juxtaposed against the faces and bodies of flawless models as the focal points. Our clients seem to love it. But aren't those images a replica of real life—hidden behind the façades of our own creation? Beauty and tranquillity superimposed on the cruel realities of the world. Me and my trusty Nikon. Maybe this is why fashion work appeals to me so, the ability to structure the essence of that beauty, recreating an emotion or mood to capture the fancy and imagination of the viewer. Much like Gordon Parks, Helmut Newton, Horst, Irving Penn, or Cecil Beaton. My faves. Fabrics, flesh, nature, and drama.

Like this place, for example, this reception on a gorgeous June afternoon—all the beautiful people propped up against the real world beyond: the secrets, the hurts, the hunger, homelessness, the fear, the love, hate, the betrayals, and the poverty.

I see everything in frames, held in the blink of an eye for all time. Like now. As my eyes sweep across the yard, they click, locking the print inside my head. They catalog the empty space beside Lisa and Ross where his parents should be, the barely contained resentment in the eyes of Lisa's older, very divorced sister Sandra, the look of expectancy and hope in the smile of her younger sister, Tina. Ross, outwardly serene but probably churning inwardly, on his second drink. And Lisa—yes, Lisa, the vision of perfection: smile radiant, eyes glowing, body full of life, totally unaware of the shapes, the discontent, the hopes and fears that surround her in the frame.

I sigh and head across the lawn trying to spot the cute waiter with the champagne. I need a refill. I know that over time the pictures will yellow, the edges will fray, and the once perfect images will no longer hold their focus. The image will dim and only memory will remain.

Smile, Asha, smile. So I smile and nod at the two women who pass by. They look like people I should know, but I can't place them. What I really want to do is kick off these heels and curl up somewhere and sleep for about a week. The past six months of preparing for Lisa's wedding have been an unending stream of nonstop activity: fittings, rehearsals, lists, lists, and more lists . . . and Lisa.

Mind you, I'm not complaining, not at all. I'm just thankful that it's finally over and we can all begin to move on, squeeze into this new lifestyle suit and see if it fits—unlike these shoes.

I shift uncomfortably from side to side after finding a lone spot under the shade of a maple tree. My feet are killing me, really killing me. I've never been one for heels, and Lisa knows that, especially at my height. But she insisted. *Insisted.* She said she wanted us to look *statuesque.*

Statuesque is fine for Lisa Holden-Davis, who barely touches five feet five inches. They call women like her petite, a characteristic that gives people the feeling that she needs to be taken care of, that her feminine veneer may crack if she's not handled delicately.

I, on the other hand, sometimes wish that I could cut off about three inches of my five-foot-nine-inch height, lighten my skin by a half shade, and soften the texture of my hair just a crinkle. It's not that I don't love who I am or what I look like. I suppose it's wanting to be different somehow, wanting to embody the qualities that others . . . that men find endearing. For once, I would love to meet someone who wouldn't automatically assume that I have it all together, that I'm tough and don't need anyone but myself to get through my day. Don't they know that you can't judge a book by its cover—that things are never as they appear? *Take a moment and look at me—Asha Woods. See what I need, what I want.* Or maybe it's a simple case of the gene flaw in human nature, believing that the grass is always greener on the other side. Fantasizing about what could be rather than what is. Who knows?

I smile as I watch Lisa dancing with her husband. She is beautiful, and always the true lady, the romantic, living in a world of perfection and illusion, steering clear of ugliness and hard-core realism. And whenever she happens to tumble into it, her shock at being removed from the magical world that she's created is almost comical. But I never laugh. It's just the way she is. Focusing through my lens, seeing her there so lovely, innocent almost, I wonder as I often have what Lisa would do if she ever looked around her. Really looked at life as it is without all the artificial hearts and flowers.

Smile, Asha, the camera is pointed your way—and so is Clifton. He kisses my cheek in time with the snap of the camera—us, framed forever in that moment of greeting.

"Great job, Asha. You should be really proud of yourself." He looks around as if to convince himself and assure me that his observations are true.

"Not bad," I agree, sliding my arm around his thickening waist.

I like Cliff. I always have, ever since we were kids. He's a really a great guy—stable, steady, a real family man. Lisa worships the ground he walks on. I wonder how he feels about Ross taking his place in Lisa's heart.

"Can I get you anything, Cliff? Have you eaten?"

"I'm fine and full."

He begins snapping his fingers to some beat other than the one playing. I raise my brow skeptically.

"But you can have this dance with me. Lynn refuses, says I step on her toes."

I laugh, nearly spilling the warm champagne I've been nursing. "So, you're going to step on *my* toes instead?"

"Hey, it's tradition, Asha. The best man and the maid of honor always share a dance."

He gives me a hangdog look and I know instantly that I can't say no.

I wag my finger close to his nose, and give him my best menacing stare. "I'm doing this for Lisa. You know how she is about tradition. But Clifton Joseph Holden, I swear, if you step on any one of these toes, you *will* be the headline in tomorrow's paper. Are we straight?"

"Lynn exaggerates," he says, trying to sound offended.

I'm not convinced. "Hmmm." I step into his embrace as the band segues into Billie Holiday's classic, "Good Morning Heartache," and I wonder briefly if there's some significance.

"Do you think they'll make it?" Cliff suddenly asks me.

I nearly stumble, but don't miss a step. I admit I'm surprised by his question, especially knowing that Ross is Clifton's closest friend. Is this a test? Does he expect me to reveal some secret knowledge that Lisa and I may have shared? Or is this his roundabout way of trying to offer me a clue?

"I'm surprised you would ask something like that, Cliff. They seem happy. Lisa says she's crazy in love with Ross, and he treats her like a queen." I step back an inch to look into his eyes, searching for the true answer to the question he posed to me.

Cliff's glance slides away, intentionally avoiding the question in my own eyes. "I'm sure you're right," he hedges, and chuckles. "Guess I'm still being the overprotective big brother."

"Is that really all, Cliff?"

The music draws to a close, and he releases me. The right corner of his mouth curves up slightly as if he wants to smile but can't. I'm unable to read his face, and for some reason, that bothers me.

"Yeah, of course. Don't mind me."

He releases a long breath and slides his hands into the pockets of his tuxedo slacks. "I just want this to work out for my sister. She deserves some happiness with a good man."

"What is it that you're not saying, Cliff?" I search his sudden, tense expression. "You're mouthing all the right words but—"

"—It happened too fast, Asha," he confesses. The heavy lines of his brows draw slowly together above his dark brown eyes, reminding me of clouds gathering momentum just before the storm.

"Too fast? What do you mean?"

"*I've* known Ross longer than Lisa has. I just wonder if Ross happened to come along at the right time—when Lisa was still vulnerable, getting over that last idiot she was engaged to." His jaw clenches for an instant, hardening the lines of his face.

"I'm sure Lisa didn't base her decision to marry Ross on anything that happened in her past. She finally found the one for her. Third time's the charm, right?" With the light of my smile, I try to wash away the graying images that begin to surround us with brewing doubts. "You don't think she's made a mistake, do you?"

"Hey, forget it. This is what Lisa wanted." He stares at me, almost daring me to contradict him and at the same time find a way to dispel the misgivings that underscore his words.

He glances across the expanse of lawn. I follow his gaze and spot his wife, Lynn, standing alone, waving at us, or maybe it was just at Cliff. Lynn Holden is an enigma I can never figure out. Nice enough but distant, almost vague, like a photo that's been airbrushed or double exposed—there but not.

"Lisa was always a dreamer, you know," Cliff adds, almost to himself. "She was the one with the grand ideas, always made everyone believe that any wrong could be righted, that nothing was as bad as it seemed." He blows out a long breath, then looks at me. "Thanks for the dance, Asha." He pauses, then brusquely kisses my cheek and adds, "Be there for her, all right. I'd better go and keep my wife company." He squeezes my hand and weaves through the bumping and grinding bodies, heading toward Lynn.

I start to walk away, find some refuge for my aching feet when Lisa, practically skipping across the grass with Ross in tow, calls out to me.

I paste a big smile on my face as they approach. "Hey, you two. How's married life?"

Lisa turns to Ross and giggles, then takes my hand. "So far, so good," she says, her voice brimming with happiness. "Thanks for everything, Asha. You helped to make this all happen."

"What are friends for, sweetie?"

"I'm the luckiest woman in the world." She plants a kiss on Ross's clean-shaven cheek. "Now I have two best friends: you and Ross."

Ross flashes an awkward smile. "I have a lot to live up to," he says, looking directly at me. "You probably know Lisa better than anyone."

"That happens when you've known someone as long as Lisa and I have. But before you realize it, you'll know her as well as I do. Better, probably."

He glances briefly at his new bride. "You'll have to fill me in on all of her secrets one of these days. I'm sure I have a lot of catching up to do."

"Oh, I'm sure Lisa will be more than happy to do that herself." I take a sip of my champagne. "Right, Lisa?"

"We have the rest of our lives to get to know each other," she says, a tightness suddenly forming around her eyes and mouth.

"That you do," I murmur.

"Hold that pose!" Vincent calls out.

We all turn our eyes toward the camera and smile. *Snap*. The three of us, chronicled for all time.

"Well, come on, sweetheart, we'd better mingle or our guests will think we are being rude," Lisa sweetly instructs.

"Take care, Asha," Ross says as Lisa gently pulls him away.

I nod as the couple turn to leave.

I take a long sip of my warm champagne, letting the dying bubbles come to rest in my belly. Moving away, I see Cliff drape his arm around Lynn's shoulders, the picture of familiarity, security. His words tumble around in my head, bumping against my own unspoken thoughts. He'd actually said out loud what I'd only wondered, what had been confirmed in that brief, almost awkward conversation with Ross and Lisa. But it's like Cliff says, *this* whole shindig is what Lisa wants, and Ross is *who* she wants.

Maybe those other two idiots she was engaged to really did a number on her. More than I realized. More than she admitted—even to me. I thought she would get over it, move on. Sometimes I forget that Lisa is not like me. She can't compartmentalize her feelings, her life—separate the two. One merges and blends with the other, creating startling bursts of color, yet one is indistinguishable from the next.

TWO

What More Can I Want?

LISA

"It was a beautiful ceremony, Lisa. You must be so happy," my cousin Vanessa says.

I link my arm through hers as we walk together across the lawn. "I am happy, cuz. Everything is just the way I always imagined it would be." I turn to her. "And you worked that song." She gives my arm a squeeze.

Laughter draws our attention to the line of dancers forming on the opposite side of the lawn.

Vanessa lowers her voice. "Now you know Aunt Pearl don't have no business doing the electric slide in that tight-ass dress."

I cover my mouth to stifle my laughter and nudge Vanessa in the side. "Van, you need to stop."

"It's true!"

We both giggle in agreement.

"So where to on your honeymoon?" Vanessa asks as she swipes a glass of champagne from a passing waiter.

"Hawaii."

"You go, cuz!" She kisses my cheek. "Be happy, you hear?"

"I intend to," I reply, and a flash of the conversation with Asha and Ross jumps into my head. I force a smile.

"There's my sweetie," she says, referring to her husband, James, of ten years. "Let me scoop him up before one of these single hussies get him hemmed in. Now that you're a married lady, you gotta watch out for the hungry single women on the prowl. There are only so many good men out here. They're at a premium," she adds, wagging a finger at me.

"Vanessa, you are still crazy."

"As a bed bug. You take care of that handsome hubby of yours."

I glance quickly around the crowd for a sign of my husband, who I see talking with his sister, Karen. "I will," I say to Vanessa's receding form. For a moment I watch her as she steps into her husband's embrace. I sigh and shake off the odd momentary sensation of uncertainty, and I focus instead on all the joy around me.

Everyone seems to really be enjoying themselves. I knew an outdoor reception was the thing to do, though Asha didn't agree with me. The weather is perfect; the food is delicious. I can't eat a thing, but everyone tells me that it is. I gather my gown into my hand and move around the swirling crowd, accepting kisses, envelopes, and congratulations along the way.

I wave to my mom and dad, who've been dancing nonstop. Everything is just the way I'd always imagined that it would be—a fairy tale come true. And Ross is my knight in shining armor. What more could a woman ask for? I spot Sandra, sitting alone under one of the canopies. Maybe a smile for her younger sister, a kind word of congratulations, perhaps. Sandra has avoided me all afternoon, almost as if she's afraid that my happiness will somehow rub off on her. How long can she remain locked in that bitter place of loss? It hurts me that she cannot seem to shake off the pain of her divorce and make peace with her choices. We all make mistakes. Many days I think mine was loving Steven.

"A drink, Mrs. Davis?" a waiter asks.

Absently, I take a glass of champagne from the tray. "Thank you."

I did love Steven, maybe too much. So much at times it felt as if I was losing a part of myself in order to have him love me back. He made every man I'd ever known pale in comparison. He was a visiting professor in the Actor's Studio at the New School University where I still work, and where he doesn't.

The day we met is still as clear as the diamonds sparkling on my finger.

It was late January 1998. I was on my way home, loaded down with term papers and a million things on my mind: arranging the baby shower for my younger sister, Tina, and the trip to the department store to pick up a gift for my parents' anniversary. Forty-five years, I was thinking. What was it like to be married to the same person for that long?

With that on my mind, an armful of term papers, and my need to get out of the frigid cold, I didn't notice Steven Phillips until we were nose to nose, on our knees gathering up my papers from the gray-tinged snow.

"Sorry about this," he mumbled, tapping the ends of the papers against his thigh as he collected them. "I didn't see you."

"It's my fault, really. I had everything on my mind except where I was going."

He chuckled. "Seems I've had a bad stretch of those in a row."

It was then that I noticed his accent—British. I took a moment to look at him. He wore his hair dreaded, something that was becoming more the rage, especially in the arts and music crowd. I immediately envisioned reefer pipes, incense, and rolling paper cluttering his coffee table. Silly and judgmental, I know, but it was my first thought—and it intrigued me.

"Are you . . . working here?" I asked.

"Yes. Only for this semester and next. Teaching classes in the Actor's Studio."

Slowly we both stood.

"Really? You're an actor?"

He smiled. Gentle dimples flashed. "So I've been told. Steven Phillips."

"Lisa Holden. I teach in the English Department. Creative Writing."

"Really? You're a writer?" he said, straight-faced.

I was just about to justify myself when he began to laugh.

"Sorry, I couldn't help myself," he teased.

"Maybe there's some hope for you as an actor after all," I tossed back.

"Clever. I like clever." He handed me my damp papers. "Hope they're not too badly ruined."

"I'm sure they'll be fine once I get them dried out." I stuck out my hand, which he took. "Thank you."

"Maybe we'll run into each other again," he said, sliding his hands into the pockets of his black shearling coat.

I gazed at him for a moment, took him in. I liked what I saw. All of it.

"Maybe we will. Good night."

As I turned and headed for my car, I hoped it wouldn't be the last time I'd see Steven Phillips. And it wasn't.

About a week later as I was leaving my last class for the day, Steven was standing outside of my classroom door. He was leaning against the wall, flipping through a magazine.

"Hi." I was really happy to see him. I didn't realize how much until he stood right there in front of me.

"Hey, there." He rolled the magazine and stuck it in his jacket pocket. "Are you done?"

"Yes. How about you?"

"Hours ago." He answered the question in my eyes. "I was waiting for you. I thought we could go for a bite. If you don't have plans, that is."

"Uh, no. Nothing at all. Did you have someplace in mind?"

"I've found I've taken a liking to this small restaurant, Dojo's. It's in the area."

"I know the place. I go there a lot with my friend Asha. I love the tahini dressing," I added.

"So do I."

We both laughed.

"Dojo's, then?" he asked.

"Great."

We saw each other often after that. We sat up for hours, talking late into the night about literature, analyzing movies, debating what made great books and lousy actors. Before I could put a name to it, I knew I was in love with Steven.

It wasn't just the sex, which was wonderful. But his mind constantly challenged my own. His wicked sense of humor and his gentleness touched my soul.

When he asked me to marry him, there was no doubt in my mind. Yes. Yes. I was in love, not "in sex" the way I had been later with Carl. This was real, this was forever—until Steven announced that he was returning to England. He had a job he couldn't refuse, he'd said. He would send for me, he'd said. I believed him. But I didn't hear from him for almost six months. He'd vanished from my life as magically as he'd appeared. Then I received a Dear Lisa letter. He'd found someone. He was sorry. He hoped I could forgive him. He wished me all good things. Fuck you, Steven Phillips. Fuck you!

I made a decision that day as I tore up the letter into tiny shreds and washed it away with my tears. I wasn't going to let what he did turn me bitter, turn me into my sister Sandra. I was better than that. Bigger than that. I deserved more.

And so does my sister. She just won't let the past go. Here she is in the middle of *my* wedding reception looking as if she smells something awful. If I didn't know better, I'd think that she enjoyed suffering and regret, relished in being miserable. Well, I won't have it. Not on my day. She's going to put a smile on her face whether she wants to or not.

"Sandi, honey, isn't everything lovely?" I slide my arm through hers, and I feel her body tense.

"As long as you're happy, that's what's important." She blows a puff of cigarette smoke into the air and cuts her eyes at a couple dancing to a Luther Vandross ballad.

"Of course I'm happy. What woman wouldn't be with a man like Ross?" She exhales more smoke. "You really should stop, Sandi. It's bad for your health."

"So are lousy relationships," she says with a nastiness that startles me. "They all seem perfect in the beginning. Don't be fooled, little sister. I've been there, remember."

"Not every man is like Dennis, Sandra. You can't base my marriage on what happened in yours."

She turns to me and puts her wineglass down on the table. "Grow up, Lisa. They're all like Dennis, at some point or another. If you're lucky, you'll be prepared when they change up their act. Don't be fooled like I was."

"Why can't you be happy for me, for once?"

"Lisa, you're happy enough for the both of us. And besides, you're so busy making everything right with the world, you can't see what's wrong in it." She stares at me, a deep sadness in her eyes, but it feels as if she's looking straight through me. "Little sis, I wish you the best."

She turns, leaving me standing here with her words echoing in my head. I don't want to hear them. I won't listen. Not today. This is my day. And Sandra can just go to hell!

I feel a hand on my shoulder. It's Tina. "You okay, sweetie? You have such a pinched look on your face. Must have had a dose of Sandra."

We both laugh, knowing all too well our sister.

I take a deep breath. "Yes, and I'm determined not to let her bother me with her gloom-and-doom forecast."

"That's my girl." She kisses my cheek. "You are so lucky, Lisa. Ross is a dream. I think you make the perfect couple."

"Do you really?"

She looks at me curiously, her tiny face squeezing into a frown. "Of course. Don't you?"

I glance quickly around and spot my husband in the throes of conversation with Cliff and my dad, the two men I've known all my life. For a moment I match that against the short time I've known Ross, the time it took to reach today, and I hesitate.

I force a smile and hug my sister. "Of course I do. Ross is the man I've been waiting for."

"You two are going to have a great life together, Lisa. Just like me and Alan. Watch and see. Sandi will be eating her words."

I certainly hope so.

THREE

Ties That Bind

ROSS

"Ross, you've been like a son to me for years. Now it's official," Mr. Holden says, slapping me on the back. I take the slap in stride, try not to choke on my drink. Mr. Holden's hands are like catcher's mitts, large and beefy. Hands that have seen a hard day's work. Everything about Mr. Holden is big—his body, his voice, his personality. I can't imagine him being intimidated by anyone or anything. For a man in his mid-seventies, he is in great shape. And although I match him in height, he outweighs me by a good twenty pounds. I wouldn't want to tangle with him. But at the same time, there's an openness about him that makes him easy to talk to.

He points his cigar at me. "Lisa has been hurt before, bad choices. But she's happy now, and I expect her to stay that way." He glances at Cliff then back to me. "We all do." He gives me one of those "you get my meaning" looks.

Cliff lowers his head to hide his smile.

"And I won't let you or Lisa down, Mr. Holden. I promise you that."

"That's what I like to hear." He stops a waiter with a tray of drinks and hands one to each of us. He raises his glass. "To the future, Ross, yours and Lisa's. Be prepared for it, and it won't take you by surprise."

"I will."

We touch glasses in a toast, sealing our bond.

Mr. Holden slings his arm around my shoulder, and we begin to walk across the grounds as he tells me about his wedding—a civil ceremony nearly fifty years ago. "Lisa is just as beautiful as her mother was," he says in faraway voice, but one filled with fatherly pride. "I gotta tell you son, I thought this whole thing between you and Lisa happened kinda fast. Worried me for a while. I know how high-strung Lisa can be sometimes, even with all her good sense."

High-strung? He obviously has a completely different picture of his daughter from the one I do. But of course, he's still thinking of her as his little girl, not the woman I know.

"I thought she mighta been . . . well . . . you know. But I feel that you're a decent young man, with a bright future. I believe you love my daughter and she loves you. But love doesn't always put food on the table, Ross. It doesn't always answer all your questions or solve all your problems. It takes more than that. Believe me, I know. So I want you to understand, that you're my son now, too, just like Cliff. You can come to me with anything, anytime you need to talk, anytime you . . . need anything. Understand? Don't forget that."

"I won't, Mr. Holden."

"Call me Dad." He slapped me on the back again. "You're part of the family now."

"Thanks . . . Dad."

It's been a long time since I've been a part of a "real" family. Longer than that since I've uttered the word *dad*. The past ten years it's only been me and Karen. Now I have a brother, two more sisters, and a mother and father. It feels good, really feels good to be part of something outside myself, my job, and my responsibilities. I'm going to live up to their expectations. I'm going to give my marriage and my new family the best that I have to offer.

Like most men, I'd made friends with my solitude and loneliness, settled into a comfortable rut, each day resembling the last. That is, until I met Lisa. Sometimes it takes a good woman like Lisa to make a man realize what is missing from his life. A woman like her holds a mirror up to you, and finally you understand that just making do, sleepwalking through your days, is not enough. Her patience, goodness, and optimism are catching. It affects everyone around her. I know Lisa can be single-minded at times, thinking about what she wants to the exclusion of everything else. Sometimes it gets to me, but it's so minor compared with all she brings into my existence. We'll work it out over time, because I can't imagine my life without her in it. Even though Lisa and I have known each other only a short while, each day is a learning experience. I'm looking forward to the future.

Standing here, drinking champagne with my new father-in-law, and watching my new bride charm all our guests with her smile, I know how lucky I am. Probably most men would have taken some of her father's words as a veiled threat. But I know better. To me, his words mean love, concern, and responsibility. He's holding me responsible for his daughter's happiness and that's all right with me because I know what's involved in making a marriage work day-to-day. I won't fail him or her. I can't, or everything I pride myself on as a man will be no more than a façade. I'm part of a family now, and that means the world to me.

FOUR

Breathing Space

LISA

I knew Hawaii would be like this. Better than the ads, the brochures, or anything a travel agent could tell me. The salty smell of the ocean, the grainy feel of white sand—like a scene from a tropical movie. But it isn't a movie. This is our new life. It truly is paradise. Volcanoes stand in the distance. Palm trees and pineapple plants embrace them. Perfection.

The half-hour ride from the airport to the hotel—actually the private bungalow—is breathtaking. The emerald green lushness of the landscape splashed with brilliant multicolored plants, fruit so ripe it looks as if it will simply fall from the trees, and the rushing waterfalls are an assault on my senses. I can almost see Asha completely mesmerized by the island's beauty, her photographic eye on a constant prowl for the ideal shot. I'll have so much to tell her when we get back.

"We're actually here, Ross. Can you believe it?" I ask as he helps me out of the taxi.

Suddenly, he hugs me tight, kissing me long and slow. I can't explain to you what this feeling is like, this completeness. I know I've had my doubts, concerns that perhaps I was rushing things. But I thought everything through, weighing the pros against the cons. Of course, there are some issues that Ross and I don't fully see eye-to-eye about, but we'll work those things out. Every couple has differences. It's to be expected. The main thing is, we're both committed to marriage and making it work.

"I think we're causing a scene," I whisper against his mouth, before giving him one last peck on the lips. His warm fingers wrap around mine, and suddenly he looks at me as if he's about to tell me it's over before it begins. My stomach instantly tightens in alarm.

"This is the beginning of our new life together, Lisa. You and me."

I nearly laugh out loud with relief and stroke away the worry line that runs between his brows. Ross can be so intense at times, taking the world and all its problems on his shoulders. I admire that trait in him, his strength. Some people may think him stoic. But it's only that he's had to be responsible, relied upon, and clear-headed for so long that it's taken some of the spontaneity out of him. But I'll fix all that.

"And I can't wait for it to get started," I tell him, already thinking ahead to the evening I'd planned for us. Many women today balk at the idea of allowing the man to be just that—a man. She wants to compete with him on every level, in the workforce and in the bedroom. Not me. I'm willing to support my husband and let him be the man in our house. It's what kept my mother and father together all these years. They're partners. And that's what I plan to be for Ross, his partner.

When I was growing up, our family was one of the few in our neighborhood that had both parents living in the house. I suppose I took it for granted. It never occurred to me that life should be any other way.

I think what made me fully realize how lucky we were was meeting Asha and her mother, Denise.

I used to watch Ms. Denise drag herself home from work. She was a nurse. But even in her starched, white uniform, she always looked bent and beaten. What really struck me, however, was the change that would come over Asha when she spotted her mom. The joy would squeeze right out of her. Almost as if Ms. Denise drained Asha of vitality in order to put one foot in front of the other.

"How come your mother never smiles?" I asked Asha one day when we were walking to school. I guess we were about fifteen-sixteen at the time.

Asha shrugged. "Guess she ain't got nothing to smile about."

"Why?"

She turned and stared at me with a look in her eyes I'd never seen before: anger, pain, and jealousy.

"Maybe 'cause everybody ain't like Mr. and Mrs. Perfect Holden."

"What's that supposed to mean?"

She turned away and began walking faster. I reached out and snatched her by the arm. "Answer me. What's that supposed to mean?"

She swung toward me, and for a minute I thought she was going to hit me.

"It means that she doesn't have anybody to depend on but me and her. It means that she can't look me in the face when I need new shoes, money for a class trip, or when I stand next to her and listen to her lie to the bill collectors to keep them off her ass until payday. It means when she lays her head down on the pillow at night, ain't nobody on the pillow next to her. It means she's pissed off five days out of seven, and she blames it all on the man who's supposed to be my father. So what does that make me? A friendly everyday reminder that pisses her off the other two days out of the week." She smiled a twisted smile. "Satisfied?"

Asha stalked off, and we didn't speak for nearly two weeks. When we did, I never mentioned it again. But I looked at Asha and my life with new eyes.

Asha Woods was a survivor, and so were my parents. Asha chose to take her life by the horns and wrestle it to the ground. My parents chose to adhere to the vows of marriage, against all the odds, and make it work.

That summer changed me. I gained a new respect for commitment, tradition, values, and individual strength. And I knew that one day all that I believed, the choices I would make, would be tested. Like my parents, like Asha, I would find what I needed inside me to pull me through whatever adversity. On my own terms. In my own marriage.

"I know how much you love tradition," Ross is saying against my mouth, snuggling me close against him, as if he were reading my mind. "And nothing is more traditional than a husband carrying his bride across the threshold. Even if she did have a hearty lunch on the plane."

I try to slug him in the arm, and he nearly drops me.

"See what I mean?" he taunts, his eyes sparkling with merriment.

"Don't you dare drop me, Ross Alan Davis!"

His face stretches into a grimace as he groans in feigned agony. Giddy with joy and laughter, I wrap my arms tightly around his neck. Ross carries me as if my weight in his arms is no more substantial than a feather, and we reach the door and cross our very first threshold.

When he sets me down, for a moment I catch my breath as I quickly take in our accommodations. Relief slowly washes through me. The layout is exactly the way I wanted it. Exactly. I'd called months in advance to make sure that there would be chilled champagne, a private pool, fresh fruits, and a beachfront view—for starters. I know the hotel staff, the travel agency, and the caterers must have thought I was crazy. But I had no intention of leaving anything to chance. I didn't want Ross to have to worry about all these little details. My diligence paid off, and according to my watch, the waiter will arrive with our seafood dinner in one hour. That gives us just enough time to shower and change.

"So what do you think, sweetheart?" I know that Ross is a stickler for design and detail, but I can't imagine him finding fault with anything.

He turns to me, a half-smile playing around his mouth. "It's fabulous, babe." He pushes open the sliding doors that lead to the deck and the boulder-enclosed pool, which resembles a tropical wonderland.

The faint scent of chlorine drifts into the open space, the only element that defies the myth of paradise. But I can't wait to dive in. I love the water: pool water, ocean water, tub water. Loved it for as long as I can remember. My brother taught me to swim when I was six. I've been hooked ever since. I can already see myself cutting through the water . . . playing strip tag with my husband—

"You know . . . I never learned how to swim." Ross chuckles.

My bubble bursts, and I blink to bring the room back in focus. "Really?" I cross the room to stand next to him at the sliding doors. "It never occurred to me that you couldn't swim." Gently clasping his arm, I turn him to face me and look into his eyes. "We have two long, glorious weeks in heaven. You'll be swimming before you know it. I'm sure I can get you set up with some lessons."

He looks upward at the clear blue sky and shakes his head. "Oh, no. Not me. It's a little late in the game to be teaching this old dog new tricks. No, thanks." He pecks me on the tip of my nose. "You can do the swimming for the both of us. How's that?"

Ross eases away from me and goes back inside. I can't quite put into words how I feel right now. It's nothing I can put my finger on—just an unsettling feeling.

As he moves through the rooms, I watch him picking up seashells from the rattan tables, putting them down, checking the bar and the well-stocked mini refrigerator, the bedroom and bath; I think both are beautiful, and I wonder if he does, too. It isn't so much what Ross said about not knowing how to swim. It's that I didn't know that he couldn't. And I suddenly wonder what else I don't know about this handsome, self-contained man who is now my husband.

I want to ask him what he's afraid of, why he believes that it's too late for him to learn, why he isn't even willing to take the chance and try. But at the same time, I don't want to rock the boat. Not now. Not on our honeymoon, our wedding night. We have the rest of our lives to discover things about each other. It's such a small thing, anyway.

"Babe, I was thinking we could leave the unpacking for later, change clothes real quick, and take a tour, maybe have dinner at one of the local restaurants—"

"But . . . Ross . . . I'd planned something special. Just for us." I approach him, slowly, almost cautiously, and take his hands in mine. "Don't you want us to be alone?" I press my body against his. "At least on our first night?"

His hesitation takes me by surprise. "Sure, babe. I guess I wasn't thinking." He releases my hands and steps away from me. "Whatever you want to do is fine with me."

Whatever I want to do? "It's for *us*, Ross. Not just me. I did all of this because I thought you'd want it, too."

"I know, I know. Listen." He runs his fingers through my hair, looking at me with an almost pained expression that I can't understand. "I'm just tired, babe. These last few weeks—hell—these last few days have been crazy. Between work and getting ready for the wedding . . . I guess it's finally catching up with me. That's all." He pulls me close, resting his head atop mine. "So stop looking like something horrible is about to happen."

I can feel my body slowly begin to relax, the teasing pitch of his voice chasing away the shadows that had begun to encircle us. "I just want everything to be perfect, Ross. You're right, these past few weeks have been maddening. We've barely had an hour alone together in ages. I was only thinking of us finally having some private time." I again rub the worry line from between his brows. "But if you really want to go out . . . we can. I can cancel everything. It's not a—"

"No. I'm sure whatever you've concocted will be great." He laughs—finally. "And if I know you, you're ticking off the minutes to countdown in your head."

I step back and pitch a taunting glare his way.

"Well—aren't you?"

I watch the corners of his mouth flutter as he tries to suppress a smile. His knowing gaze holds mine, and I can't help the laughter that bubbles up from my stomach, the relief that fills me as the final strains of tension leave my body. I move into my husband's arms and rest my head against his chest. Closing my eyes, I listen to the steady beat. Everything will be fine.

FIVE

Out of Step, Out of Time

ROSS

Lisa! Have you seen my denim shorts? I'm sure I packed them."

"Check the bottom drawer in the armoire," she calls out from the bathroom.

I cross the bedroom to the armoire, and sure enough, my shorts are in the bottom drawer.

"Got 'em."

I pull out a white T-shirt and toss the shorts and shirt onto the bed.

You know, I was sure this weird feeling of unreality would disappear after the wedding was over. I figured everything would get back to normal. But I'm standing here, in the middle of one of the greatest locations on earth, a beautiful woman—*my wife*—is in the next room, taking a shower, and I can't seem to get myself together. I feel outside myself, like some other force is controlling my life and I'm standing on the sidelines, watching.

I know Lisa must think something is wrong with me, that I don't want to be with her because of what I said about going out and touring the island. Don't read anything into that. It's not that I don't want to be with my wife. That's not it at all. I just need to get my feet back under me.

I step into my slippers and head for the back garden to wait for Lisa. The warm, tropical air feels great against my bare chest. I can hear Lisa singing in the shower. It brings a smile to my lips. From the beginning, I was enchanted by Lisa, for lack of a better word. When I look at her, all I want is to make her happy, make her dreams come true. I don't know the whole story of her broken engagements, but I know it hurt her deeply—that much she told me. "I felt so betrayed, foolish . . . violated," she confessed to me one night over dinner. "All I wanted was to be loved, to love in return, to make someone happy," she'd said. The look in her eyes asked a simple question: "Will you hurt me, too?"

I knew what it felt like to love and lose, to give your all and have it tossed in your face, intentionally or otherwise. And all I could think about at that moment was protecting her from hurt and disappointment, making her happy. In the process, I put my own wants and priorities in the background. Maybe that's what love is about: thinking of your partner first. But at what cost?

I lean against the railing and watch the tropical fish in the man-made pond.

As much as Lisa is trying to make everything good for us—it's like . . . too much. But I can't blame Lisa. She means well. I suppose it will take some getting used to, having someone else involved in the decision making in my—our life. We'll just have to find a way to work those kinds of kinks out.

Maybe if I'd had some say, been involved in the wedding plans, the honeymoon, where we were going to live, from the beginning, I'd have a better grip on things. But I didn't. And to be truthful, that's not something I'm accustomed to. It was almost like being on a boat without oars. I just went along, not wanting to rock the boat. I should have spoken up, but I didn't.

It's times like now when I really wish I had my dad around to maybe ask his opinion, get some male advice. I can't ask Cliff or Lisa's dad. The first thing they would think is that something is wrong. I don't want to start out this marriage with their confidence in me shaken. On the other hand, my father was never a man for much talking, anyway. He was a doer, a take-charge kind of guy. "Anybody can run their mouths, talk a good game," he once told me, "but it's a man of action that gets respect. Don't you forget that." My father was the type of man who never seemed unsure about anything. Once he made up his mind about something, that was it—no questions asked, no turning back or second-guessing.

What would he have done if Mom had totally taken his choices out of his hands, made all the decisions without him? That's a stupid question. Mom would never have done anything like that. She simply wouldn't have. The bottom line is, if my dad was around, he'd consider me weak, a punk.

Funny, but the truth is I can't even remember him sometimes. Certain faint things come back to me, like the sound of his voice or the way he walked, or how far his shadow could stretch down the street in late afternoon. There are things that I do remember clearly: the fact that he never hugged me the way other fathers hugged their sons, never took me to a ball game or taught me how to drive when I turned sixteen. But he made up for it in other ways by teaching me about responsibility and hard work, the value of doing what was expected of me. "Spending your free time learning how to swim isn't going to prepare you to take care of your own family one day, Ross," he'd said to me while I hauled boxes and debris out of the garage. It must have been close to a hundred degrees that afternoon. "I know you may think it's important now because you're young. And that I'm just being hard on you. But you'll thank me for it."

That day I remember. I remember the blistering heat, the feeling of being let down and alone, of disappointment. I was twelve years old, and I wanted to go play with my friends. For once, I wanted to be like all the other boys, have a father like their fathers. I wanted to be carefree, with no responsibilities. I wanted to drape a towel around my neck and put on a pair of swim trunks. I wanted to jump in the water and learn to swim.

"The bathroom is all yours, sweetie."

I close my eyes to squeeze away the memories before turning to face my wife. I don't want her to see that little boy when she looks into my eyes.

When I emerge from the shower, the dining area is laid out with every kind of seafood, fruit, and vegetable imaginable. My wife has done a quick change into one of those flowery wraparound skirts with a halter top. Warm brown flesh is everywhere, more appetizing than the meal. Just looking at her, seeing her smile of hope and anticipation, the sparkle in her eyes, settles me down a bit, pushes those earlier feelings aside.

Watching her rise from her space on the floor and come to me gives me the same rush I felt the first time I'd met her at the office. Will it always be this way?

"I got all your favorites. Soft-shell crab, lobster, mussels in wine sauce, broiled shrimp . . ." She glances back at the table, then at me, an almost anxious look on her face.

"So this was the big surprise." I join her at the low table, take her hand, and bring it to my lips, hoping to chase away that frightened look in her eyes. "It's wonderful, babe. Better than any restaurant."

"Really? Are you sure you're not disappointed?"

Her mouth plays with mine while her fingers stroke my bare back, and I'm pretty sure that dinner will have to wait. This is our honeymoon. Everything will be fine.

SIX

Just My Imagination

LISA

"Need any help in there?" Ross asks from the living area as I prepare our first breakfast together.

"No. I'm fine. Just relax. I'll have everything ready in a few minutes."

I turn off the coffeepot, pour two cups of coffee, and place them on the wicker tray. I'd ordered fresh fruit, but the rest of our meal I wanted to prepare myself.

At least for the time being, maybe the busywork of scrambling eggs and frying bacon can take my mind off last night. I tighten the belt of my lace robe, a gift from Asha, and lay the strips of bacon on the platter.

I don't think I've ever been afraid of making love before, especially with Ross. The juicer squeezes out the last drops of nectar from the oranges. I pour two glasses and place them on the tray. By no means am I an expert on sex, and I have never considered myself a femme fatale, but I've never been afraid of it before—until last night.

I suppose I thought the level of expectation was higher. I felt as if I needed to be better, different somehow. The me I'd always been in bed with Ross had to be eclipsed. I imagined that the magic wand of the wedding vows would somehow make our first night as man and wife an awesome experience. It wasn't. That realization bothers me. Marriage is more than a vow. It's a bond. It's sacred. And the two people who stand before man and God and pledge their lives and their hearts to each other are blessed. Knowing all these things, it would seem that the love, the passion, the need would transcend the ordinary somehow. And it didn't. At least not with us.

The first time Ross and I made love was exactly two months and two days after we'd met. I was glad he wanted to wait. I needed the time, not only to know Ross better but also to get used to the idea of sleeping with a man after Carl. It had only been six months since our breakup.

I'd met Carl about a year and a half after the fiasco with Steven. Truthfully, I was still raw from the experience and very leery about getting involved again. Asha said I was being silly, that relationships were like riding horses—you fall off, bust your butt, and get back on and ride. Easy for her to say. I wish I could be as cavalier about love, my body, and commitment. I wasn't, and I'm still not.

I guess I was searching for what I saw at home, what my brother, Cliff, had with his wife, Lynn, or Tina and her husband. These were everyday examples that good, long-lasting relationships were possible.

In any event, Asha convinced me to go with her and Matt—her beau at the time—to a screening and after-party for an independent film. She'd shot some of the stills for the advertising and had gotten complimentary tickets. Vincent was there, as well, with his lady friend—a model, I think.

It was pretty exciting to see some of the stars up close. Most of them were much shorter than they appeared on the screen. All the women were a size two. Petite. Asha was totally unmoved by the glitz and glamour. She chatted with Blair Underwood, Ben Affleck, and Alfre Woodard as easily as she did with the bartender.

"I'll be right back," Asha had said. "I want to talk to Spike about his next film. I've been dying to get an assignment on one of his projects, even though his stuff is usually local. It'll still look good on my resume." She put her drink down on the bar. "You'll be okay?"

"Sure."

"If you need some company, just look for Vince. He's around somewhere. I think I saw him with Vanessa Williams."

She hurried off, and I tried to look as if attending movie premiere parties on a Wednesday night was something I always did.

"Enjoying yourself?"

I turned toward the voice on my left and looked up. Eyes the color of maple syrup greeted me, and the kind of perfect, clean-shaven face that you see only on magazine covers, on men like Tyson Beckford or Denzel.

"I'm trying." I took a sip of my wine. I could feel the heat of his body radiate toward me.

"Mind if I take up some of this space with you?" His voice was low, comforting.

"Be my guest."

"I hope you don't mind me saying this, but you're quite beautiful. Actress or model?"

"Neither. English professor."

"Today's my lucky day. I was thinking about going back to school. Now I'm convinced I should."

I had to laugh, it was so corny. "What brings you here?"

"Press pass. It has its perks."

"Oh, a journalist. That must be exciting." The intoxicating fragrance of his cologne floated around in my brain, making everything seem hazy, a bit surreal.

"It can be," he said. "I work the hard-edged news mostly. Investigating. I like uncovering things."

A shiver ran along the column of my spine.

"Have you done anything really interesting?"

"Depends. I've covered murders, corrupt politicians, police brutality, con games, consumer frauds. Things like that."

"This is a little off your beat. You really are far from home." His hand accidentally brushed mine, and I nearly screamed from the surprise thrill of it.

"Yeah. But a change in atmosphere is always good for the mind. You write enough about crooked people and you're bound to start believing everybody has something up their sleeve. At least in a place like this, you figure ninety percent are fake, and the other ten are phony."

I laughed. "A bit of a pessimist, huh?"

"No. Just being real." He leaned his slender frame back against the bar. "Look around you. This is all bullshit, excuse my French. Some of these folks are no better than the wheeling-dealing crooks I write about. They just dress better."

I almost sputtered out my drink. "You're bad."

He snatched a napkin from the bar and dabbed away the wine from my lips and chin. "So I've been told."

"Thanks," I mumbled. All the while he held his body inches from mine, and his eyes dragged over my face as if it were an appetizer. I held my breath.

"What brings you out tonight?"

"My friend, Asha. She's a photographer."

"Asha Woods?" His right brow rose.

"Yes. You know her?"

"I know her work. Some of it is pretty wild."

I smiled. "That's Asha."

"Okay, so now I know how you got here and who you're with. What's your name, and are you married?"

"It must be the journalist in you. Straight to the point," I said not unkindly. "Lisa Holden. And no, I'm not married."

I'm not sure why I let him take me home, or why I let him kiss me that first night, or why I let him slip his hands beneath my coat and caress my body.

Maybe it was loneliness, desire, pent-up passion. I couldn't be sure.

The only thing I was certain of was that I missed a man's touch. I missed being held, caressed, kissed, looked after.

I thought I could fill the emptiness with Carl, as if filling my body with another man would make the emptiness go away.

Yes, I would wake up in his bed or mine, physically satisfied and emotionally unfulfilled. Carl was incapable of truly giving himself to anyone, I soon discovered. Sure, the words—I love you, marry me—the touch, the moves were all there, but his heart was missing. At first I thought I could change him, make him warmer, make him open his heart to me.

The night we finally said good-bye, eight months after we'd met, he told me, "I've seen too much ugliness, too much evil, heard too many lies. It does something to you after a while. It steals your humanity, Lisa. And sometimes I believe that some of the horror I've seen, the trickery, has slipped into my pores somehow. Seeped into my soul." He looked at me with such sadness in his eyes that my heart felt as if it would break. "And I know if I open myself up to you, you'll be eaten alive, too."

I didn't want to believe him. I didn't want to hear that he didn't want me, didn't want us. I could change him. I could bring joy and gentleness into his life, but he wouldn't let me. Maybe it was best.

Asha said it was a "crock of shit." "He was probably getting scared of commitment like a lot of men and he panicked. Simple as that. Forget all that mess he was talking. You're better off without him. One of these days you'll find someone you can love and who will love you back. Just don't give your heart over so easy next time."

Now, sitting across from Ross, watching him eat his grapefruit and sip his morning coffee, I wonder if he feels the same way that Carl did. Was Ross suddenly afraid of letting me in last night? Was that what I felt—the distance? Are there places in his heart, in his soul, that he doesn't want me to reach? Had I given my heart over too quickly once again?

Last night we did what we usually do, touched what we usually touch, made all the appropriate moves and noises. On any other night, any other day, I would have rolled over sated and totally satisfied. Instead, I lay on my side with my eyes closed, feigning sleep until the sun rose, listening to

Ross's even breathing, the tumbling of the waterfall, the cawing of tropical birds, and the rustle of palms in the cool night breeze.

So many times during the night I wanted to turn to Ross and ask him if he felt the same strangeness, if something between us had changed, if what I felt was only temporary.

I know I'm probably having new bride jitters, as Asha would call it. I'm sure everything will be fine and that I'm getting all worked up for nothing. Besides, if something were wrong, Ross would definitely tell me. I know he would.

"Are you, okay, babe? You have such a worried look on your face." A spoonful of grapefruit is suspended between his mouth and the wooden bowl.

"No, honey, I'm fine." I reach out to take his free hand, assure him that I'm okay. There's no need to dump my crazy thoughts on him. Not now. Not on our honeymoon. I don't want anything to dampen our joy. Everything will work out. "Just thinking about how lucky I am. How lucky we are."

The touch of his lips on my knuckles sends the familiar tingle running along my arm, and I silently pray that tonight will be different—better—more.

"How soon do you want to get out of here and get our day started?" he asks, chewing thoughtfully.

I'd already crossed off at least a dozen things on my list of activities that had anything to do with water or swimming. "We could take the tour and start picking up souvenirs for everyone back home."

"Yeah, sounds like a plan."

As I watch him prepare for our first full day as a married couple, I wonder what's really on my husband's mind.

SEVEN

The Dark Room

ASHA

Watching images slowly begin to take shape, colors bloom, and shadows become light is as amazing as the art of capturing the moment, the look, the gesture.

Here in the cool, chemical silence, with darkness as my companion, I am in total control, my sole sanctuary in the world, the one place where I feel certain of my worth. It is here that I can choose how vivid I want that moment to be, if I will even let it survive.

Frame by frame, Lisa's wedding comes alive: from our time in the dressing room to the moment she and Ross stepped into the limo and sped off to their new life together.

I can't help but admire Vincent's handiwork. I couldn't have done a better job myself. I'll have to tell him, if he doesn't tell me first.

His surprise kiss on the back of my neck feels like the brush of butterfly wings and reminds me of what once was between us—beautiful but fleeting.

"I didn't hear you come in."

"Then I haven't lost my touch. So what do you think, boss lady? Pretty damned good, huh?"

He comes around to stand beside me, examining the evidence of his creations with a critical eye. "I should have gotten a better angle on that one," he says, pointing to the picture of Lisa and her mother sitting beneath a towering maple tree.

The photograph has the feel of a portrait, stylized, nearly perfect. Lisa will be pleased. "The lighting could have been a bit better, but it is beautiful," I admit.

He turns and rests against the sink, folding his arms. "So, when are you ever going to settle down, especially now that Lisa is all married off? You two aren't going to be able to hang out like you used to."

He takes a pack of cigarettes from the pocket of his denim shirt and taps one out, slipping it between his lips without lighting it. Vincent quit smoking about a year ago, but he said he still liked the image.

"So does that mean I should get married, too?" I hang another photo up to dry.

He shrugs. "No . . . but you ever think about it?"

"Not really. There's no room in my life for marriage. I travel six months out of the year and spend much of my free time in a dark room with you. What man in his right mind would put up with that?"

"Is that still the reason?"

I cut my eyes in his direction to see how serious he is. "Where's all this going, Vince? You getting all sentimental on me after taking a few wedding photos, or are you asking me to marry you?"

He chuckles and shifts his cigarette from the right corner of his mouth to the left. "I tried that, remember?" He attempts to hold me with his gaze, but he can't.

"You know you and I would be no good for each other. We're too much alike."

"Was that the reason, Asha? You never really said why, just *no*."

I push out a breath, try to gather my thoughts, a quick retort. How can I ever explain to him or to anyone the demons that plague me, the sensations of insecurity that send me running from one relationship to the next, one country to another, steeling myself behind my camera lens, creating my own reality? I can't, not until I can get it straight in my own mind. Until then, the moment will have to be enough.

"Because it wouldn't work, that's all. You know it, and I know it. I'm not the settling-down type, Vince. Never was and probably never will be. Marriage is for women like . . . Lisa."

"What kind of woman is that?"

The quiet sincerity of his question pulls me up short, and I know one of my pat responses will not suffice today. "The kind of woman who sticks, toughs it out, builds her hopes and dreams on someone else, whose happiness is based on the happiness of another. Who is willing to give herself totally to another human being—*all for love*." Our eyes meet. "Am I that type of woman, Vincent?"

He hesitates, and I can almost see the images of our times together flash in his eyes, each experience, every burst of laughter, every climax, held fast on the permanent film strip of his mind.

"No, you're not," he finally answers, his voice giving way to acceptance.

I should be relieved, let off the hook, but instead a wave of sadness washes over me.

Vincent reaches out and gently twirls one of my short twists between his blunt fingertips. "No, Asha Woods, that's not you at all."

Vincent kisses my lips, lightly, the way he always does before we part, but for some reason this time feels different, as if we've crossed some imaginary line into no more land, the end. I want to grab him, hold him, hold on to the familiar, tell him I can change, that I'm no longer that way at all. I *can* be like Lisa.

But I don't. I simply watch him walk away. The door opens, then closes quietly behind him. The moment of light is extinguished, and the room is once again submerged into darkness, cocooning me in my thoughts. The scent of him lingers in the air, and for an instant I wonder, what if. What if things had been different, if I had been different? Where would we be now, the two of us? But why speculate? Things would be no different from what they are.

A relationship between Vincent and me was inevitable, as predictable to begin as it was to end. We met during my early years of fashion photography. We were in Paris. Yes, the city of lights and love—totally cliché.

I was assigned to photograph the new spring collection from the fashion who's who of designers, beating out several other photographers for the coveted spot. I'd been to Paris before as a student during my final year at Parsons School of Design. But this was different. It would mark the turning point in my career.

The shows themselves were always held in grand style, with all the pomp and circumstance due the renowned masters of *haute coutre*. The photographers, however, the ones who are responsible for capturing these designers' visions and bringing them to the world, were generally relegated to the cheap hotels by their sponsors, with minimal expense accounts. But in Paris, even the worst dives had a sense of *vitalité*. So many of the photographers would wander into the low-budget cafés for morning croissants and twilight sips of Pernod.

It was during one of those evenings, after my first drink of the night, that I met Vincent.

Vincent is attractive in an understated way; the cut of his clothes, the casual appeal of his walk, the smooth assurance of his mannerisms, all put together make an eye-catching picture. Average in height, Vincent doesn't take over a room when he enters it, but rather allows himself to become part of the atmosphere, as if he belonged there. Vincent is never out of place even in some of the farthest reaches of the world.

I still believe it was the simple paradox of his ability to blend yet remain distinct that drew my attention to him.

He was sitting alone at the bar, dressed simply but totally French in a black silk shirt, pleated black silk pants, and customary beret. His ankles were bare. And the tiny diamond in his ear sparkled intermittently in the muted lighting of the café. A beacon.

I excused myself from the group of photographers I'd been palling around with for the past few days and eased up beside him.

"Mind if I sit here?" I asked.

He took another sip of his drink before he turned to me and responded. "I'd like the company."

"What are you drinking?"

He grinned. "Are you buying me a drink, Ms. From-Somewhere-in-Brooklyn, New York?"

I laughed. "You're good. Is my accent that noticeable?"

He quickly scanned the room, then lowered his voice to a teasing whisper. "Any accent other than French is noticeable to me. Vincent Durant." He stuck out his hand.

"Asha Woods."

"Pretty name. It suits you."

"I'll take that as a compliment?"

"Good." His gaze connected with mine, and a lazy smile spread across his mouth. "It was meant as one."

The waitress momentarily broke our connection when she asked what I'd be drinking.

"I'll have what he's having," I said.

His eyebrows rose in what looked to be admiration and he said, "I can truly appreciate a woman who knows a good liqueur simply from the look of satisfaction on a drinker's face. A Pernod for the lady. And another for me, *s'il vous plaît*." His French accent was as bad as mine, but I didn't comment, because his eyes and the curve of his smile held me this time, and we sipped our drinks, snapped pictures in our mind, shared stories and visions of our mutual love of photography. We sipped and talked until we held each other up along the Champs-Élysées, beneath the tease of the rising sun, tumbling by daylight among the twisted sheets of his bed.

Vincent was and I'm sure still is an incredible lover, that once-in-a-lifetime combination of animal lust and tear-rendering tenderness. If I were ever to marry, it would be to a man like Vincent Durant, who could make my body weep.

And it was always that way between Vincent and me; if we met on the shores of Virginia Beach, the mountains of Colorado, along the banks of the Nile, the avenue of Montmartre, or among the ruins of the Roman Coliseum. We were like a lit match, a burst of flame—hot, bright, and momentary—and if held too long you risked being burned or worse, watched in sorrow as it was extinguished.

We fell into some sort of pattern, I guess you could call it. We had spots we'd designated as "our place"; like hotels, shops, cafés, nightclubs in each city of the world. So when he'd call and say "Meet me at three in front of Harrods," or I'd wire him a note saying DINNER'S ON ME AT THE PARROT CLUB ON PEACHTREE. There was no scuffling for phone numbers, endless calls to confirm, checking ahead for reservations. It was simply understood that we would arrive at "our place."

But just as easily as it went and how simple it could be, the same furious desires that drew us together from across the oceans could erupt into firestorms of creative mayhem that would leave us seething with rage, vowing never to speak to each other again.

Vincent's edgy energy and sweeping passions on everything from politics to Sunday brunch competed with mine on every level—from the bedroom to the darkroom.

We were too much alike to be able to last without combusting, and would ultimately risk losing one of the greatest partnerships of all time—especially when our employers of the moment began to see us as a team—sending us out on the same accounts. We both knew why.

Vincent and I fed off each other like racehorses who need running mates to get them to full speed.

If he took a shot of a model dressed in a Dior gown set against the twisted metal of an abandoned shipyard, my shot would be of a nude draped only in silk scarves juxtaposed against a burning building.

We'd laugh at our daring, our ingenuity, critique ourselves and each other, then tumble into bed to make fierce carnal love, hoping that in the throes of passion we might drag from each other the coveted secrets of our next creation.

Everything would have been fine and could probably have gone on forever, until Vincent asked me to marry him.

It was September, I believe, the tenth to be exact, 1998. We'd just finished shooting stills for an upcoming movie ad campaign in Vallejo, California. We were both exhausted. The heat had been brutal. We went to this great Japanese restaurant and ordered everything we thought we could consume.

After his third cup of sake, Vincent leaned across the white, linen-topped table and took my hand. "Asha, how long have we known each other?"

I squinted my eyes and tried to bring him into focus. "One year, six months, and ten days," I muttered triumphantly.

"Exactly! And don't you think it's time we did something about that?"

"We do. Every time we see each other we have an incredible time, fuck to make the earth move, and then share some of our most embarrassing moments."

"Aren't you tired of seeing each other only every six weeks in some foreign country, in some strange bed?"

"No. Are you?"

He paused for a moment and for the first time in our relationship I felt suddenly uncomfortable. My mellow high began to wear off.

"Yes. I want more than this, Asha."

I laughed outright from nervousness. "You're getting much too serious—"

He squeezed my hand. "Marry me, Asha."

For a moment, I couldn't breathe, certain that I'd eavesdropped on someone else's conversation. "Wh-what?"

"Marry me. Let's cut out all the bullshit. We work well together, you and I."

"Exactly. We work together, Vincent—and sleep together on occasion. That doesn't equal marriage."

Slowly he released my hand. "What's your answer, Asha? Just say it."

I searched the depths of his eyes and saw the sincerity in his soul. I was never more terrified in my life. I had no yardstick, no graven image to hold up and measure what happiness, fidelity, love-everlasting, or forever meant. It did not exist in my world, and hadn't since before I was a teenager. I'd seen what love and marriage could do to you when you were suddenly stripped of it. It robbed you of your spirit, your joie de vivre. And you wound up like my mother. That's not what I wanted for me. I wanted to be a lot of things, but my mother was not one of them. But I carried her genes: her walk, the way she angled her head while in deep thought, the sweep of her brow, even the texture of her hair. And I was afraid that I would be as unworthy as she.

I pulled in a deep breath and pushed out the pain and uncertainty. "No."

Vincent nodded his head, quite matter-of-factly as if he'd just listened to an explanation of the day's menu. He tossed down the last of his drink and stood.

"Feel like walking down to the beach? I have an idea for a shot for tomorrow's session. I'd like your eye."

"Sure," I answered, not certain how to take his nonresponse to my refusal.

Things changed after that night. We still saw each other often, but the physical union that we'd shared slowly tapered off. We remained fierce competitors until we realized that the competition was futile and joined forces instead. And for all the late-night talks we shared since then—about his love life and mine, our careers and goals—we'd never again discussed that night.

Until today.

It shouldn't unsettle me so. But it does. I wonder how much I've changed, if at all. A part of me believes I have, but the old fears remain, lurking in the background of what appears to be my wonderful carefree life.

But it's simply easier this way. Isn't it?

EIGHT

Coming Home

LISA

I look out the plane window and notice that the cluster of islands are already becoming no more than green dots in the ocean. Our two wonderful weeks in Hawaii, one exquisite cloudless day after another, are rapidly disappearing like vapor. I couldn't have prayed for better weather during our stay. And Ross—well, Ross has been great. Watching him play the role of dutiful husband was quite cute, making sure that I was always comfortable, that whatever little trinket I wanted I would have. He seemed pleased that he didn't have to worry about anything, that our activities, meals, and everything else were all taken care of. I'm happy about that. I wanted that for him, and still do. I want to make his life easier.

I wish I could hold on to our time in Hawaii. At least there I knew what to expect every day, from activities to meals. Everything is planned, taken care of. You don't have to worry about anything, and if something is not to your liking, there is someone at your beck and call to fix it. Well, almost everything.

I can't quite put my finger on it, but there seems to be an underlying thread of uneasiness between Ross and me, and I don't know why or where it stems from. Especially at night. Nothing specific. Nothing that was said or done. Just there, like a third person.

For the past few days, I've wanted to ask him if he has been feeling it, too. But I'm not sure how to put it into words, and I don't want him to start thinking that I'm imagining problems.

I can barely see the islands now. Soon they'll disappear totally. All that we'll have left are our memories. I wonder what Ross's will be.

"Did you have a good time, sweetie?" I ask, snuggling as close as the armrest and seat belts will allow. I'm so glad I got us first-class seats. They're so much more comfortable and roomy, especially on these long flights.

"Of course, babe. How couldn't I? Beautiful island, fabulous weather, my every need met. I think I must have gained at least ten pounds with all the food I ate."

His deep chuckle warms me. "I'm heading straight for the gym when we get back. I can feel the food settling in all the wrong places." I lean over and gently kiss him. "I want to look good for you, sweetie. Make you proud of me."

His silence surprises me. I expect him to say all the right things like, *I am proud of you, babe.* Or, *you have a great body*. But he doesn't say anything at all, just squeezes my hand and looks up at the movie that's beginning to play.

Forrest Gump. I'd seen it three times, twice with Ross. I can't imagine how he could be so interested in it—again. I wish I had a remote control—

"We need to work on moving when we get back and get settled, Lisa," he says, out of the blue. His eyes remain fixed on the screen.

"Moving? What—where did that come from? I thought we decided to stay in my condo until we were ready to buy our house, hon."

"I've thought about it. It's not going to work." His voice has this tone of finality that I don't like, as if any opinion I may have wouldn't count.

"You've been thinking about it. How long? And why haven't you said anything to me?" I know I sound like a shrew, but how dare he just up and decide something this important without discussing it with me first? I'm his wife. His wife! "Ross?"

"It hasn't been that long."

"You sound annoyed that I'm even asking you."

"No, I'm not, Lisa," he says, each word clipped and precise.

"Then how long *has* it been that you've been thinking about this?"

"A few days."

"A few days? While we were on our honeymoon?" I can't believe it.

He turns to me with a look that goes right through me, as if I've slowly vanished from view like the islands had, and he was staring out the window looking for me. Suddenly I feel afraid.

"Yes, it has been a few days. I'm sorry I didn't talk to you about it. Maybe it wasn't clear in my own head. It's not that I wanted to leave you out of the decision, Lisa. Honestly."

"Well, you did." I don't want to sound sad, hurt, or disappointed. But I know I do. I want to sound as firm and decisive as Ross. But I feel betrayed, and I shouldn't. Not by the man who pledged to love and honor me.

I can't even look at him or return the comfort of his hand in mine. I don't want him to see the tears that are burning my eyes. I don't.

"Lisa. Babe, look at me."

The clouds are all I can see now. I can almost lose myself in them if I focus really hard.

"Lisa, I'm sorry. I was wrong. Lisa, look at me—you're crying. Oh, Lis, come on, I'm sorry. You're right, I should have talked to you."

He unfastens his seat belt and then mine. His hands on my body feel foreign. I don't want him to touch me, stroke my back, or try to comfort me. I don't want to hear his heart beat against my ear.

"Please, don't cry, Lisa. I can't stand it when you cry. Please, come on, babe. If it's that important . . ."

My head rises and falls with every swell of his breath.

". . . if it's that important to you, we can stay in the condo. I'll see if I can get some freelance work. Besides, Mr. Morgan has to notice all the time

I've been putting in. The next promotion is mine. We'll have enough for a down payment in no time. All right?"

All I can do is nod my head, because for a moment Ross is Carl. Ross is Steven. Ross is disappointment. I don't trust my voice. I don't trust the words that will surely come from my mouth if I open it now: *selfish bastard, insensitive jerk, chauvinist dog. Liar. Creep*. But of course, I can't say any of those things. As a professor of writing, I know the power of words. I know that once spoken they are as indelible as red ink on white silk. The stain of them will never truly go away. So we'll hold hands and watch *Forrest Gump*.

"You okay?" Ross turns to me and asks.

Hell no. "Fine."

He squeezes my hand again before lightly kissing my forehead. "We'd better buckle back up."

My acknowledgment is a faint smile, all I can manage at the moment. I go through the motions of clicking the seat belt's lock in place and hope to lose myself in the puffs of white clouds on the long flight home. But my mind won't let me rest.

I wanted this so desperately. I wanted these two weeks to be idyllic, fairy-tale perfect. On the surface it was. There was nothing out of place—except me and Ross. And that has never happened before. Never. Ross and I clicked from the beginning—on every level. There has never been a doubt in my mind that Ross was the man I would marry. I believed it then, and I still do.

Granted, it's true that my brother, my sisters, and Asha questioned the fact that we were marrying so quickly.

"What's the rush?" Asha asked me one evening over after-work drinks. "You're not pregnant, are you?"

"Of course not. Why would you even think that? Ross and I are very careful. I—"

"All right, all right. Take it easy," she said, holding up her hand. "Just asking. Knowing you, if you *did* get pregnant, you *would* get married. Simple as that."

"And you wouldn't?"

"Hell no. Not just because I was pregnant. Single women successfully raise their kids every day."

"Not me."

"My point exactly." She took a sip of her martini. "What I'm saying, hon, is knowing the type of woman you are, and your personal beliefs, it seems logical." She paused for a moment. "So, in other words, you're really in love with Ross?"

"Yes."

"Like you were really in love with Carl . . . and . . . Steven?"

For an instant, my breath stopped in my chest. "What's that supposed to mean?" I asked, stunned by Asha's cynical tone, her verbal attack on me.

Asha leaned toward me, and I had the momentary urge to smack her. She lowered her voice.

"You wanted to marry them, too, remember? You swore to me that each of them was the love of your life, how happy they made you. Remember?"

"Why are you doing this? You're supposed to be my friend. You're supposed to be happy for me."

"I am your friend, Lisa. If I wasn't, I wouldn't give a shit about what you did, who you slept with, or who you married. I want you to make the right decision. I don't want to see you get wrapped up in an illusion of love, only to be hurt again."

I couldn't look at her. I didn't want to see the truth in her eyes. She knew me too well. Knew my weaknesses and my fears. My needs. How I wish I could be like Asha. Fearless. I wish I could take the world by storm, live carefree, never worry if I was doing the right thing because the right thing was whatever I decided was right for me. But I wasn't like Asha. I never would be.

"I do love Ross," I said in my own defense. "This is different. He's nothing like Carl or Steven." Carl's soul was dark and wounded. He was a man in hibernation, afraid of the elements, afraid of being rescued. Tempted by possibility but unable to take the fruit. And Steven . . . Steven was blinded by the "here and now" with no desire to exist beyond the present. Capable of love—but only for the moment.

"Then if he's nothing like them, Lisa, he'll wait. He'll want to make sure this is what he wants, as well."

"He does want this. He told me he does. What are you saying—he doesn't love me?"

"That's not what I'm saying at all. And you know it."

"I want to marry him, Asha. I want to spend the rest of my life with him. I can't put it any more simply than that."

She pushed out a breath. I couldn't tell if it was frustration or resignation. "Fine, Lisa. If you're sure." She polished off the rest of her drink. "So when is the big day?"

"The second weekend in June."

"That's barely six months. Can you get everything together by then?"

I grinned. "With your help, I can."

She began to laugh, and the tightness in my chest slowly eased. We were back on track.

"I knew there was a catch," she said over our laughter. "Where do we start?"

Sitting here now, watching my husband's total absorption in the movie makes me question my decision. Would there have been things we would have discovered about each other had we waited, dated longer?

I honestly can't see what it could be. Marriage is a learning experience. Everyone knows that. What does it matter that our honeymoon didn't turn out exactly as I'd pictured it? Nothing in this life is perfect. We can only try to do the best we can. And that's what I intend to do.

As I reach for Ross's hand, he turns to me with the most wonderful smile on his face. Everything will be fine. I know it will. He can watch the movie, and I think I'll take a nap.

NINE

Guilt Trip

ROSS

I pull open the closet door in the bedroom to hang up my suits, only to realize that it's lined with dresses and skirts. *Lisa's closet*. I slam the door shut.

"Everything okay, Ross?" Lisa calls from the front of the condo.

"Yeah. Fine." I move to the next closet and shove my clothes inside.

"I'll be there in a minute, hon."

"Fine."

I shouldn't have given in to Lisa so easily about this whole living indefinitely in her condo thing. I just shouldn't have. I'd made up my mind. But I backed out like someone had a knife to my throat. I've never been this way before. Once I think things through and make a decision, that's it. That's the way I've operated all these years, and it's worked for me. What has happened to me?

I take a seat on the side of the bed, juggle a pair of socks in my hands, and try to remember which drawers she said were mine. Looking around the perfectly kept space, I see nothing here that resembles me. The colors are all soft shades of mauve and off-white. Even the bedspread is floral. Nothing I would choose. I feel like a houseguest instead of the man of the house. Nothing's out of place in the entire apartment, as if it's a photograph for a catalog instead of a home where people actually live. I don't even feel comfortable leaving my shoes by the bed because it might mess up the perfect picture.

I know Lisa means well, but she has this uncanny way of making me feel guilty. Like my actions have hurt her in some way that I don't understand. Or that I don't appreciate the things that she does for us, like on our honeymoon and my wanting to go out that first night and she didn't. I'm sure it's not intentional on her part. It's just the way she is, so vulnerable. And it kills me to see her hurt or upset. It reminds me so much of my mom and my sister after Dad died. Seeing the pain in their eyes did something to me inside. I don't ever want to see that look in Lisa's eyes. I don't ever want to feel as if there is something I can do to prevent it and don't. I don't want to feel that guilt. Not again.

Like with *Dad*.

Maybe if I hadn't been so angry with him. Maybe if we had talked, if I'd explained my feelings, he would still be around. He wouldn't have taken on the extra job. But my dad was not the kind of man you could talk to that way. His word was law. His decision was final.

If he'd had his way, I would be a bar owner now. He couldn't see that I wanted more for myself. I'm not saying there's anything wrong with owning a bar. But it wasn't my dream. It was his. He couldn't understand that. From the moment I told him I was going away to college, things changed between us.

He was sitting in his favorite chair, his work boots dusty and mud-caked from his day at the construction site. His head was back against the cushion of the lounger. His size thirteens splayed out in front of him.

My father was an imposing man. Big in every respect, from his height of six-four and bulk of 240 to the rumbling timbre of his voice, which when riled had the strength of a hurricane ripping through everyone in its path.

I came into the living room with my acceptance letter from M.I.T. I had every reason to believe that he would unleash his fury on me.

He slowly opened his eyes and turned his head to focus on me. When he did, everything inside me that had good sense told me to crush the letter of freedom in my fist and just ask him how his day had gone.

"How ya doin', son? Good day at school?" He yawned long and loud.

I eased farther into the room. "Yeah, everything's okay."

"You know I was thinkin', son, you should come down to the bar with me this Saturday, see how things go. It's gonna be yours one day." He yawned again. "With graduation coming, you'll be out of school in a minute. Figured you'd work there for the summer, learn the ropes."

"That's what I want to talk to you about, Dad."

He sat up a bit straighter. "Sure, son. What is it?"

"I, uh, got my acceptance letter from M.I.T. today. I got the scholarship."

The sudden silence grabbed me by the throat. I watched his thick jaw flex. His voice came from the pit of his stomach. "We talked about this months ago, Ross. We decided you'd stay here and go to the local community college. Work at the bar and help out with these bills."

"You decided, Dad. You never listened to me when I told you what I wanted to do."

"What did you say, boy?"

His eyes were reduced to two slits as he glared at me. I could see his entire body tense, the muscles, from years of working construction, contract.

"You . . . never listened to me. I don't want to stay here and go to school. I don't want to own the bar and work there for the rest of my life."

Suddenly he stood, and his height and bulk seemed more overwhelming than ever as he moved toward me. "This is my goddamned house! You live by my rules. I bust my ass every day to take care of this family—your mother, your sister, and you! And as long as you live under my roof, you do as I say. I bought that business so you could have something to call your own one day, and this is the shit I get from you."

He was in my face then, so close I could smell the sweat and dust rise from his pores. He snatched the paper from my hand and read it, then ripped it to pieces and walked out.

Later that night I heard them arguing—my mother and father. His voice was unrelenting; my mother's, wet with tears.

For weeks after that, my father ignored me, working longer and longer hours. He'd leave his construction job and go straight to the bar, coming home in the early hours of the morning.

My mother walked around with a wounded look on her face, and my sister Karen didn't know where to look or what to do. All she knew was that I had somehow caused some terrible thing to happen in our house.

As the day of my departure grew closer, the tension mounted. I went alone to the airport that summer. My father wasn't even home. My mother and sister stood in the doorway of our Atlanta home with the solemn looks of those who are burying a loved one.

The image stayed with me. My father's obvious absence was just as potent as my mother and sister's presence.

The next time I saw my father was one year later, at his funeral.

Had I stayed and taken some of the pressure off, instead of insisting on "doing my own thing," would he still be around? That question constantly haunts me. The weight of his loss never leaves me. All I want is to make it go away. Make it stop creeping into my life, freezing me in place and leaving me silent, frustrated, and angry.

"Ross?"

I look up, and Lisa is staring at me with a pained expression on her face. She comes and sits beside me and takes the socks from my hands.

"Are you okay?" She strokes my brow.

I lean over and kiss her lightly on the lips. "Yeah, I'm fine."

TEN

To Be or Not

ASHA

"Give me all the juicy details. I know you and Ross had a ball in Hawaii. Did you wear all the lingerie we picked out, or did you even get a chance to put them on?"

I wait for Lisa's shy smile that never comes. She picks up her cup of herbal tea and takes a sip. She's been back from her honeymoon for a little more than two weeks, and this is the first moment we've had a chance to talk—to see each other since the wedding. I expected her to be bubbly and glowing. She isn't, and I can't imagine why.

I stretch out on my couch and watch the images race across her expressive face. Finally she looks at me, and hundreds of questions dance in her eyes.

Her mouth forms a tentative smile. "It was absolutely wonderful," she says, and I immediately know she's lying. "Hawaii was better than I could have imagined. You would have loved it, Asha. The service was great. The weather was perfect, and our rooms were right out of the catalog." She laughs lightly. "I couldn't have asked for more."

I let her litany of Hawaiian attributes hang in the air to dry. Then I pick them off one by one like a laundry woman gathering clothes from the line. "Sounds great—the Hawaiian part, the service and the weather part, but what about the honeymoon part?"

"It was fine," she says, sounding almost as if she's trying to convince herself more than me.

"Did Ross have a good time?"

"Of course. Who wouldn't?" She looks away.

"And what about you?"

"What about me?"

Lisa buries her gaze in her teacup as if the answer is swimming in the lemony warmth there.

"Want me to refill that for you, or would you like something stronger? I have that wine you like."

"Yes. That sounds good. Some wine."

"Be right back."

While I take the wineglasses from the cabinet and pour the chilled wine from the mini-fridge behind the bar, I try to fill in the blanks of what Lisa isn't saying. It's obvious, at least to me, that she's hiding something. Why, is the first question; the second is, why from me?

But if I'm honest with myself, I'll admit that I already know the answer. Pride. Stubborn, stupid pride.

Lisa will never readily admit that something is wrong in paradise. At least not right away. And I can appreciate that, understand it even. I'm very much the same way. There's no phrase that pisses me off more than "I told you so."

And based on previous experience, I have a strong feeling that this is going to be a long afternoon. It's going to take time and patience before Lisa opens up and says what's bothering her.

Then again, I could be completely off base and reading the wrong signals, seeing shadows that aren't there, setting up my own background for this photograph. But I doubt it.

But when she's ready, she'll talk. She always does.

"Here's your wine."

I hand Lisa her glass and reclaim my lounging position on the couch—the willing patient ready to be probed by the doctor in a search for answers. When she gets me to open up, so will she. I close my eyes and wait.

"Have you had a chance to develop any of the wedding pictures yet?"

An image of Vincent flashes briefly in my head. "Yes. Most of them. Vince did a great job. You'll love them." I open my eyes and glance at her. "I can take you to the studio and show you what we have so far, if you want."

She shakes her head. "No. I can wait. Anyway, I want Ross and me to look at them together."

"Ain't that sweet?" I tease, hoping to loosen her up, make her smile.

Lisa cuts her eyes in my direction and laughs—sort of. "It is nice, you know."

"I suppose for some. Seems to be treating you good. You look well."

"Hawaii is conducive to rest."

"Rest? Weren't you on your honeymoon? There shouldn't have been time on your agenda to rest."

I reach for my glass of wine from the black lacquer coffee table that separates us—and wait. Over the rim of my glass, I watch her intently, as the random images play out on her face—one frame after the other. I'm not liking what I see: flashes of doubt, concern, sadness. Why, I wonder? What could possibly be wrong so quickly?

"I hope you two took some great pictures," I finally say, breaking the chain of silence. "I can add them to the wedding album. I'm definitely going to have to finagle an assignment to get me to Hawaii. Everyone I know who's been doesn't want to come home," I continue, still watching the distracted look on her face that's losing the battle of trying to look anything but.

Lisa sips her wine and then suddenly confesses. "Ross can't swim," she says as if it were a cardinal sin, and I hope the bewilderment that emerges in my mind doesn't register on my face. I want to laugh with relief that it isn't something truly awful, but I don't. I know how she can be if she thinks I'm not taking her seriously, no matter how ridiculous it sounds.

"When did you find that out?" I finally manage.

"Our first day. I was telling him all about the plans I'd made, all the things we would do, and he just blurted it out."

"It's not the worst thing in the world. Hey, if you threw me in the water, I'd have a helluva time getting out. Plenty of folks can't swim."

"I know that, Asha," she says in that reprimanding teacher tone. "What I'm saying is that I didn't know it about Ross. It took me by surprise."

"Oh," is all I can think to say. I want to ask her, What's the big deal anyway? I want to ask her, Why are you only finding this out on your honeymoon—on a tropical island, at that? It's such a small thing, really, but basic in those get-to-know-you conversations. "So Ross didn't do any swimming. I'm sure there were plenty of other things to do."

"Yes. But I had everything planned out." She finishes her wine and then refills her glass. "It just threw everything off." Lisa's expression turns petulant, like that of an adolescent who is denied the family car on Friday night.

"Everything can't be planned, Lisa. Sometimes shit happens, you know. Life can't always be an orderly to-do list."

"Thanks for the update."

"Just stating the obvious. You have got to loosen up. Let go of the tight rein you have on life and just enjoy it for what it is, take it as it comes. Been telling you that since we were twelve." I toss a rectangular pillow that bounces off the top of her head, causing a thread of wine to dribble down her chin. Lisa jumps up and spills some more down the front of her pale green T-shirt.

"Damn it, Asha! You play too much."

"And you don't play enough." I toss her a cloth napkin. "That's what I'm talking about."

She stops her dabbing and looks across at me. "What?"

"I'm talking about not always being prepared for everything. Taking life as it comes and dealing with the surprises."

"I like to know what I'm doing," she snaps. "Maybe you can walk blindly and boldly through life," she adds, dabbing some more, "but I can't."

"Well here's the million-dollar question: Why in the hell not?"

Her hand stops inches from her shirt that now sports a circular spot between her breasts. "Why?"

"That was my question. Why? Why are you so fucking afraid of risks, of taking chances, of doing something spontaneous?"

"That's not who I am. It's what works for me."

"But it didn't work in Hawaii. . . . So, what did you do?"

She folds her arms in front of her as if she can protect herself from my questions.

"Well?" I know I'm being a bitch, pushing her like this, forcing the words out of her mouth, but if I don't, she never will. Nothing will change for Lisa Holden-Davis. Nothing.

"I made do."

"What does that mean?"

"It means that I . . . worked around it," she says almost in resignation.

"What about Ross? Did he enjoy himself?"

"He said he did."

"So this is really about you. You were disappointed that things didn't work out *exactly* as expected, as *you* wanted. Ross messed up the plans because of his confession—"

"It . . . was more than that," she says suddenly, cutting me off, and I know we are about to get to the heart of it all.

I sit back and listen.

"It . . . was more than just the swimming thing, Asha. I think it bothered me because I didn't know. We'd never talked about it. But . . ."

"But?"

Lisa sighs and searches for some place in the room to rest her gaze other than on my face. "It was the whole . . . sex thing."

"Sex thing?" Now my interest is truly piqued. I lean forward as ugly images take shape in my head. "He didn't get strange with you or anything?"

"No. Nothing like that. It was just different."

"Better? Worse?"

"Neither. It was . . . it wasn't the same. I don't know how to explain it. I thought it . . . I was going to feel changed somehow. That Ross was going to love me differently."

A million questions run through my head. So many things I want to ask, but I know how sensitive Lisa can be, especially when it comes to sex. For the most part, she's always been pretty closed-mouthed about her sex life. And I can respect her privacy. But now I wish we had been more open in the past. Perhaps she would be more willing to share her feelings and anxieties now. And maybe I could help in some way.

"Did he hurt you?" I ask tentatively, praying that was not the case.

"Nothing like that. Ross was sweet, the way he always is. But I . . ." She looks at me, "I didn't . . . feel anything. I didn't feel . . . him."

"Physically?"

"No. In here." She points to her heart. "Inside."

"It could have been a lot of reasons, Lisa," I say, hoping that my tone can somehow soothe her fears even if the words can't. "Jet lag, being over-anxious, just the stress of the past few months."

"Maybe." She doesn't sound convinced.

"What do you think it is, hon?"

"I just thought it would be something spectacular. That being married, having said those words would have . . . made . . . it better somehow."

The look in her eyes is so innocent, so full of hope, as if she truly believes that my agreement with this illusion will somehow make it all better. Does she believe that because my life, my love life, appears so open and free that it contains some magic formula I can share with her?

I've never had what Lisa has, that thing inside her that takes people and life at face value, that wraps it all up in pretty paper and pretends that what's inside is just as wonderful as its covering. Life doesn't work that way. It plays dirty tricks on you, pulls the rug out from under you, makes you believe in the unbelievable, steals your innocence. That's real life. My life. I don't think Lisa really wants to see what's under my wrapping paper. It's easier for her to accept the image that she has of me, ignoring the qualities about me that are unpleasant and unacceptable to her. But maybe if I could be more like her, maybe, just maybe the background of my life would lose some of its hard edges.

"Everything will be fine, Lisa. I'm sure of it. This is an adjustment period for the both of you. Give it a chance."

"He said he wanted us to start making plans to move," she says as if she didn't hear me.

"I thought you two were planning to stay at your place until you were ready to buy a house."

"So did I."

"Ross just said it out of the blue—no reason?"

"Only that he'd been thinking about it."

"Lisa . . . call me dense, but I'm not understanding what's going on here. Didn't you two talk?"

"Of course. I suggested that we stay at my place. It's a much easier commute than coming all the way in from Long Island every day. I have plenty of room for the two of us—"

"But what did Ross say?"

She hesitates, looking as if all the conversations she and Ross ever had are replaying in her head and she's searching for the right one.

"He said . . . fine."

"Did he? Honestly?"

"He didn't say no," she concedes.

"It's not the same thing as saying yes."

She looks at me as if she wants to smack me or at the very least tell me to go to hell. Instead she puts down her glass and gets up. "I'd better get going. Ross is working late, but he should be getting home soon."

"Working on a Saturday?"

Lisa picks up her purse as I peel myself off the couch.

"He's been putting in some extra hours hoping to get the next promotion. He's taken on a freelance job, a really big one, for this young wealthy couple on the upper east side of Manhattan. That should help out some."

I walk her to the door. "Sounds great, Lisa. You'll have that house in no time."

She turns to me with that famous win-you-over smile of hers and states, "You'll help me decorate, right? I know just the kind of furniture I want. I've been collecting all sorts of fabric and wallpaper catalogs. I know Ross will love it."

"I'm sure he will."

"So, you'll help, right?"

"Of course. What are friends for?"

Lisa kisses my cheek and checks her watch. "Gotta run. I'll call you during the week."

"I'm only here until Thursday. Then I'm flying to England for a week, maybe more."

She shakes her head and smiles. "One of these days something or someone is going to keep you in one place. See you."

As I watch her through the window heading for her car, I know one thing for certain—change and evolution are who I am. The thought of being held in place by an idea, a situation, or a person frightens me, and that fear will always keep me running.

ELEVEN

Don't Explain

ROSS

I turn on the lamp on my drafting table. The evening shadows begin to cut across the open floor plan office. The models of works in progress around the office give the space a surreal feeling, like being tossed onto a miniature movie set.

I take another look at the design I've been working on all day. I just can't seem to get the damned thing right. Can't come up with anything that I'm pleased with. Hours of work for nothing.

A phone rings in one of the offices down the walkway, and I catch of glimpse of Marty—the senior partner—darting to catch it. Marty is only thirty and already a senior partner in one of the most successful architectural companies in the city. That's what I want, my own office one day. But that dream is definitely on hold, at least until we find a house, pay that off, and get settled. At this rate, it will be at least another ten years before I can see my reality.

Disgusted, I rip the page from my drawing pad and crumble it into a ball. The other designers always tease me about how I work—the old-fashioned way—with pen and paper. There's something satisfying about the process. It makes me feel as if I'm the one really creating, not a computer. To tell the truth, at heart, I'm an old-fashioned guy with old-fashioned values. I spin around on my swivel stool and aim for the stainless steel wastebasket on the opposite side of the floor. Two points. Big deal.

I study the specs for the guest house and start again. I don't want the entire day to be a bust.

"Still working, Ross? I thought you'd be long gone by now."

I glance up from my drafting table as Cliff pulls up a stool and sits.

"Yeah I'll be finished soon. Just wrapping up."

He picks up one of my pencils and twirls it between his long fingers. "You've been putting in a lot of hours since you've been back, man. Everything cool at home?"

"Yeah. Why?"

"Generally when a man works overtime *and* Saturdays, and he's married, it's usually because he's in no rush to get home."

I chuckle. "What about you? You're here on a Saturday," I say, stalling for time. Under other circumstances, I would sit back and run it all down for Cliff. I would tell him about what's been bugging me since before the wedding: having a place that's ours, not Lisa's; fulfilling *her* dreams at the expense of my own; being afraid of failing her and everyone. I want to tell him that I wake up scared shitless, feeling like I'm going to come up short. That no matter what I do, I'm never going to make Lisa's dreams come true. And most of all that somewhere along the way, I gave up a piece of myself—as a token of my love—and now I can't get it back. But I can't tell him any of it. Things are different now. I'm married to his sister, and that changes everything.

"But I don't have a new bride at home," he says. "Lynn and I are moving on ten years. You're still in the blush stage." He pauses and looks at me curiously. "At least you should be."

"Hey, just trying to stay on Morgan's radar, which means putting in the hours. I want that promotion. It will give me the kind of salary I need so we can seriously go house hunting. I want to take care of your sister the way I promised her, you, and your father." I chuckle, hoping to ease the mood. "I don't want to find you and your father on my doorstep. I plan to keep my word."

Cliff nods slowly, but looks at me like he's expecting more. "Don't work too hard," he finally says, pushing himself up. "New brides need attention. Take it from one who knows."

"I'll remember that."

He slaps me on the back, moves away, then stops and turns to me. "If you ever need to talk . . ."

Cliff's offer lingers in the air. I want to reach out and take it. I want to tell him to meet me in a half hour at the bar. I want to toss back a couple of beers and explain to him what's going on in my head, the growing uncertainty I have. "Thanks. I'll remember that, too," I say instead.

"See you Monday, Ross."

"Yeah. Tell Lynn and the kids I said hello."

"Will do."

The office is quiet now. The last of the Saturday worker bees are gone. This is usually a time when I can do my best work. I turn on my computer and pull up the specs and preliminary designs for a beach house I'm working on for one of our only individual clients. Personally, that's the kind of work I like best—working one-on-one to create a personal space for someone. Unfortunately, it's the cold, corporate jobs that keep these firms afloat.

Building things, creating beauty from scratch, was something that fascinated me since I was a kid. I love the entire process: concept, design, reality. Architecture is so much like life, like relationships— at least to me. It's a matter of assembling the pieces in the right places, making them fit, building and creating that image in your mind. You can shape life the way you want it. But the least little mistake—taking shortcuts, cutting corners, overlooking things you wouldn't overlook if you'd had the time—may not cost you during construction, but it will—somewhere down the road. Just like life.

It can happen with relationships, too. You get caught up. Caught up in the excitement, the thrill of something new and different: the concept, the design, the reality.

Is that what happened with me and Lisa? Did we get caught up in the process, leave out some of the necessary materials, take shortcuts? I don't want to see what we're trying to put together begin to crumble. I don't want that to happen to us.

Standing, I flex my back to work out the kinks and turn off my lamp. My work area slips into darkness, except for the glowing computer screen.

Hey, I don't even know why I'm thinking crazy like this. I love Lisa. That much I do know, that much I believe. It's been only a few weeks. Everything is still new, a bit uncertain. Our foundation needs to settle, just like a building does.

That's probably all it is.

What I need to do is get out of here. I shove my papers into my briefcase and turn off my computer. Go home to Lisa. Stop thinking crazy. I'll go home, have a good meal, a hot shower, and make love to my wife. Forget all this bullshit, stop worrying so much and just relax. Yeah, just relax.

The aroma of chicken baking in the oven greets me as I step through the door of Lisa's condo—*our* condo. I need to get that through my head. *Our* condo.

I can hear Lisa humming off-key in the kitchen, as usual. But the sound is comforting in a way. I can feel my body unwind, relax. My thoughts slow down to something manageable. That tight feeling in my chest begins to loosen.

Home. At least temporarily. I can put my issues aside and ride it out. Maybe I've been overreacting. It's just the whole idea of losing my independence that has me by the short hairs.

I toss my briefcase onto the chair in the foyer and put my leather jacket in the hall closet.

See, I grew up believing that it's a man's duty to take care of his wife—his family. It's his responsibility to put and keep a roof over his family's head. It's what I saw my father do. I may not have agreed with his methods or his choices, but I had to respect him as a man who took care of his family. It's what I saw myself doing one day, as well. Now that the day has come. . . .

Anyway, I suppose when it finally sank in that I would be living in Lisa's house, under her roof, "moving in with my wife," it undermined all that I believed in, what I saw of myself as a man. I'm the one who should be the provider, the king of the castle, not the prince.

I know that if I say these things to Lisa she'll say I'm overreacting, being too sensitive. Shit, maybe I am. But it's how I feel. And the sooner we can get "our" place, the better I'll feel.

"Ross? That you?"

Lisa appears in the doorway of the kitchen. Her face is flushed from the heat of the oven. Right now she looks about eighteen, bright-eyed and eager. The faded gray sweatsuit and ponytail only add to the effect.

Home.

"Hey, babe. Sorry I'm so late."

"Don't worry about it. I know where you are when you aren't with me," she says almost like an invitation. She kisses me, and all my doubts seem to evaporate. "I understand," she says, and steps back. "You look tired. Why don't you go take a shower and relax for a few minutes? Dinner should be ready in about a half hour."

"What did you do today?" I ask, not quite ready to do what I was told.

"Went to see Asha."

"Yeah. How is she?" I head toward the kitchen, pull open the fridge and grab a beer. I turn to glance at her and catch the flash of something in her eyes that I can't quite make out. "What?"

Lisa shakes her head. "Nothing." She moves toward the oven, checks the contents.

"So . . . how is she? You two have a good visit?" I take my first long swallow of the ice-cold brew.

"She's fine. Getting ready to go to England at the end of the week."

I down the last of the beer, think about another, then change my mind. "She sure gets around."

"I think it's her way of escaping a real life."

"A real life? What does that mean?"

Lisa shrugs, something I notice she does whenever she doesn't really want to answer you, or is figuring out what to say. She shuts the oven, then checks a pot on top of the stove.

"You know," she hedges, "running from one end of the world to the next. No permanent relationship. Sometimes I think it's her way of not having to deal with anything concrete. It keeps her from settling down, from committing to anything or anyone. I don't want her to wind up alone and lonely."

"Maybe she likes what she does, the travel, the excitement, her work."

"That's part of it, I'm sure."

"Believe me, Asha doesn't seem to be the kind of woman who would wind up alone and lonely." I chuckle at the thought.

"Why do you think that?"

"Just the kind of woman she is, that's all. Asha has a zest for life. Excitement. Maybe she's just not ready for anything more than that."

"Maybe."

I watch her as she crosses the room to stand in front of me. "Do I have a zest for life?"

The sudden question stuns me, challenges me. It isn't so much the question itself, but the intensity of it, the almost feral look in Lisa's eyes.

I chuckle, try to put off the question and regain my footing, because underneath the simple inquiry is really a request for validation, that I must somehow confirm for my wife something about herself that she is uncertain of, a quality that her dearest friend has and that she may not.

"You have everything that I want," I tell her. "That's what's most important."

Her expression slowly relaxes, and she smiles. "I want her to have what I have. Someone to look out for her, love her."

I rinse the beer can and toss it into the recycle bin. "I'm pretty sure Asha can look out for herself, babe." I kiss the tip of her nose, ready for my shower now. "Be back in a few."

Standing here in my birthday suit, I'm still trying to get used to finding my stuff. Lisa did most of the unpacking. She insisted that she'd find the perfect spot for everything, assuring me that there was more than enough room for my clothes. That's a matter of opinion.

Take my socks, for example. I like them tied in a knot and tossed, not arranged, in the same drawer with my shorts and T-shirts. Makes sense to me that all the things that go under your clothes go together in the same drawer. But no-o-o, that's not what Lisa figures. "There's a drawer for everything," she'd said when I complained about having to go through six drawers before I could find a lousy pair of socks.

"What's the point?" I'd asked her. "This isn't a department store."

"Things will stay organized. You can find your clothes much easier once you get used to it, sweetie."

She looked at me then as if she'd just revealed the secret of eternal youth, and that I should be as excited as she was.

"I put your suits, shirts, sports clothes, and shoes in the second closet. I know you'll love it."

I went to the closet, pulled open the door, and everything was lined up and color coordinated like the men's department in Saks Fifth Avenue.

I know she wanted to make me happy. I know she thought she was helping. But it pissed me off, and I'm not sure why.

I guess it's because little by little I feel like I'm losing bits and pieces of myself. I know it sounds silly, but that's how I feel, and I don't know how to explain it to Lisa without hurting her feelings. But things will change when I buy our house. I'm sure they will. It'll be ours. I won't feel like a tourist. Yeah, when we get our house, things will be different. I just have to give this some time.

Drying off, I gaze at my reflection in the foggy bathroom mirror. *"Do I have a zest for life?"* The question nags at me, demanding an answer—an answer I cannot give.

TWELVE

More than This

ASHA

In the past six months—pre- and postwedding—I've been to London, Madrid, Caracas, Ankara, Sydney, Stockholm, Copenhagen, and a sleepy little town outside of Birmingham, Alabama. I've taken some of the best photos of my career. I even met some interesting men along the way. At least interesting enough to hold my attention for my short stays.

Had there been more time, I think something could have come from the brief affair with Marcus.

Marcus Cain. We met in London near Westminster Abbey. Not my ideal for a backdrop, but it's what my clients wanted.

Marcus was seated on a bench across from the Abbey. At first I was able to catch only a profile of his face, as it was partially obscured by a five-foot canvas.

My crew had been out since sunrise, our goal was to capture the renowned Abbey in all variety of light and shadow. And Marcus had been there the entire time—painting the Abbey, or so I believed.

When I'm involved in my work, searching for the perfect angle, I can be obsessive, driven, blocking out everyone and everything except what I see through my lens. But that day was different. I found myself more often than not glancing in his direction as if I wanted to assure myself that he was still there.

I couldn't explain my fascination then and can't now. All I remember thinking at the time was, I hope he stays until I'm done.

There was something about his intensity that was almost pure; his single focus on the task at hand attracted me. I understood that much.

We broke for tea, as the Brits call it. I would have preferred to keep going, but with a predominantly British crew, there was no breaching the rituals of tradition.

I packed up my equipment, slung my bag over my shoulder, and headed toward him.

"Aren't you going to break for tea?" I asked by way of introduction. He was obviously not from England.

Slowly his eyes rose from the canvas and settled on my face. A strange sensation swept through me: a tingling warmth, a sudden surge of electric energy. I don't know what to call it, but it was there.

He put down his brush and rubbed his fingers along the length of his paint-splattered thighs. The move was simple, ordinary but at the same time deceptively sensual, and I wondered if he knew that, wondered if it was something he'd fine-tuned to an art.

"Not really my thing," he said with an accent that was clearly urban American.

I smiled, the ring of a familiar accent like music to my ears. "Asha Woods," I announced.

"Asha. I knew a woman named Asha once." He stuck out his hand. "Marcus Cain."

We shook hands, quickly sizing each other up during the brief exchange.

"What's with all the photos?" he asked, lifting his chin in the direction of the Abbey.

"I'm working on a tourism catalog for a new design company, a sort of 'what to wear, where' book."

He laughed. I liked the sound.

"So you're in charge?"

"You could say that."

"Hmmm." He nodded. "Travel much in your line of work?"

"More often than not, but I love it," I said, thinking of the emptiness of the place I called home, the sameness of it. "Travel has its merits."

"Like what?"

"All my expenses are paid. I get to see the world, try exotic foods, meet interesting people."

"Sounds like a good deal."

"Like I said, it has its merits. What about you? Are you a full-time painter?"

He laughed again, a good old-fashioned belly laugh. "I only wish," he said, slowly sobering.

"Can I see what you've done?"

His gaze held mine for a moment as the corner of his wide mouth curved upward. "I think I should warn you. I paint things the way I see them."

"Oh, abstract," I said, coming around to face the canvas.

For an instant, I was stunned, speechless. He was right, he did paint things the way he saw them, and what he saw was a naked version of me—supine on the Abbey steps, one leg bent at the knee, smoking a cigarette.

Once the initial shock wore off, I have to admit I was utterly flattered, especially with the enhancements of my attributes. Beauty as viewed through a fun-house mirror.

I began to laugh, and he joined me. "Totally irreverent," I sputtered. "I love it. It's just the type of shot I would try to capture with my camera."

It's hanging now over the fireplace in my living room. A surefire conversation piece during dinner parties. Everyone always wants to know how I had the guts to pose for it. I never answer, just laugh. I let them think what they want. They will, anyway.

I asked Marcus one night when we were lying in bed together what made him think to paint me that way. And he said, "The moment I saw you, I felt a recklessness, a desire to shock, disturb. I felt a sense of a fierce yearning within you to have someone look at you, beyond the surface. That longing was in your body language, the glint in your eyes, the pitch of your voice."

Lying here now, stretched out on my couch, I know how right Marcus was. He came as close as anyone to turning the key to unlock my secrets. Secrets, dreams, and fears that I don't even whisper. It's probably why I left him, left him without a note, without a good-bye.

The fear that keeps me running never diminishes. It took me away from Marcus, away from Vincent, away from all the others. Sometimes in the hours just before dawn, that quiet time when nature is at total peace, shadows and light are in perfect unity, I cry—when no one can hear or see me. I become that discordant background, my existence incongruous with the beauty that surrounds me. I am the howl that can be heard as the sun crests the horizon. I am the pain cry that can never be soothed. Vivid, sharp, and fierce, the aloneness of my soul echoing across the rooftops and mountainsides, skimming the oceans and the depths of the valleys.

My secret.

But upon awakening, the shadows recede. Asha Woods emerges, vibrant, flippant, energized, driven. I will never submit to my demons.

Odd, but mostly I can never recall why the tears come, why the cries sear the night, why the aloneness engulfs me. All I know is that I don't want to hear the sound, don't want to feel the terror. So I seek comfort, a balm for my soul, in my work, in the arms of a man, my legs locked around his muscled back, riding away the loneliness. There my cries are muffled by passion, my solitude circumscribed by another's need for me. And for a time I don't feel like a stark black-and-white image with nothingness as my background.

The picture hanging over my fireplace is so me, apparently brazen, attention seeking, yet its backdrop is the high seat of purity, godliness, sanctity, holiness. How true to life.

The last time I saw Marcus was at the airport in Rome. I was returning home from a shoot, dead tired and travel weary. I barely recognized my name when he called me as I was on line to board.

I turned toward the familiar voice, both anticipating and dreading the first moment. A million questions floated in his eyes, hovered on the curve of his mouth. I wanted to explain. But I would have needed a lifetime.

Marcus smiled a sad but accepting smile that I returned. I handed the blue-and-white clad woman my ticket; when I looked again, he was gone.

I often wonder if that one moment when he was there and then not, if it was Marcus's way of hinting at what he'd felt like that morning he'd found me gone, with nothing but an empty space on the pillow and a damp spot on the sheet to prove that I had ever been there.

If so, it worked, at least a little.

I never told anyone about Marcus. Not even Lisa. I mean she knows how we met, but not the details, not the reasons. She thinks she does. She thinks she knows all about me, better than I know myself. I find that impossible to believe. There are too many mornings that I stare into my bathroom mirror and wonder who is staring back at me.

Each day I try to make sense of it all, examine the pieces of my life, the roads I've chosen. One of these days, I'll figure it all out.

The half-filled bottle of wine sits on the center of the table—calling me, asking me to reach for it, take another taste and relax. "It's Saturday night," the wine seems to be saying. "You don't want to work tonight. Relax."

Just as temptation has secured a firm hold on me, the phone rings. I swear, if I didn't know better, I'd bet money that the bottle cussed me.

"Hello? Hi, Mom."

"Haven't heard from you since you've been back," she says, accusation rippling through her voice.

"I've been a little busy since then. I'm sorry. I should have called."

My mother has the singular ability to make me feel so guilty. Guilty about waking up in the morning, guilty about any piece of happiness I can snatch, guilty about being me.

"Did you enjoy yourself?"

"It wasn't a pleasure trip, Mom. It was work."

"You always seem to find time to squeeze in some sort of entertainment."

If I shut my eyes, maybe when I open them this conversation and my mother will be gone.

"Are you going to stop by this weekend?"

"I really don't know, Mom. I have a ton of work to do."

"I'd fix dinner. . . ."

My stomach shifts, and I feel my heart knock hard in my chest. It's not so much what she says, but the tone, the inflection, the implication. My mother is a master of manipulation, has been for as long as I can remember. I always wondered, if she were so good at what she does, then why did my father leave? Why couldn't she have found the string to pull him back, tie him fast to her hip? Perhaps she wasn't as good at it then as she is now. After all, practice makes perfect.

"Sure. What time?" I finally concede, as I'm sure she knew I would.

"I thought a Sunday brunch would be nice. About eleven."

"Great. I'll see you then."

"How's Lisa, by the way? Settling into married life?"

"She's fine."

"Hmm. I always liked her." She sighs, the weight of the world apparently on her shoulders. "I hope you find somebody one of these days and settle down. You can't keep—"

"Mom, there's someone at my door. Gotta go. I'll see you Sunday." I quickly hang up before she can get a full head of steam going about the quality of my life.

It may sound as if I don't love my mother. That I dislike her as a person, a human being. It's not true. Not really. My mother gave me life, put a roof over my head, provided me with an education. She fulfilled all her motherly duties. But I never felt that she loved me beyond the fact that I was her flesh and blood, or for who I am, or for all the things I could become. Loved me for my mind, my sense of humor, my smile, the joy that I might possibly bring to another or to the world.

Those things, those love things, I never received from my mother, my first source of validation in this life. So I sought it elsewhere, continue to search for it, an endless, relentless search of self.

Many nights I lie awake and try to assemble the pieces that make me Asha. Try to discover when the pieces no longer fit, but were instead forced into place.

The closest I can determine was the winter night, a week before Christmas that my father left us. I was ten.

He and my mother had been arguing for days. Nothing unusual by ordinary circumstances. They always argued. But that time felt different. I'd never heard my mother cry before. But during the week, at night, when my father would storm out of the house, I could hear my mother's sobs through the thin walls of our apartment.

I remember standing outside of her bedroom door, wanting to go in and ask her what was wrong. Her sobs, strong and heartfelt, sounded as if they were being torn from the fabric of her soul.

The ringing phone stopped me. I could make out only every other word. But what I did hear stopped my young heart.

". . . He says he's leaving. . . . He's in love with her . . . his assistant at the office. . . . I can't believe it. . . . I've been a good wife . . . tried to make a good home. . . . The bastard . . . I hope the both of them rot in hell for what they've done. . . . I don't know what I'm going to tell Asha. . . . She adores her father. . . ."

I tried to put it together, even as my stomach turned over like it was being stirred with a hot spoon. My daddy was leaving. He was in love with that lady in his office. He was leaving us. Leaving me. Who would kiss me good night, check my homework, ask me, "How's my big girl today?"

I remember sliding down the off-white wall as if my legs were no longer able to hold my weight. I drew my knees up to my chest and cried. I guess I must have cried myself to sleep right there on the floor, because the next thing I remember was my mother's voice telling me to get up and go to bed.

"Where's Daddy? When's Daddy coming home?"

"Go to bed, Asha," my mother said in a voice so worn and weary that I barely recognized it as my mother's. "We'll talk in the morning."

I clung to her waist, needing her to reassure me, to comfort me. She peeled my thin arms from around her and led me down the hall to my room. "Go to sleep," she said in that strange voice, turned, and walked away.

Christmas never came that year.

The next time I saw my father was about a month later. In the days preceding his return, I hadn't been able to sleep or eat without throwing up. Every afternoon following school, I would sit at the window and will his sky blue Buick 225 to turn the corner and park in front of the house—like before.

One day he did, and I knew everything would finally be like it was before. I longed for the arguments, the shouting, the sound of the squeaking bed and my mother crying out my father's name in unbridled passion. Anything was better than what it had been without them. The silence. The absence of his male presence. The void.

But he didn't come to stay.

I ran to him as soon as he stepped through the door.

"Daddy! I knew you would come back. I knew it. Mommy's sorry she made you mad."

He lifted me up in his arms, and a warm sense of peace washed through me. For the first time in weeks, my heart slowed to normal and the twirling in my stomach ceased.

I inhaled his familiar scent—Old Spice—pressed my head against his shoulder, and felt the tickle of his beard brush against my cheek.

"Listen, princess," he said, carrying me into the living room. He set me down on the couch. "Daddy has to go away."

My body stiffened.

"Things aren't working out between me and your mother, and it's best that I leave."

"Nooooo!"

"It'll be all right, princess. You're gonna stay here with your mother, and I can visit you."

I looked up at him, tried to see the truth in his eyes, to see if the things my mother said about him could be found on his lips, in the way he held me, the deep timbre of his voice.

"You love that lady," I said, suddenly emboldened by my pain, making me no longer afraid of what was true. "You gonna leave us and live with her," I accused, sounding like my mother even to my own ears.

"That's not for you to concern yourself with, Asha. This is between me and your mother."

"I hate you! I hate you!" I jumped off the couch and ran to my room, slamming the door like I'd heard and seen them do.

I never saw him again after that. He didn't keep his promise to come and see me. He disappeared into the streets, into the world. All I knew was what I'd overhear my mother say: "Men are bastards at heart, they get you to love them, and then they leave you with a broken heart and a kid." She swore she'd never love again.

And she didn't—not even me.

Shortly after that, we moved. That's when I met Lisa and watched as the series of "uncles" passed through my and my mother's lives. Faceless men who stayed only for the night and vanished with the sunrise. Some would last longer than others. In each of them, I tried to find the comfort and security that I'd once had with my father. It never happened. They never stayed. Nothing and nobody are permanent. It was a lesson I learned at an early age.

I wish I could envy women like Lisa, but I can't. My mother wishes I were more like my best friend, had the life that Lisa has attained. In truth, she wishes it for herself. In one breath she says I should settle down, and in the next breath tells me how unfaithful, how shallow, how selfish men can be, and not to tie myself to any of them, not to wind up like she has. At first, that contradiction in her opinion about men confused me, but it doesn't any longer.

I have no desire to settle down, to love, to live out forever in some fantasy born of *Ozzie & Harriet*, or *The Cosby Show*. I've seen real life up close and personal, and I don't want any part of it.

I really don't.

My life is fine just the way it is—an image of my own making. And as long as that image is what people see and believe, I will never wind up like Denise Woods—or even Lisa Holden-Davis.

I must believe that.

THIRTEEN

The More Things Change

LISA

With dinner finished and Ross in a mellow mood, I figure it's as good a time as any to broach the subject of our financial future. "Ross, I was going over our savings today and working out the bills and—"

"Why? I just went over them two weeks ago. Did you think that something was going to change, or that I didn't know what I was doing?"

"That's not it at all, Ross. I was only trying to figure things out. See where we are, that's all."

"Where we are is about a half inch from where we were when we started six months ago."

I watch him lower his head, his body relax, almost as if he'd been confronting an enemy. I know how tired he is. It must be the stress of the long hours he's been putting in at the office. I hardly see him anymore. But maybe it's something else. Something he's not saying.

"Ross . . . honey . . . What is it? I can't believe you're upset about me going over *our* finances."

Slowly his lids raise and his gaze settles on my face. Suddenly, he looks so unfamiliar, like a stranger. The notion startles me.

"Just tired," he mumbles. "Sorry." He reaches for his glass of iced tea and takes a long swallow before speaking again. "It's just that I want to be the one to handle things. You know. I want to take care of you, of us. The way it's supposed to be."

"But we're in this together. We want the same things, don't we? My money is part of this process, too, Ross. I contribute."

"Like I said, just tired. Sorry for taking it out on you." He pushes up from the dining room table. "I'm going to watch some television and relax," he says before kissing the top of my head like an afterthought and walking away.

I watch him leave the room, and I want to snatch him back, make him talk to me, really talk.

It's been only six months since we said "I do." But it feels like an eternity ago. I can't help but wonder what could have gone so wrong so soon. What happened to the two people we once were? I want them back. I want Ross back.

I want the man I could make smile by just walking into a room. I want to hear his laughter again. I want to feel his passion for me rise late at night and into the morning. I want the light back in his eyes.

When I reach the bedroom door, my intention is to seduce my husband, rekindle the flames by any means necessary. What I find is Ross, stretched out on the bed, fast asleep, the remote flat across his chest.

Something inside me softens, pushes away the urge to shake my husband back into the man he was before our wedding day.

I cross the room and ease down on the bed beside him, careful not to disturb his sleep. He looks so innocent, so vulnerable, so exhausted. Ross has done no more than lie down. He's still fully clothed, right down to his red power tie.

Gingerly I remove his shoes, then unfasten his belt buckle, the buttons of his shirt. As his smooth cocoa brown skin becomes visible beneath my fingertips, I remember the first time I touched his bare flesh.

We'd been dating for almost three months—well, two months and two days, to be exact. We'd gone to see a late spring Wynton Marsalis concert at Lincoln Center. It was mid-May. The evening was warm. The stars lit up the sky like a blanket of diamonds. It was perfect.

From the day Ross and I officially became a couple, I made certain that he knew I cared, that I took our relationship seriously. Something my dad always stressed to me was that as much as a man may balk, he appreciated a woman who took care of things, took care of him. So, I devoted myself to *us*.

Each day I would make sure that I called Ross, even if it was only to say hello or ask how his day was going. I knew how hard he worked, how devoted he was to his craft and the financial and parental responsibility he felt for his sister, Karen. Often his schedule was erratic, so I remained flexible, accessible to him. I let him know every chance I got that I was committed to building our relationship, and to him. Buying the tickets to the concert was my way of showing him that I thought of him, remembered how much he liked Wynton and that I understood how hard he worked.

I won't lie. There were more times than I can count when I was disappointed. When his work or a family commitment would cause him to cancel dates at the last minute, or back out of dinner because he was too tired.

I remember one evening in particular. We'd been talking about having a special night, just the two of us, for about a week. I wanted it to be private, not in a fancy restaurant, where he generally took me. But an intimate, home-cooked meal—a little wine, nice music—just us. Ross was all for it, and I went out of my way to make sure that it would be special.

I'd had a pretty bad day at the job. One of my white students and I had really gotten into it when I gave him a failing grade on a paper he'd handed in. The student was a tall, rangy, well-dressed son of privilege who was used to getting his way, and any resistance to his arrogant behavior was met with snide remarks and angry looks. His paper on the populist themes of Steinbeck's *Grapes of Wrath* was lousy, poorly written, with no depth or texture, no imagination. He claimed that my harsh appraisal of his sloppy homework was a case of reverse racism. Because I was a black professor and he was a minority white male, he felt that I'd singled him out, to make a political, feminist statement. What a crock. In any event, he actually had the nerve to report me to my dean, attempting to turn the tables on me with a host of discrimination claims.

The better part of an hour was consumed by my defense of my abilities as a capable professor, a woman of intellect, while fending off his allegations of my bigotry.

"Dean Hargrove, I was hired in this position because of my background, my experience, and my credentials. The guidelines established in my class are for everyone, not a selected few. I've never shown favoritism among my students."

"Perhaps we should do a review of your class records and interview some of the students to see how they feel about how you handle the class," the dean said, one eyebrow arched. He flipped through my employee folder and then looked across at me. "Your evaluation is coming up in about two months, Ms. Holden, isn't it?"

His meaning was painfully clear. But what was most disheartening was hearing my dean tell me what a good family that student came from, unlike many of my other students who were there because of laws outside the school's purview—in other words, my black students—he was there paying full tuition. And that perhaps my expectations were too harsh and that *I* should reevaluate my course. In other words, pass him or I fail.

I'd never been so humiliated in my life as when I turned to leave and saw the smug smile on my student's face. In his mind, he'd won the first battle in the war.

What I wanted to do was go back to my office, pack my belongings, and get out, find some other means of employment—perhaps at another university, where integrity meant more than dollars and cents. But who was I fooling? At least I knew who and what the enemy was. There's nothing more unsettling than the unknown, which is what I would be walking into if I went elsewhere.

The balance of the day felt like one defeat after another, from a cold lunch that was supposed to be hot at a local restaurant to the parking ticket I received at its end. All I could think about as I made the trip home was seeing Ross. Having a chance to recover my balance, share my frustration with him, be held, and let him take my blues away.

I'd already picked up everything I would need for dinner earlier in the week. I'd planned a menu of shrimp pasta with Spanish rice, a mixed green salad, and chilled wine. There was raspberry sorbet for dessert and *The Best of John Coltrane* in the CD player for background music.

I'd taken a shower, determined to wash away the effects of my miserable day and was right in the middle of setting the table when the phone rang. It was Ross.

"Lisa, I'm sorry, but I'm not going to be able to make it tonight. I have a stack of work that must be ready by tomorrow morning. I know we've been planning tonight for the past week. You don't know how bad I feel about this. But I swear I'll make it up to you."

I couldn't even speak. The words knocked me into the nearest chair, and I simply sat there, staring at the flames on the tips of the two white tapers.

"Lisa . . . are you there?"

"Yes. I'm here."

"I'm sorry, babe. Really I am. I was so involved in what I was doing I didn't even check the clock until a few minutes ago, or you know I would have called you earlier."

"I know."

"I'm sorry."

"Don't worry about it, Ross. I was a little tired, anyway. I'll just turn in early."

"Are you sure? I mean, I can stop by whenever I get out of here—"

"No. Really. It's okay. Forget it. We can do this another time. Things happen."

I could hear his sigh of relief on the other end while the tears I'd held at bay for hours slowly rolled down my cheeks. "I'll call you later, okay?" he said.

"Sure."

"Thanks for understanding, babe."

"Hmm, umm."

In a daze, I hung up the phone, pulled myself up from my seat, got my purse and my car keys, and walked out. On the ride across town to Park Slope, I vacillated between fury and emotional exhaustion. By the time I pulled up in front of Asha's apartment, I knew that if she wasn't home, or if she had company and couldn't talk, I would probably lose it right there on her stone steps.

"Hey, Lisa. What are you doing here? Please don't tell me I forgot an appointment or something," she said when she pulled the door open and saw me standing there. "Are you all right?" She pulled the belt of her short, white satin robe around her waist. "Your eyes are all red and swollen." She looked past me, then up and down the quiet tree-lined block as if the answer to her questions rested somewhere beyond her front door.

"Can I come in?"

"Of course, I'm sorry. I'm standing here babbling. I was doing my toenails. Come on up."

I followed her up the one flight of stairs to her second-floor apartment. Actually, she had two floors, the second and the top, which had been converted into a duplex several years earlier. Somehow, she'd talked the owner down from $1,250 per month to a lower $1,000 rent. To this day, I have no idea what she did or said, and I don't want to know. I'd hate to find out that it was anything more than fair, unrelenting negotiating.

"Sit, sit," Asha ordered as soon as we were inside. "Relax. You look a little beat."

"Thanks. I feel better already." Asha was always good for a slap in the face with a bit of cold reality, whether you wanted or needed it.

"Well, maybe if you tell me what the hell is wrong, I can gauge my responses accordingly."

"I will if you just give me a minute." I sat in the love seat, but what I wanted to do was curl up in it.

"Fine. I'll shut up."

Asha cat-walked over to the paisley-printed chaise longue and stretched out, her mini-robe hiking up to her hips. Idly, she began filing her nails and humming some off-beat tune as if I wasn't there.

"Can you at least offer me something to drink?" I snapped.

Slowly she turned her head in my direction. "Lisa, how many times have you been here? More than we can both count. You know your way around in my kitchen better than I do, and if you want something stronger, help yourself at the bar."

I swore I heard her suck her teeth.

"Fine." I got up and headed to the bar. "Vodka and cranberry juice?" I asked, knowing that was our favorite we-need-to-talk drink, an old tradition we'd started in our college days.

"Sure. And if it's really bad, make yours a double."

I laughed, the first time I'd laughed since my lousy day started. I laughed until I cried, until the sobs consumed me, until they shook my body, until Asha took the drinks, led me to the couch, and sat me down.

"Drink it. All of it," she said. "And wipe your face." She pulled a tissue from her robe pocket and handed it to me. "It's clean."

I sniffed and smiled weakly through my tears.

"Just relax for a minute, Lisa. Catch your breath."

I nodded and sipped my drink until it was gone.

"Want another one?"

"No. Thanks. That one was enough." My head was swimming. "What did you put in there?"

"Just what the doctor ordered. Now . . . what happened?"

Bit by bit I unfolded my day right up until the final straw with Ross.

"Damn," was all she muttered.

"I don't know what to do, Asha."

"About what part? The job? If it were me, all that would remain was my smoke trail. You have plenty of talent. Any college would be happy to snatch you up. Hell, you can write. You're a writing teacher, for heaven's sake. Take some time off and write a book or something. Go to work for yourself. Fuck them." She rolled her eyes. "That's exactly why I will never work for someone else again. I'm not going to allow myself to be at the mercy of someone else's whim, their issues. Heck no. I can't have my life dictated to by someone else." She was shaking her head the whole time she talked as if to reaffirm each word. "As for the lunch . . . no tip. The ticket . . . suck it up and pay it. You were in the wrong. Sorry. Ross . . . Well . . ."

"Well, what?"

Asha got up and went back to the bar. She refilled her drink . . . with more cranberry juice than vodka, I'd noticed.

"Well . . . what about Ross?"

She turned toward me, stared deep into my eyes for a long moment, and then looked away. "I don't think you really want to hear what I have to say, Lisa. Not really."

"If I didn't want to know, I wouldn't ask you. Tell me. Tell me what you think I should do."

She sat down, studied her red toenails for a minute, then eyed me. "I think you need to get out while you can."

I sprang up from my seat. "Get out! Why, because of one broken date?"

"One?" she asked in that supercilious tone that said, "You know I know better."

I turned away. "It doesn't happen that often. Ross works hard. It's not as if he breaks a date with me to run around with some other woman. He takes his work seriously. He's responsible."

"Ross is all that, and a token will get you on the subway, but the fact remains that Ross has tunnel vision. He's not in the same place in this relationship that you are, and you don't even see it."

"What's that supposed to mean?"

"It means that yes, he cares about you. But not enough to stop him from what he needs to do first. As hard as this may be for you to accept, Lisa, you haven't reached the level where you're number one in his life yet, and maybe you never will."

"You don't know what you're talking about. You—"

"Right. I don't know what I'm talking about, and that's why you came to me to ask me what to do. If we're going to be anything with each other, let's be honest. Okay? You make it too easy for Ross, Lisa. He screws up your day, and you send him roses."

"I do not."

"You know what I mean. "Don't let him take you for granted. Don't let him think that he can break a date and break your heart and it's going to be okay with a phone call and a movie. He has to want what you want, and you have to want what he wants. If you're not on an even playing field, it'll never work. It's as simple as that."

"It's not as simple as that. I care about Ross. I really do. I don't want to blow this, Asha. Not again."

"I understand that. But relationships can't be scorecards with win and loss columns. So what if past relationships didn't work out. You move on, and hopefully learn from the mistakes."

"But this is different. I know it is. It feels right to me. I want it to work."

"I want it to work for you, for all the right reasons, and not at the risk of yourself. No one is worth that. Not even Ross Davis."

"I love him, Asha," I said softly, needing her to understand, to validate it somehow.

"Not even that thing called love. Love is what love does."

Sitting here now, watching my husband sleep, Asha's words ring in my head like a church bell. Loud and clear. How right is she, if at all? But Asha is always skeptical about everything, especially when it comes to men and women. She inherently believes that it is all transient, something that is here and then gone. I don't. I can't. I just can't. If I did, all the beliefs that I've built my life and convictions upon would crumble.

Sure, we've had some ups and downs and false starts. All couples do. It's part of the growing pains, as my mother would say. But that doesn't mean you should walk away when things get tough, or when you get bored. And I knew from the first time Ross and I made love that I could never feel that way, be that way again, with another man.

Actually, it was the night of the concert. There was something about the whole evening—the sky, the music, the very air we breathed, the tender way that Ross treated me—that told me the night was special. That it was going to be "the night."

"You're really amazing," he'd said as we walked through Lincoln Center to the parking lot to pick up his car.

The rushing fountain, the stars, the soft breeze, and the glittering people all made it feel like magic. I know he felt it, too.

"How did you manage to get tickets? I heard they were sold out for weeks." Ross slipped his arm around my waist and pulled me close.

"Working at the university has its perks," I said. "We're always getting tickets to one thing or the other, or someone has extra ones."

"Hmm. Maybe I need to change my line of work," he said chuckling. "Well, however you did it, I really appreciate it. The show was great, babe."

"I'm glad that you enjoyed it. I know how much you like jazz and—"

Suddenly he stopped walking and turned me toward him. He looked at me with such intensity that my heart started racing.

"I've never known anyone like you, Lisa. Most women would have waited for me to get tickets, to make plans." He smiled a crooked smile. "Not you."

"It's nothing. I like doing things for you, for us," I added, relieved that it wasn't something else.

"Yeah, you do." He kissed me long and slow, right there in the middle of Lincoln Center Plaza. "Come on, let me get you home."

When we reached my condo, he walked me to my door, something he always did. "Thanks again for a great evening, Lisa."

"I enjoyed it, too."

We stood there for a few minutes, awkward almost.

"Are you in a hurry? I could fix us some coffee if you like."

He shrugged slightly. "Sounds good. I don't have any early plans for tomorrow."

Coffee turned into a glass of wine, to conversation about our evening, to talk about us. The progression was steady, inevitable. We moved from my living room couch to my bedroom.

Ross took his time with me, explored my body, let me explore his. The instant I felt him enter me, I knew something magical had happened. My soul seemed to open up and let him in. We connected, more than physically. He felt it, too. I know he did. And that first morning we awoke together, I knew that forever was in our future.

Everyone commented on how happy we seemed, how perfect we were for each other. And I believed it. With Ross, I could forget the past, the hurts and miscues. He gave my day a purpose, gave me a reason to smile.

Ross had known my family for a few years on different levels through his friendship with my brother, Cliff. But the dynamics changed when I reintroduced him as the man I loved.

". . . So you and little sis are really an item," Sandra commented dryly. My sister tapped a cigarette from her pack and lit it.

"I really wish you wouldn't smoke in here, Sandra," my father said.

"Oh, Dad. I've been smoking for years, and you've been saying the same thing for years."

"It's obvious you don't pay any attention to what I say. If you did, you wouldn't be in the fix you're in now. No husband and two kids to support."

Sandra sprang up from her seat. "At least I had sense enough to get out while I could. Forever isn't for everybody, Dad. We all can't be picture-perfect like you and Mom. You both have Lisa and Tina's heads so full of that fairy-tale bullshit they'll never know what hit them when it does."

"Sandra! You won't talk to your father that way," my mother said, her face flushed with uncharacteristic anger.

My sister turned hard, cold eyes on my mother, then suddenly began laughing hysterically. "Mom," she said over her laughter, "do you know that this is the first time in thirty-eight years that I've ever heard you raise your voice, say something like you actually meant it?" She grinned and blew a plume of smoke into the air. "Maybe if you had stood up, spoken up years ago, we wouldn't be having this asinine conversation now."

Sandra then proceeded to douse her cigarette in her glass of lemonade, snatched up her purse, and walked out.

For several moments, the room was locked in an embarrassed silence. I wanted to fall into a hole. I knew Ross must think awful things about us, and I was furious with my sister for causing a scene when she knew how important the day was to me.

My father was the first to make a move. He walked quietly into the kitchen. I looked around at the closed faces.

"She didn't mean it, Mom," I offered. "You know how Sandra can get sometimes. She talks without thinking." I patted my mother's shoulder. "I'll talk to her."

My mother's lips pinched; then she raised her chin and turned to Ross as she held my hand. "Can I get you anything, Ross?" she asked as if the ugliness of the past few minutes had never occurred. That was my mom, always able to make lemonade. She had a way of dismissing traumas, upsets, disagreements, and the like with a tilt of her head, the lilt of her voice, or a meal that could soothe your troubles away. She never made a scene, never raised her voice. Always the lady.

"No thanks, Mrs. Holden. I'm fine," Ross said.

"I'll be right back," I whispered to him, and walked to the kitchen.

My father's back was facing me when I entered.

"Are you okay, Dad?"

"Yes, I'm fine. Never could understand why she always needs to fight me, challenge me on every level. Told her when she met Peter not to marry him. He wasn't the marrying kind. He was weak, let her run all over him. Did she listen? No."

Slowly he turned around, and for a moment he no longer appeared the six-foot-plus burly maintenance worker with the voice that could raise the roof. He was a man well past middle-age who looked frayed at the edges.

"She didn't mean it."

"Of course she did. Sandra is an unhappy woman. She wants everyone else to be as unhappy and miserable as she is. Simple as that."

"Dad, Sandra's been through a great deal. She hasn't been the same since the divorce. She has a lot on her."

"Like you don't! You think I don't know how broken up you were after Steven . . . and Carl? Of course I do. It wasn't easy for you. It's never easy for a woman to lose the man she loves. But it didn't turn you ugly. That's why I know you and Ross are going to be fine. Ross is solid, honest. A hardworking young man. A man of values." He looked off for a moment. "Reminds me of myself in a lot of ways. Guess that's why I like him so much. You made a good choice, baby."

A tender smile moved across his wide mouth. "You always were my special one," he said, the words I'd heard all my life in the quiet of my bedroom, in the warm cocoon of the kitchen, on the porch on a hot summer night. "Never gave me or your mother a bit of trouble. Could always depend on you to do the right thing, make the right decisions. We always expected the best from you, and you've never let us down, never disappointed us."

He reached for me, and I stepped into his embrace.

"I know I disappointed you with . . . Carl . . . and Steven. But I won't this time. Not with Ross."

"I know you won't, sweetheart. He's just what you need. I see good things for you and Ross. You do right by him, like your mother's done by me."

"I will, Daddy. I promise."

"You go on back out there. I'll be out in a minute."

I kissed his cheek and did as he asked. Passing through the living room and seeing that some semblance of normalcy had returned, I went in search of my sister. I found her on the porch, sitting on the bench swing, nursing a new cigarette and a bottle of beer.

"Don't start, okay, Lisa. I don't want to hear it," she began before I could open my mouth. "It's always the same bullshit with me and Dad. Always has been. Don't expect it to change now."

"Why can't you two be in the same room without fighting? Just apologize."

"Lisa, Lisa. Always the peacemaker. Always trying to smooth things over. You and your mother are one of a kind. Neither one of you ever deal with the real issues or say what's really on your minds. I do, and Dad can't stand it because he can't control it. Did he send you out here, or did Mom?

"Neither one of them did."

"Mmm." She gazed up at me from beneath her lashes. "Not directly. Not directly."

"What's that supposed to mean? I couldn't have come out here on my own? Did it occur to you that you embarrassed me in front of Ross?"

She put down her bottle of beer and stared at me as if she'd never seen me before.

"Embarrass you? Ross is no baby. He's been around, and he's been around our family before. You were the missing link."

"So does that excuse your behavior?"

"I'm not one of your students, Lisa," she said from between her teeth. "My behavior does not have to meet with your approval."

She retrieved her beer and took a long swallow. "Look, I'm sorry. All right? I didn't mean to screw up your day."

"Forget it," I mumbled.

Sandra released a sigh. "I know everyone thinks I'm angry and bitter since Peter and I divorced. Maybe I am. Maybe I'll get over it. Maybe I won't."

She looked up at me. A combination of sadness and wisdom hovered in her eyes. "You may not want to hear any advice from someone who apparently couldn't hold her own marriage together." She chuckled sadly. "But I let things happen, Lisa. I saw things and didn't say a word. I suppressed my happiness, my needs for Peter's. And I lost. Lost everything."

She reached for my hand and held it, the first sisterly gesture that had passed between us in years. "Don't take marriage and life sitting down."

Suddenly she stood. "I gotta go. Tell everyone good-bye for me. Not that they'd care one way or the other." She stepped off the porch, got in her car, and drove away.

Ross's deep breathing penetrates my thoughts, pushes the images aside. Funny that I should think about that day now. But what's so wrong about wanting tranquillity, harmony? Regardless of whatever problems my mother and father had or have, they never put it on display. The years of living at home I watched how my mother dealt with my father's moods, how she dealt with her children. She didn't make a fuss. She didn't try to do battle for every bit of ground, but she was still able to get the things she wanted simply by allowing my father to feel that it was his idea. There is a silent strength about my mother that many might take as weakness. Sandra certainly does, and believes that I am cast in my mother's image. Perhaps I am. I hope I am.

One thing I do know, I don't want to wind up like Sandra, full of bitter opinions, controlled by resentment, and alone. But now my father's advice and my sister's counsel war in my head. Between a rock and a hard place, I must find a middle ground.

Looking at Ross, I know how much I want the magic to return, the oneness of it. But it seems as if we're moving in opposite directions, pulling for the same things, but in different ways and against each other.

Resigned, at least for tonight, I'll let him sleep, leave his flesh untouched, my heart unsettled, soul unfilled.

FOURTEEN

Like a Circle in a Spiral

ROSS

Damn, I'm glad the day is finally over. Getting into my car I hope the drive home will ease my mind. All day at work I thought about last night. I thought about how I felt when Lisa told me what she'd done. I know this may sound stupid, or petty, but I feel emasculated. I feel useless, less than the man I know myself to be.

All my adult life, I've prided myself on my sense of values and responsibility, the knowledge that I could be depended upon. I've always looked after the women in my life. Maybe too much and too hard. But that's the way I am. I want to give all of me. And that's why it's so difficult, even painful to realize that the core of who you are, isn't needed. This isn't the first time I've felt stripped, exposed, but this time is the worst. This time it isn't a girlfriend, a maybe, as Michelle had been. This is my wife.

Michelle. Damn. Where did that come from? I've fought not to think of her. But she still slips in from time to time. Ten years later, and the memories are still raw.

I suppose you could say that Michelle was my first love, or at least my first adult love. We'd met during our second year at M.I.T. We were in the same design class. Since I'd had to drop out of college for a couple of years after my father died so that I could work and take care of my mother and Karen, and then Karen after Mom passed, I was a few years older than the rest of the students in the graduate class. But that only made me work harder, to prove to them and to myself that I had what it took to compete with the rest.

I pretty much stuck to myself, preferring my own company to the college-boy preppy crowd, who were always on the prowl for women between classes. Competition was fierce, as the majority of the student body was male with a few women sprinkled among us.

I'd seen Michelle around campus, watched her sometimes in class, but so did every other man in the vicinity.

There's no question, Michelle was and probably still is a beautiful woman—by anyone's standards: slender but shapely, a comfortable height of maybe five-five or so, with a killer smile. But the thing that was most startling about her features was her gray eyes set against sand-toned skin with a cap of sleek auburn hair. Wherever she went, there was always some guy at her side—always a different one. But it wasn't only her looks that attracted men to Michelle; the woman was also brilliant. She could talk about any topic with authority and ease, and she had the uncanny ability to work out dimensions in her head, proposing some of the most innovative design concepts in the class. And she actually seemed like a nice person.

All that being known, the last person I expected to sit beside me on the campus quad was Michelle Carter. Mind you, I'm not saying I wasn't worth her time or didn't deserve a second look. I'm confident about my appearance. It was more of a surprise that she was actually alone long enough to notice me in the swarm of people.

"You're Ross . . . Davis, right?"

I looked up, shielding my eyes from the glare of the sun with my cupped hand. By degrees, her image began to take shape. Her body became outlined by the glow of the sun behind her. For a moment, it appeared as if she were carved into the background. All I could register at first were her long, bare legs. The incredible image was suddenly replaced by a pair of faded denim shorts that only accented what they'd tried to hide. There was no doubt Michelle Carter was food for the eyes.

"Yeah, I'm Ross."

"Mind if I sit down?"

"Help yourself." I picked up a stack of books that were next to me on the bench and put them between my feet on the grass.

She sat a little closer than she really needed to, but that was okay with me. "I'm Michelle . . . Carter. We're in the same design class."

"I know. You're one of the professor's stars." I smiled, hoping she'd know I was saying it in admiration, not envy.

"I don't know about all of that," she said, and I actually saw her blush. "I just like what I do." She turned those gray eyes on me and grinned. "Maybe *love* is a better word."

"So do I. There's no greater feeling than seeing your ideas come to life from a few lines on a piece of paper."

"Exactly!" she said, excitement heightening her voice.

We sat and talked for hours about our goals, missing our homes and families, where we wanted to be in five years, what it was like for her growing up as a biracial child.

"For the most part, I never really thought about it much," she said in a vaguely accented voice, a mixture of British and French, remnants of places she'd lived most of her life. "Mom was Mom and Dad was Dad. I suppose living in Europe helped. Folks there don't seem to be as annoyed and put off by mixed marriages as much as they are here in the States."

"How old were you when you came here?"

She pursed her lips thoughtfully. "About fifteen. That's when I noticed that I was different. But by sixteen, I didn't give a damn." She laughed. "I decided I was just as smart, just as funny, looked just as good as I always did, and the hell with what people thought."

And that's exactly the way Michelle lived life—with vitality, making every minute count, and doing things her way. You couldn't help but become infected by her zeal.

I'm not sure when I fell in love with Michelle—if it was all at once that first day or over the countless minutes that she was a part of my life for almost two years.

I'd never been happier in my life. Each day with Michelle was like getting a surprise birthday gift: you unwrap it, never sure of what you're going to get. Michelle opened my world, forced me to live in it and not merely walk around its perimeter.

We tried new foods, took spontaneous trips to the Caribbean for long weekends, danced at clubs with kids half our age until the early hours of the morning. We designed what I thought would be our dream house. I knew Michelle would be my wife and that the rest of my life would be spent unwrapping one gift after another.

But Michelle had other plans, plans that didn't include me.

We were having dinner at one of our favorite restaurants, a week before graduation. I'd pretty much spent the bulk of my savings on the perfect ring, knowing that I wanted her to wear it forever.

We were finishing up the last of our wine. She looked so beautiful in the glow of the table's candlelight. She was chatting about some really challenging design project when I placed the box on the table.

Michelle froze in midsentence.

"Open it," I said.

"Ross—"

"Go on, open it." I guess in my excitement I mistook her look of terror for surprise.

Slowly she reached for the box and opened it. For several seconds she just stared at it.

"I want to marry you, Michelle. I want to spend the rest of my life with you." But even as I said the words, meaning them with all my heart, something dark and foreboding sat down at the table between us.

The box snapped shut, and to me it sounded like a gunshot.

"I can't."

I couldn't speak. It seemed as if everything had suddenly come to a standstill.

"Why?" I finally managed to say.

"I'm moving back to Paris after graduation. I've been offered an incredible job that I couldn't turn down, Ross. It's . . . a great opportunity for me."

I couldn't believe what I was hearing. She'd never said a word. Just made her plans that would alter both our lives, and she didn't say a fucking thing!

"Why didn't you tell me?" My emotions were swinging between devastation and rage.

"Because I knew if I did, you'd try to talk me out of it. I know how committed you are to your sister. You'd never leave, and I can't stay."

Her matter-of-fact rationale felt like a series of below-the-belt blows. The truth was, she was right.

"What about us, Michelle? Did you think about us at all?"

Briefly she glanced away. "You could always come to Paris. Bring Karen," she added feebly, unable to look me in the eye.

I swallowed hard. It felt like that diamond was suddenly stuck in my throat. I nodded, unable to speak, afraid of what I might say. Slowly I stood, looked at her one last time, and walked away.

"Ross!"

I stopped, kept my back to her.

She came to my side. She had the box in her hand. "The ring," she whispered.

"Keep it."

I caught glimpses of Michelle throughout the graduation ceremony surrounded by circles of friends, admirers, and her parents. I kept my distance, even when we made brief eye contact. There was nothing more to be said between us.

"Do you want to talk about what happened with you and Michelle?" Karen asked me as we walked arm-in-arm across the campus grounds after the ceremony.

That knot was still in my throat. "No. Not really. Maybe some other time."

She tiptoed and kissed my cheek. "Whenever you're ready. You know I'm always here for you."

Karen *had* been there for me as I've been for her. As I know she will be now. It's what brings me to her front door, needing her clear head to help me unclutter mine.

"Ross, what a surprise. I didn't expect to see you," Karen says as she steps aside to let me into her apartment.

"Didn't really plan on dropping in until I found myself pulling up in front of your building."

"What's wrong, Ross? Did something happen? You might be a lot of things, but impulsive isn't one of them."

"Nothing. Just came to see how you were."

"Well, you know I love seeing you, no matter what the reason. Come on in."

Walking into the living room, I'm surprised to find that my sister is not alone. He stands, and I quickly calculate that he has me by a good two inches. He has the look of a young buppie professional, from the stark white shirt and deeply creased slacks to the clean-shaven face and perfect haircut. He sticks out his hand.

"You must be Karen's brother, Ross."

I return the handshake and wish I was as informed about him as he apparently is about me. "Yes, I am."

Karen steps up and slides her arm—almost protectively—around his waist. It takes all I have not to ask her what the hell she thinks she's doing. Even now with Karen being twenty-five and on her own, it's still hard for me not to think of her as my little sister, someone I have to protect and keep an eye on. Standing in front of this guy, it seems like the last thing she needs or wants is protection from big brother. And all at once I feel this sadness and loss. I can't explain it. I just do.

For the past ten years, Karen has been my responsibility. Looking out for her, teaching her about life and responsibility, seeing her through school was my life—that and my work. And now . . .

"Ross, this is Brian Campbell. Brian, my brother, Ross."

He gives me one of those big glad-to-meet-you smiles. "Karen has nothing but great things to say about you, how you took care of her and everything . . . after your folks passed." He turns and gives Karen this look as if he really understands. No way. He could never understand the bond between Karen and me.

"Well, sit down at least," Karen says to me. "Can I get you something to drink? Some dinner?" She grins, and it reminds me of the little girl she used to be. "We just ate. But I could heat something up for you."

"No, I'm cool. Thanks."

They both sit on the couch—close. Brian drops his arm across its back, and his fingers play with Karen's shoulder.

Several moments of silence pass. Then Karen and Brian both speak at the same time. They laugh and that look passes between them again.

"You first," Karen says to him, then pats his thigh.

"Karen tells me you're an architect. That must be a great job."

"What do you do?" I ask instead of answer.

"I work on Wall Street."

"Brian is a broker," Karen announces proudly.

"Really?" He obviously has my sister fooled. He's a kid. Twenty-six at best. He was probably someone's clerk in some back office. "Pretty tough job to get for someone . . . so young. You work on the floor?"

"No. I have my own office."

"And a staff," Karen pipes in.

Brian turns to her and grins. "Just a secretary and two assistants," he says.

"That's a staff. Ross, would you tell him that's a staff? He's so modest."

I force a half-smile. He's lying. I know he is. "How'd you get into the business, Brian?"

He shrugs. "Since I was a kid, I was always trying to figure out how to multiply my allowance, my part-time job money." He shrugs again. "When

I was in my junior year in high school, I had this great math teacher. One of our class projects was to come up with a product that we thought consumers would want to invest in. I chose real estate in the Poconos." He grins. "If I'd had the money, I would have followed my own advice and invested. It's one of the fastest-developing areas in the Northeast corridor. Ever since then I had the bug. Majored in economics and finance at Princeton, got a job on the Street right after graduation."

"Hmmm. A meteoric rise."

"Not at all. If you want to get ahead, you have to put in the time, be willing to sacrifice. I have no intention of working all my life. I want to enjoy it while I'm young. I'm planning for my future." He turns to Karen. "Maybe ours," he says a little too intimately, "if Karen will have me." He smiles and Karen blushes. He turns back to me. "How's your portfolio, Ross? Hope you went for diversification. The profit margin is so much greater than simply going for the safety of bonds."

"I, uh . . ."

"Do we have to talk business?" Karen cut in—intentionally or not, I'm not sure. But I'm grateful. "I hear shoptalk all day."

"You know what, on second thought, a beer would be great if you have one."

"Sure." Karen gets up and heads for the kitchen.

"So, how long have you known Karen?" I ask, wanting to get to the bottom of this.

"Seems like forever," he says, and then smiles. "About six months. We met at a club in Harlem. Right after your wedding, as a matter of fact. Yes, I remember her telling me you were on your honeymoon. Congratulations, man, big step. I'm sorry, what's your wife's name again?"

"Lisa."

"Right, right," he says while nodding his head. "So how is it?"

"How's what?"

"Being married. Is it what you thought it would be?"

His question completely stumps me. It's so unexpected. He's looking at me with such open anticipation. What I want to tell him is, Hell no! It's nothing like what I expected. But the truth is I'm not sure what it is I *did* expect. But I don't want to disappoint him, so I lie.

"Yeah, pretty much."

He nods again, just as Karen returns with my beer and a glass.

"Thanks."

"So, how's Lisa? I haven't talked to or seen her in weeks. Maybe you guys can come over for dinner. And bring Asha. She's always so much fun. That's Lisa's best friend," she says, turning to Brian to fill him in. "They've been friends since they were kids. Asha's great. She's been all over the world and has more stories to tell." She shakes her head and laughs.

"Oh, right, the photographer," Brian recalls.

"Right. Yes, Ross, you and Lisa, Asha and her latest, and me and Brian. I'll cook."

"I'll talk to Lisa about it."

"Tell her I said no excuses. And that I miss her."

I set my half-finished glass of beer on the coffee table and stand up. "I better get going. Lisa will be wondering what happened to me."

Lisa and Brian stand—in unison. Brian extends his hand. I notice the neatly clipped nails.

"Glad to finally meet you. Hope we'll get a chance to know each other better."

"Yeah me, too." I know I don't sound very convincing, but I don't really care.

Karen walks me to the door. I kiss her on the forehead, like I used to do when she was a little girl. "Take care. I'll talk to you soon." She takes my arm.

"What's really wrong, Ross? You seem so . . . I don't know . . . distracted. Is everything okay at work?"

"Yeah, yeah, everything is fine." I try to smile.

"I know you and Lisa are doing great." She smiles. "You guys must still be honeymooning. It must be wonderful to marry the one you really love."

"Yeah, it is. And I better get home to her." I turn to leave and head down the corridor.

"Don't forget about dinner," she calls out.

"I won't."

On the drive home, my abbreviated visit to Karen's apartment plays in my head. My intention was to have a candid talk with my sister, the one person in the world who knows me better than anyone. I figured if anyone could talk me through all the stuff I've been dealing with, she could make some sense of the feelings I've been having. But the truth is, seeing Karen and Brian only made matters worse. I should be happy that she has someone in her life, even if she's never told me anything about him. He seems like a decent enough guy. But I feel as if everything is slipping out of my grasp. That everything I've always been sure of, could count on, is no longer a certainty. And I don't know what to do.

FIFTEEN

Sunday Brunch

ASHA

The blare of a car horn behind me is a potent reminder of just how slow I'm driving. Delaying the inevitable. The driver of the black Cadillac whips by me, and I'd swear he gave me the finger. It still doesn't make me pick up any speed. What I'd really like to do is go home. Brunch with Mom—definitely not on my list of favorite things to do for a Sunday afternoon or any other time, for that matter. I wish I could wiggle my nose like Samantha in *Bewitched* and make this forty-five-minute drive morph into a cross-country trip to somewhere else. My hands tighten around the steering wheel. It doesn't matter where, just anywhere other than my mother's house.

It's sad to say, but I don't enjoy my mother's company. We're like an accident waiting to happen. I'm not being callous or unfeeling when I admit this, but the truth is she doesn't like me very much and I don't particularly care for her, either. She gives me no reason to do so. I've spent the better part of my life trying to please her, make her love me. I guess I'm simply tired. I've decided that no matter what I do, what I say, or how I feel, things between us will never change. It's just the way things are. How absolutely horrible is that?

I can't count the number of times when I wished I had a real mother, someone who talked to me, taught me about life, about myself, listened to me when my heart was broken or when I had my period in school and was completely humiliated.

I guess you could say I had to raise myself. If it hadn't been for Lisa and her family taking me into their home and their hearts, I don't know how I would have made it through adolescence.

Most of my holidays were spent sitting in Lisa's living room with her family. They celebrated my birthdays with me, and Lisa's mom always baked me a cake from scratch. I always call her Ms. Carmen, and Lisa's dad Mr. Louis. I wish I could call them Mom and Dad, but . . .

It didn't seem to bother my mother one way or the other that I spent so much time in someone else's home, that I thought of Ms. Carmen as my surrogate mother and the main influence on my young life. I suppose it took the pressure off my mother for me to just go with it.

Yet as much as I cared for Lisa and her family, there was a part of me that resented them, and what they had. I would lie awake at night and pray that my mother would love me as Lisa's mother loved her, that one day my father would come back home and take care of us the way Mr. Louis took care of his family.

Finally I just stopped praying, stopped wishing for things to be different, and accepted my life for what it was. At least I tried to. Yet, even now, years later, there's still a part of me that clings to the childish fantasy that my mother will love me, finally make me feel worthwhile.

I guess that's why I keep agreeing to these get-togethers. As much as I hate them, I long for them. There's still the little girl in me that hopes against hope that things will be different this time.

"So . . . how've you been, Mom?" I ask as she moves from one end of the kitchen to the other, preparing our Sunday brunch.

"That's what I should be askin' you. You're the one runnin' from one end of the world to another. One bed to another," she says under her breath, but loud enough for me to hear her.

"Let's not go there, all right, Mother?"

She laughs a dry, harsh laugh. "*Mother*, huh? Are you supposed to be reprimandin' me with that tone of voice?"

I push up from the table. I've been in my mother's house all of fifteen minutes. "I'm not going to do this. Not today." I grab my purse and start for the door.

Her palm connects with the table, rattling the glasses. "Do what! Listen to the truth? Look at you, Asha," she says, something mean and unnamed in her voice. "What have you done with your life? What do you have? Nothin'. Nothin' but a bunch of pictures of other people. You run from one man to the next, never staying long enough to give anything of yourself—"

I whirl toward her, ready for battle. "What could I possibly have to give to anyone, Mother?" I yell, stepping closer to my reflection. "You've made me feel like crap damn near all my life. Worthless, unlovable. What could I possibly have to give to anyone?"

"Me! Your life is *my* fault?" She tosses her head back and laughs nastily, then stares at me with a look that chills me. "You made your own choices, Asha." She steps toward me. The invisible line is now crossed. Her voice lowers to a hiss. "You're the one who lays on her back and spreads her legs for any man who strikes her fancy."

The shock of her declaration freezes me. I feel as if all the air is being sucked from my body. The pain inside my chest is so intense that I'm certain if I don't expel it, it will consume me like a careless match tossed onto dry wood.

"Like you, Mother!" The words are out of my mouth almost simultaneously with the backhand that rocks me onto my heels.

Searing tears sting my eyes, white light flashes behind my lids.

From somewhere deep in the soul of me, a cry rises, wrapped in a sound I've never heard before. A howl, like that of a wounded animal reverberates through the small yellow-and-white kitchen. It pushes my mother back against the sink, pins her there.

I capture the picture in my mind, file it away before I turn to leave.

"You're just like your father!" she screams at my back. "Just like him. No good. You'll never be any good."

She sounds hysterical now, her words collapsing one atop the other like a building that's been imploded, her sobs making her words almost unintelligible—that much more painful. "Do you hear me? Nothing, Asha. Nothing!"

I slam the door behind me and stumble toward my car, barely able to make out the shapes in front of me through my tears. This pain is something inexplicable. I can find no words to describe what's going on inside me, the desolation I feel. How can you put to words the emotions that convey the disdain your own mother feels for you—and what that knowledge does to you?

Time and again she has broken me, beaten me down with her wicked tongue, a withering look, the absence of affection. But still I rise. Still I survived.

Today, this moment . . . I . . . don't think I can. Not again.

Getting behind the wheel of my car is the last thing I should be doing. But I need to put as much distance between myself and *her* as quickly as possible.

Is it feasible to hate your own mother? If it is . . . then I do. God help me, I do.

Somehow I find myself, hours later, pulling up in front of Lisa's parents' home. *Fate or instinct?* I'm not sure how long I drove through the streets of Brooklyn. But I'm here now. It is twilight. I have come to the one place in the world where I know I can find comfort and not be judged. *Please be home*, I chant as I walk to the familiar front door and ring the bell.

Moments later, Ms. Carmen comes to the door, and before I realize what's happening she holds me in her arms, ushering me inside, telling me that whatever it is will be all right.

She guides me into the kitchen, and from the corner of my eye I notice Ross, Cliff, and Mr. Louis, and briefly I wonder if Lisa is around, as well. The men start to get up. I hear muffled voices of concern. Ms. Carmen waves them off, creating a safe space for me. We keep going.

"Is Lisa here?" I mumble over my tears, a part of me hoping that she isn't. I want some time alone with "Mom."

"No. She has some special meeting with the professors at the university. Come. Sit." She pulls out a chair for me and then closes the kitchen door.

I stare at my hands, lacing and unlacing my fingers. A cup of herbal tea magically appears in front of me.

"Drink up. You'll feel better," she says gently, and brushes my tightly coiled twists. The tender, motherly gesture opens the floodgates again.

"Let it out, sweetheart," she coos, gently stroking my back. "Let it out. It's all right."

"It'll never . . . be all right, Ms. Carmen. She hates me . . . and I hate her."

"No, you don't, Asha. You love your mother desperately," she says, instinctively knowing of whom I spoke. "Or else you wouldn't be here crying. What it is, is that you want her to love you back."

"She called me a whore. A whore. Her own daughter." Another wave of tears overwhelms me.

"She didn't mean it. You know that. Your mom is a very lonely woman. A part of her resents your resiliency, your ability to take on the challenges of life, to live it to the fullest and not let it get you down—as it's done to her. She doesn't hate you. She's simply lost her capacity to show love. It's her own fears, sweetheart."

"But what have I done? What makes it so hard for her to love me, show me that she cares that I even exist?"

"It's not you, baby. It's her. It's your mother's demons that she must battle. Sadly enough, it's often the one we love most whom we hurt."

I glance up at her and can feel the heaviness of my swollen lids. "So, what can I do?"

"Find a way to let it go. I know it's hard, and it may be impossible. But you must. You have to go on. Live your life, under your own terms, whatever they might be. But you have to let the hatred go. If not, it will destroy you and everything and everyone that comes into your life."

"I don't know if I can, Ms. Carmen." I cover my face, ashamed of this weakness. "I'm so tired."

I feel her arms around me, holding me close, and as much as I relish the comfort and security of her embrace, there is still the little girl in me that wants those arms to be my mother's.

I reach for a napkin and wipe my eyes, then blow my nose. "Thanks, Ms. Carmen."

"You know I love you like one of my own daughters, Asha. Anytime you need me, you just come."

I nod my head, grateful. "I'd better go."

"Why don't I get Ross to drive you home? And have Cliff bring your car in the morning."

"No, that's okay. I've been enough trouble. I'm fine. Really."

"Are you sure you feel up to driving?"

"I'll be okay."

She holds my face between her hands and looks into my eyes. "I know you will, sweetheart. You're a strong woman." She kisses my forehead, and it takes all I have not to dissolve into tears again.

"I'd better go," I repeat, this time heading for the kitchen door.

Ms. Carmen follows me out. I stop in the living room and chat for a moment with Mr. Louis.

Ross is pretty quiet, introspective, and I get the impression that maybe I interrupted something important—a man-to-man talk. Cliff is nowhere to be seen at the moment, which is just as well. One less front I have to put up.

I say my final good-byes, and Ross does as well.

"Mom, Dad, I'll see you both later," he says. "Thanks for dinner."

"You know you're welcome here anytime, son," Mr. Louis says. "Kiss that beautiful daughter of mine for me." He slaps Ross on the back.

"I will."

"She treating you right?"

"Absolutely."

"Good, good, and you do the same," he says, wagging a finger of fatherly warning.

Ross chuckles lightly. "You don't have to worry about that."

"You two get home safely," Ms. Carmen says.

"I will," we chorus in unison, then turn to each other and smile.

The door closes behind us.

"Long time," Ross says as we walk to the curb. "How've you been?"

"Pretty good. Pretty busy."

"Funny I should run into you. I was with my sister the other day, and she invited us all over for dinner at her place."

"That's nice," I reply, trying to force some enthusiasm into my voice.

"So, let Lisa know what night is good for you."

"Sure. I'll give her a call."

We stand in front of my car for a moment, the way people do at the end of a first date—not knowing what to do next.

"Is everything okay with you, Asha? You seem"—he shrugs—"upset or something."

I look away, thankful for the twilight to camouflage my red, swollen eyes. "I'm fine. Really. Just a bad day. But thanks for asking."

"You don't sound fine. And it's obvious that you've been crying."

I swallow, trying to dislodge the knot in my throat, and fail in the attempt.

"Asha . . ." He steps closer. "What's wrong? Are you hurt?"

All I can do is shake my head.

"Come on." His arm is around my shoulders, ushering me toward my car. "I'll take you home."

"No. Go home to Lisa," I manage.

"After I take you home. Lisa will understand. Come on, get in."

I hear the authoritative tone in his voice and quickly realize that it will be pointless to resist. The strength of it is reassuring, comforting. I almost feel protected by it, and I wonder if that's how he makes Lisa feel when he holds her—safe and secure from hurt and harm.

"What about your car?" I mumble, and wipe the tears away with the back of my hand.

"We'll worry about that later." He holds open the door.

Reluctantly I get in. I suppose the emotional exhaustion of the day has finally taken its toll. All I can think about is how weak and needy I feel. How desperately I want to be cared about, to have the holes in my soul filled.

"What brought you over to the Holdens?" I ask after a few minutes of riding in silence.

Ross releases a breath. "Just wanted to check on the folks. Figured I'd get out of the house since Lisa was gone for the day."

"Oh," is all I can manage.

"What about you?"

I feel him snatching looks at me. "Same thing—sort of."

"Hmmm."

I haven't known Ross long, but I consider him a friend because he's married to my friend. We've had only a few opportunities to talk one-on-one. During those times, I always found him to be a genuine, caring person, interesting to talk to, with a wry sense of humor and an endless wealth of knowledge about so many things. I discovered in one conversation that he loves art, the form and discipline of it. I suppose that's why he's so good at what he does. I admire that in a man—in him—focus and determination couched with simple passion. Which makes this act of kindness typical of Ross. He's one of the few truly decent men, just the kind of man that Lisa needs. She's lucky.

But there was always something beyond the obvious that intrigued me about Ross. Perhaps it's his almost aloof manner at times. Even though he is always pleasant and kind, there's a part of him that I believe he keeps under wraps—another side of him. It's like looking at a piece of art or a photograph. On the surface, it appears whole and intact, but upon closer inspection, you find so many nuances, little pieces that you hadn't noticed before.

That's how it is now. I notice the strong line of his jaw, *resolve*; the curve of his mouth, *sensual*; the way his long fingers grip the wheel, *strength*; and the sadness in the depths of his eyes when he looks at me, the *past*.

I've seen that same look in my own reflection. I know that look and the feelings that cause it. For a moment, I push my own angst aside and focus on Ross. It's almost a relief in a way—as it always is—to turn away from myself, to forget about myself and enter the space of someone else—if only for a time.

"Are you traveling again anytime soon?" Ross asks, breaking the silence.

"Not for a couple of months, I think. I have several local projects I'm contracted for at the moment."

"You do some great work. I don't know if I've ever told you that before. I really like what you do. The passion that comes across in your photographs."

I turn to him, surprised by his revelation. Most people don't get it. But then again, Ross, too, is an artist. He *would* understand.

"Thanks. That means a lot coming from you."

He turns briefly toward me and smiles. "It's true. You're good, Asha. Really good. I know how difficult it is to master your craft, to see your vision come to life, to have others appreciate what it is you're attempting to do—convey."

I listen beneath the words and hear the almost wistful intonations. I try to be careful not to read more into them than what is there. But there is a growing feeling within me that defies description, a nagging sense of something that is both dangerous and alluring.

"I know exactly what you mean, Ross."

At the same moment, we turn and look at each other, a unique thread of understanding drawing us together. That subtle emotional spark that hints and promises something that neither of us should even entertain in our minds. I know he feels it, too. It's in his face and the sudden shift of his body in his seat.

He makes the turn onto my street.

"You know, I always meant to ask you if you really posed for that portrait hanging over your fireplace," he says.

I laugh as I always do. "What do you think?"

LISA

There's a part of me that died that day. All that's left now is to bury the remains. Sometimes it hurts so bad I can't breathe. But I'm not going to let their actions destroy the rest of my life. I'm going to find a way to move on.

I know a lot of people will think that it must have been something I wasn't doing at home that pushed him into my best friend's arms—my best friend! I could scream. I have screamed, until my throat was raw.

I don't understand how they could hurt me this way. What had I done to deserve this? What gave them the right to believe that they could do this? I hate them! Hate them.

But I've been thinking about it, going over every inch of our marriage, our friendship, trying to see if I missed the signs, if there was something I could have done to stop it from happening. . . .

And the Walls Came Tumbling Down

SIXTEEN

Things Fall Apart

LISA

Over the past two weeks Ross and I have spent more time together than we have since the beginning of our marriage seven months ago. Things finally seem to be falling into place with us. I love it. He's home by six every night, and our lovemaking is back to the way it was before we said *"I do."* Even better. All that's left to do now is to find our dream home. I decided that I would back off and let Ross handle the finances. I have to show him that I trust his judgment. I'll let him handle it if that's what it takes to keep the peace, and keep him happy.

Funny how life works. I spent so much time worrying, thinking that something was wrong, that perhaps I'd made a mistake. How could I have been so foolish? All I had to do was be patient, let us find our way through the newness of marriage and reacquaint ourselves with each other. And it paid off. Our house-buying plans aren't coming around as quickly as I'd hoped, but Ross assures me that we'll be ready by the end of the year. He seems to have made the mental adjustment of living in my condo—our condo—at least for the time being. I'm so proud of him, proud of his determination. I know everything is going to be fine.

Ross seems to go out of his way to make time for us lately. Every night we lie together in our bedroom and talk about our future, how wonderful it will be. It's almost too much for me to take in. Ross never has been one for a lot of conversation, especially about the same topic. He's more of a doer, a take-charge type of man. So much like my dad. But now, for whatever reason, he wants me fully involved in the planning of our future. He talks to me about everything.

I don't think I've ever been happier. I love my life, and I love my husband. My only wish is that I could get in touch with Asha. There's so much I want to tell her. But for the past two weeks, all I've gotten is her answering machine and one terse thirty-second conversation that was spent with her telling me how busy she is and that she will call me as soon as she gets a break.

That conversation was a week ago. I still haven't heard from her, and it's so unlike Asha. Over the years, even during her travels abroad, she made time to call, if only to tell me what a fabulous time I was missing.

Odd, but with my marriage finally coming together, and Ross and I working at being a couple, the one relationship that I had always thought unshakeable seems to be unraveling.

On my wedding day, she promised that things would remain the same between us. She said there was nothing that could change that. I believed her.

Maybe I was being naïve. Perhaps I was hoping for something solid beneath my feet as my life was being altered—forever. But I suppose it is inevitable. *Change*, that is—for all of us.

Still, it's hard to simply sit back and accept Asha suddenly distancing herself from me, and from my life. In the early days before my marriage, we talked mostly every day on the phone, or met for lunch when our schedules allowed, or after work for a quick drink. And we tried to keep up our friendship when I returned from my honeymoon. But now she barely has time to return my calls. It's almost as if she doesn't want to be bothered. And I don't know why.

Maybe I'm only imagining this feeling of distance between us. Perhaps it's no more than what she's said—*she's busy*. Yet I can't help but feel that it's something more, something I may have said or done. Or maybe she has begun to believe, as many women do when a close friend gets married, that there is no longer a place for her in my life. That she no longer fits in or that she's somehow interfering in my relationship.

What else could it be?

Maybe I'll give her another call after dinner. Karen has been bugging me about us getting together at her house. I really want Asha to be there. It'll be like old times and maybe she and I can get back on track. In the meantime, I think I'll fix something for me and Ross to nibble on while we watch the news.

"You're looking mighty serious," Ross says upon entering the kitchen. He kisses me on the side of my neck. "Anything wrong?" He snatches a cracker with cheddar cheese from the platter.

"No. Not really."

"Not really doesn't *really* mean no."

He heads toward the refrigerator and takes out a can of beer. His second for the night. He's been drinking a bit more recently, which is not like him. Maybe it's his way of unwinding at the end of the day. We're all entitled to our little pleasures. As long as it doesn't get out of hand, I'll leave it alone.

Ross sits down opposite me and pops the top on the can. "So . . . what's going on?"

I shrug. "Just thinking about Asha." I place the platter on the table between us.

He takes a quick swallow of beer and gets up from the table, moving toward the sink. "What about her?" he asks with his back turned to me.

"I've been trying to talk to her for the past two weeks, and she never seems to have time."

"Probably busy. She *does* have a business and a life of her own."

His sudden defensive tone surprises me. "I know that, Ross. Asha has the same life she's always had. She's never been too busy before."

I watch him polish off the rest of his beer and toss the can into the recycle bin. "Things change," he says, and walks off into the adjoining living room. My stomach suddenly tightens. In the blink of an eye, he switches from being interested in what is on my mind to tossing my concerns away as if they were as trivial and unimportant as his empty beer can. That unsettles me even more.

I follow him. He immediately turns on the television with the remote.

"What do you mean 'things change'?" I ask, blocking the remote control's signal to the screen.

"Nothing, Lisa. Forget it. No big deal. Just a figure of speech."

I stand there a moment longer.

Finally he looks up at me. "What? What did I say, Lis, huh?" he asks as if he's completely baffled by his own attitude.

I plop down on the space next to him on the couch. "I only wanted to talk, that's all, and you just dismiss me. I was trying to tell you about Asha and how she's been acting lately, and you walked out on me."

"No, I didn't. You made a comment. I made a comment. I figured that was it. Is there more?"

"Forget it. You wouldn't understand." I fold my arms, trying to contain my mounting annoyance.

"Aw, come on," he says, the exasperation in his voice putting me on the defensive. "Don't go there and make this more than what it is. What is it that I'm incapable of understanding? You called your friend and she's busy. That's not rocket science." He tosses his hands up in the air. "Or is this some deep woman thing that my thick male brain can't understand?"

"Sarcasm doesn't become you, Ross."

"See, I can't win."

"This is exactly what I mean. If you did understand, we wouldn't be having this level of conversation."

"So what am I now, an idiot? I can't make heads or tails of a simple comment?" His shakes his head in apparent disgust. "You're blowing this way out of proportion, like you do with everything."

I feel like I've been slapped. "What?"

Ross doesn't respond. He won't look at me.

"I want to know what you mean, Ross. Like I do with *everything*? Everything like what?"

He snatches a glance at me for a moment and then looks away. "Like everything . . . a simple date, dinner at your folks' house, your students, how I put my damned socks in a dresser drawer, living here, how often we have sex . . ."

My head starts to pound.

"All I'm saying is everything isn't a crisis, Lisa. Everything doesn't need an hour-long dialogue and dissection. You could take an example from Asha. She *lives* life. She doesn't let it live her."

I look at him—my husband—and I suddenly don't know who he is. Slowly, in a daze, I get up and walk toward the bedroom. I'm certain that Ross will instantly realize how deeply he has wounded me. He will rush up behind me and tell me how sorry he is, that he didn't mean what he said, that he didn't just compare me to the one woman in the world I've ever envied.

With every step, I know that he will stop me. He'll tell me how silly all this is. He'll ask me what we're fighting about, and he'll tell me he loves me more than anything in the world.

He doesn't.

Hours later, I feel Ross's side of the bed sink as he gets in. I shut my eyes and hope that he will reach for me, close the chasm that has inexplicably opened. I lie there and wait. Too long.

The sound of Ross's deep, even breathing fills the space between us.

If anyone would have asked me, I'd say I didn't sleep a wink last night. But at some point I must have dozed off, because I didn't hear Ross leave this morning. It is so odd not to have him here beside me when I awake, especially on Sunday mornings. Sunday mornings have become our time.

On Sunday mornings, we've gotten into the routine of sleeping late, fixing brunch, and eating in bed while we watch all the news shows and give our personal take on the world events. These are some of the best times we spend together. *Our time*.

Ross has some very strong views about a great deal of things: equal opportunity, quotas, abortion, racial profiling, integration, and women in the workforce. Most of them are in conflict with my opinions on one level or the other. He is very well read, always with his nose in some newspaper, magazine, or book. I learn so much from him when we talk.

A good example is the conversation we had about two months ago during the *CBS Sunday Morning* program. The discussion was about quotas and how the country would fare without them. It was started by something a guy said in one of the show's segments, something about the tyranny of forced social programs. He hinted that civil rights laws were probably the best example of this misguided thinking. That got Ross going.

"It's about time," Ross said, washing the comment down with a gulp of orange juice.

I couldn't believe what I was hearing. I looked at him as if he were crazy. "What do you mean it's about time?"

Ross slanted his gaze in my direction. "Quotas aren't what we need. We don't need someone giving us anything because they are required by law to fill *x* amount of slots. We should get the jobs, the homes, and the seats in college because we're qualified, because we worked for it. It's like mandatory social promotion in school. You keep passing kids along whether they have the ability or not, whether they earned it or not."

"If there weren't quotas, thousands of corporations would never consider hiring a minority," I cut in.

"I agree. But quotas are double-edged swords. On one hand, they open doors, on the other, many minorities are led to believe that it should be held open for them indefinitely with no real effort on their part."

"We already have so much stacked against us," I told him. "Whatever cracks and crevices open up, we need to take advantage of them."

"Yes, take them, make the system work from the inside, and help the next person along." He slowly shook his head. "But that's not what's happening. I want to know that I got where I am because I earned it. Not that it was handed to me. That's not respect; that's charity. And a hand-out helps no one."

Ross's opinions on most things are just as firm and exacting. I'm sure it's part of my attraction to him—his focus and ability to look beyond the surface and see what's really going on. So much like my dad. Neither of them do anything, take any action, or make any decision without fully thinking through and weighing all the options. I can no more imagine Ross doing something on the spur of the moment as I could believe in the tooth fairy. Any other behavior would be out of character. Ross is as steady as a Swiss clock. That much I'm sure of.

Which is why Ross's sudden shift in attitude is so disturbing. There must be a reason. He's never been so prickly before.

After I take a quick shower and eat a light breakfast, Ross still has not returned. I have two choices: sit by the window and the phone or get a handle on my day and do something constructive.

I decide not to call Asha. I don't want to give her another opportunity to tell me how busy she is and that she doesn't have time to talk. Worst-case scenario is that she's there with someone. It wouldn't be the first time that I'd interrupted one of Asha's carnal interludes.

Another occasion happened shortly after Steven and I parted company. I'd gotten up on a morning much like this one, a bright, sunny Sunday in January. The air was crisp. There was a stillness to the day, even as couples, families, and singles moved briskly through the streets.

I'm not quite sure why I was feeling so low that particular Sunday. I had no false notions about Steven and me. Asha had previously read me the riot act about him, and I'd truly believed that I'd let it go. Until that Sunday.

I'd gotten up that morning and felt completely lost and vulnerable. It felt as if the old wound had been lanced open again. As always, whenever I had something on my mind or heavy on my heart, I turned to Asha.

When I pulled up in front of her stoop, it hadn't occurred to me that she might have company. But I knew it the instant she opened her door.

There was a soft, totally feminine look about her. I could tell by the way she tightened the belt on her short robe that she had nothing on beneath it. Her lips were puffy, lush almost, and there was a dreaminess in her eyes that was hard to describe.

"Lisa . . ."

"I should have called. I'm sorry. I—"

"Don't be silly." She took my hand. "Come on in out of the cold. It must be something important to get you out of your bed on a Sunday morning."

"Sorry I got you out of yours," I said, following her into the house.

"Not as sorry as Vincent is," she replied with a light laugh.

"Oh, Asha . . ." I clasped her forearm. "I'll go. I don't want to . . . We can—"

She looked me square in the eyes and lowered her voice to a no-nonsense whisper. "Let me say this once. No man is ever going to come before our friendship." She angled her head and waved me off. "Go sit. Let me put something on and tell Vincent to relax."

That's just the way things are between Asha and me. We're friends first and foremost. I don't think Asha realized how much that one act of selflessness meant to me. I kept that knowledge with me, especially at times when I needed her, and I knew it would be okay then, as I do now.

With that belief tucked in my heart, I ring Asha's bell and wait. But as I hear the locks being disengaged, a moment of doubt grips my stomach. I know how ruthlessly sharp Asha's tongue can be. I know how deeply it can slice. With all that has transpired between Ross and me and between Asha and me, all I want to do is talk, not hear a lecture or be censured. I want to get to the bottom of what's turning things into a page I can no longer read. I want to talk to my friend.

But instead of the open smile of surprise that I'd hoped for, I'm met with a look of barely veiled annoyance.

"Lisa . . . what are you doing here?" Her perfect brows draw together as if she'd suddenly gotten a pain.

I have half a mind to turn around and leave. But I know that I can't. Asha's response is indicative of the sudden change in her manner toward me and the rift in our friendship. I want to know why. And I intend to find out.

"I came to see you."

She laughs. I watch her tight expression slowly soften. "Well, that's pretty damned obvious." She puts her arm around my shoulder. "Don't mind me. I've been totally insane and on edge lately. I have work up the ying-yang. I was in the studio when I heard the bell. Lucky thing I was ready for a nervous breakdown or your ass would be still standing out there looking in."

She laughed again. This time the sound is familiar—not the tight, forced notes that greeted me, but the full-bodied sound that has been a part of my life since I was twelve years old.

"Hope you're not hungry," Asha announces, her pantherlike walk guiding us into her showcase living room; the stark white walls play host to many of Asha's startling photos. "My cupboards are bare," she adds, taking a seat on the apple-red leather sectional.

"I doubt that. Not as much as you love to be fully stocked."

During our adolescence and into our teens, I shared many of my lunches with Asha, and she was a pretty regular face at the Holden dinner table on Sunday nights. Asha's mother, Ms. Denise, tried. She worked hard, maybe too hard, but it was never enough.

The truth is, Asha is nearly phobic about doing without. And that covers everything from food to clothes, cars to men. When she got her first part-time job as a cashier at our local supermarket, she said to me, "I'm never gonna be hungry, shoeless, or wantin' anything ever again, Lisa. I'm gonna have everything that I want."

The hard determined look and the edge of her voice chilled me. We were only fifteen. But there was a single focus in her then that hasn't changed in all these years. If anything, she's become more driven. She's never looked back. Asha's idea of empty is that the overstuffed cabinets and refrigerator don't dump their contents on you when opened. Doing without is depriving yourself of a trip, or a dress you love simply because it's too expensive. Neediness and sacrifice amount to not experiencing that sexual thrill of a beautiful man, only because of what people might say. That is Asha.

"I'm not hungry, anyway."

"Well, you know where everything is when you are." She expansively stretches on the couch like a lazy lioness, draping her arm casually across its back.

"You know how busy things can get for me," Asha begins in a sudden rush. "Especially at this time of the year when the hours of light are so short. I feel like I have to work twice as hard. And Vincent is in Brazil on a shoot. That leaves me to do everything."

That laugh again—the unfamiliar one. And for the first time, I notice that Asha hasn't actually looked at me, something she always does. She sizes me up first thing: how my hair looks, or when did I have my nails done, how my dress or suit fits, how she loves my new makeup. But this time, *nothing*.

All she's doing is chatting nonstop about work, work, and more work. Beating me with it as if to assure me that work is the only reason she hasn't returned my calls or talked for more than a few minutes at a time. The only reason. And I know it's a lie. I know this because I know the woman in front of me. Just as it was a lie that time in the high school hallway when I *knew* I saw her with that boy and she denied it. Denied it by saying thank you—thank you for pretending to believe. Only to later confess the truth that I had always known but didn't want to believe. What is it that she doesn't want me to know now?

"You know what?" she suddenly says, cutting herself off. "I'm hungry. Can I get you something?"

Before I have a chance to respond, she's up and heading for the kitchen. I follow her across the gleaming wood floors and lean against the black-and-white marble counter while she hunts through the fridge.

"How about a healthy salad?"

She starts putting a bag of spinach, some mushrooms, tomatoes, and a bag of croutons on the counter, doing everything it seems to keep from dealing directly with me.

The realization is so swift that for a moment I feel almost light-headed. What did I do?

"Asha. Stop." I clasp her wrist to halt her flurry of movement. "For one minute, just stop." In an instant, our gazes connect, and that same unsettling feeling I had when I looked into Ross's eyes and saw the distance there halts the air in my lungs. "What is it? I swear if I didn't know better, I'd think you were trying to avoid me. Hey, if you'd rather that I leave, I'll go. Sorry to bother you."

I turn to walk away—for the second time in less than twenty-four hours—expecting the same result.

Instead, Asha stops me at the front door. I turn, and I'm stunned to find tears in her eyes. "I'm sorry, so damned sorry," she whispers.

In all the years that I've known Asha Woods, I have *never* seen her cry. *Never.* I reach out to her, and she hugs me tightly, as if she will be tugged away by whatever it is that's dragging her by both feet if she ever let go of me.

Instinctively I stroke her back, tell her it's okay. Whatever it is, it's okay. I'll help her to work it out.

Suddenly, she pulls away, turns her back to me. "You can't help me," she says in a flat tone weighed down by uncharacteristic resignation.

"Why, Asha? What is it?" My heart races with dread. "Are you ill?" I come around to face her.

She looks away and shakes her head. "It's me. It's my life. It's everything."

"Talk to me. Tell me what it is. We can work it out."

She pulls in a breath and fights back tears. "I don't think so. Not this time."

"Asha, you're scaring me."

She reaches out and strokes my cheek, a sad smile on her lips. "How have you remained my friend all these years? I'm such a bitch." Quiet sobs rock her slender body.

"Don't be silly. You have your moments, yes, but I wouldn't go that far."

She laughs lightly and wipes her eyes with the back of her hand. "You wouldn't, Lisa. Not you. I don't think you've ever had a mean thought about another person in your head. I guess you're lucky that way."

"It's not luck, it's just that I believe that at the core of everyone there's a goodness. Sometimes life and circumstances blot it out. But that doesn't mean it's not there somewhere."

"Maybe." She sniffs. "Listen, I'm sorry for acting so weepy and silly. Must be PMS or something." She laughs again. "I guess I really am burnt out."

"Are you sure that's all it is?" I say, and she looks away.

She shrugs. "What else could it be?" She drapes her arm around my shoulder. "You wanna help me fix this salad, and then you can tell me what's going on with you. That's why you came isn't it—to talk?"

"Yes, but I also came to see you."

She spreads her arms into the air, her smile just as wide. "Well, here I am. Overworked and a little crazed, but still here."

I laugh and feel the tension slowly leave the room. The tightness in my chest begins to ease. "You know what, I *am* hungry."

Over salad and a couple of glasses of chardonnay, we seem to find our way back to where we once were, like old times. Reminiscing.

"Remember the first day we met and I took that picture of you?" Asha asks.

"Yeah! I sure do. Don't tell me you still have it!"

Asha laughs. "I came across it the other day in one of my old albums."

She pops up from the couch, crosses the wood floors to a tall armoire, and opens the bottom cabinet. She returns with a large black leather portfolio.

"I've had them all specially treated to preserve them."

She takes a seat next to me and opens the book. The first photo is the one of me sitting on my stoop, my two ponytails resting on my shoulders.

"I remember what I said, just as you snapped the photo."

"Sisters," we said in unison, and laughed at the memory.

Page after page chronicles our youth: the days on the old block, faces I'd long forgotten come to life. Asha and me in pink hot pants at the roller rink. Her sixteenth birthday when she decided she needed a padded bra to make her look more like a woman. Our high school prom. Christmas, New Year's. Our double date with our first college men. Asha fixing my wedding veil. The memories were all there, forever preserved, just like our friendship.

"This is incredible," I say, closing the book. "I had no idea."

She smiles. "I call this my friendship book." She closes it. "So, talk to me. What's going on? How's the job . . . Ross?"

"The job is fine." I take a breath and ease back into the cushions of the couch. "Ross . . . well . . . that's the other reason I came." I look across at her, and for an instant her eyes dart away from me, and then back.

"Ross." She chuckles. "You have a good man, Lisa. What could possibly be wrong? It hasn't been a year yet." She gets up and refills her glass of wine.

"I know. I can't figure him out, especially these past couple of weeks."

"Two weeks . . ." She takes a sip of her wine, and then another. "What . . . happened?"

"That's what I don't know. Lately, he's suddenly so attentive and loving."

"And that's a problem? You're still newlyweds. He should be all over you. When he isn't, *then* you worry." She laughs again. "Women would kill to be in your shoes. You always were the one to worry for no damned good reason. Weren't you the one worrying after your honeymoon that it didn't seem right? Now that it is, it's still a problem. What's the man got to do to make it right?" She crosses her bare legs and takes a long swallow of her wine.

"Maybe it sounds silly standing on the outside. But it's not that simple. I mean, at first it was wonderful—and these past couple of weeks have been, as well. Ross has suddenly turned into the man I'd believed I'd married. I really love the way things are going. And yes, I was worried. But then just as quickly as things changed, they changed again."

"Why? What happened?" She takes another sip of wine.

"I was trying to talk to him about you."

Asha suddenly focuses on her pedicure. "Me?" She chuckles. "What about me?"

"Just that I haven't heard from you, and I didn't understand why. And he became totally defensive."

"Maybe he was . . . I don't know"—she shrugs—"tired or something."

"That's what he said."

"So why don't you believe him?"

"It's not that I don't believe him, it was his whole attitude toward me, as if I'd touched on a subject I had no business talking about." I try to hold on to her with my gaze, but she slides away.

"I think you're worrying unnecessarily, Lisa. Sometimes guys don't really want to hear about girlfriend issues. Maybe he just figured it was something we would work out and it didn't have anything to do with him. Ross is the kind of man who needs his space. At least that's the way he strikes me."

"Maybe." I let her comments sit for a moment. "That's your third glass of wine, Asha."

"Is it?" she asks, and finishes off the glass. "I hadn't noticed."

"Well, it is."

"I wouldn't worry about it."

"What? Your drinking or Ross?"

"Both. Just leave it alone. Sometimes when you hunt for trouble, you find it." She gets up from the couch and goes into the kitchen, only to return empty-handed, making me wonder what she'd gotten up for.

"I wish I could be like you," I confess. "Simply take life as it comes, accept things and just enjoy."

"The grass always seems greener on the other side, Lisa. Be mindful of what you wish for." She smiles and slowly nods her head.

"Yes, I suppose you're right." I check my watch. "Listen, I'd better go. Maybe Ross is home by now." I get up and take my purse. "Oh, before I forget—Ross's sister, Karen, wants us to come to her house for dinner real soon. How is next week for you?"

"Ummm . . ."

"Don't say no, and don't say you're too busy. You can take one evening off." I take her hand. "It'll be like old times, Asha. I miss that," I add, squeezing her hand.

She pauses. "Okay. Friday?"

"Sounds perfect. I'll give Karen a call. I'm sure it'll be fine."

She walks me to the door. "Thanks for stopping by."

"Thanks for listening and for putting things into perspective. I know I tend to sometimes make more out of stuff than is necessary." I laugh, but Ross's biting comments of the night before come roaring back. "This whole marriage thing takes some getting used to."

"Yeah, I guess it does. Well, I'll, uh, see you on Friday."

"Call me during the week, and I'll give you all the details."

"Sure."

I turn to leave; then I stop. "I love you, girl."

"Love you, too, Lis," she says almost tenderly. "Always believe that. Okay? No matter what."

Her intense stare creates an odd feeling in my stomach, like something unknown or unseen is around the corner.

But I only say, "Okay."

Ross is home. I can hear the sounds of Coltrane coming from the stereo, and it makes me smile. Anytime Ross puts on jazz, he's in a mellow, relaxed mood. Good. I head toward the living room with a new attitude, leaving all the bad vibes, misunderstandings, and angst at the door.

I'm glad I took the initiative to visit Asha, clear the air, and rekindle our bond. I still haven't discovered the lie. But I'm sure Asha will tell me in her own time. She always does. In the meantime, I've decided to follow her advice and and hope for the best. Just love my husband and stop worrying so much.

SEVENTEEN

Dinner at Eight

ASHA

As Vincent and I walk down the corridor toward Karen's apartment, the pop of my heels against the floor sounds like gunshots. A firing squad. Dear God. What am I going to do? How can I walk into a room with Ross and Lisa, friends and family that know all of us, and not give away what happened that night? How?

I knew the day would come: a day, a night, a time of reckoning. All my protestations about work, new projects, and being tired are bullshit excuses. How long could they last and hold up under scrutiny? A part of me senses that Lisa knows it, too, but she's too much of a lady, too much of a decent person to probe or push, to force someone to reveal too much. And if I was ever thankful for the kind of person Lisa Holden-Davis is, it's now. I'm not sure what I would have done had she pressed me for answers, if she hadn't accepted my excuses.

To be truthful, I was stunned to find her standing on my doorstep. Meeting things head-on is not one of Lisa's strengths. She'd rather find ways around issues that bother her or disrupt her life. Maybe marriage has done something to her, made her see the world differently.

I should have gone away, taken a trip, stayed for months. One night. One night!

It was all so simple, so innocent . . . so right. The inevitability of it was as powerful as the act itself. We were both so vulnerable, overwhelmed by issues that threatened to swallow us whole. And for that time nothing else mattered, except to feel better, to find a common bond with some other soul who understood. What we did had nothing to do with the act of sex itself, the release of some pent-up passion, some buried desire denied. Rather it was an act of acceptance, accepting each other for exactly who we were, faults and all. No questions asked. No compensation needed.

Ross, for the most part, is not even the kind of man that I'm generally attracted to. But that night he encompassed what I needed—the balm to soothe my wounds. I suppose I represented the same thing to him.

It was not my intention to take Ross to my bed. All I believed I needed at the time was an ear, a shoulder, validation that I was worthy, not the trifling whore my own mother claimed me to be. When he got into my car, one of the first things Ross said to me was, "You don't have to talk about it if you don't want to. But if you change your mind, I'm willing to listen."

That surprised me about Ross. He never presented himself as a man who could or would verbally empathize with anyone about much of anything. But suddenly I saw a kindness in his eyes. I heard the tenderness in his voice.

Strange, but kindness is one of the things that always seem to break me down. In my home, I grew up not knowing what it was. I saw it at a distance, through a distorted prism, as if it were some elusive photo that had been treated to give it an out-of-focus finish. My first personal experience with kindness came from Lisa's mother. And I took that sparingly. I was afraid to trust it, to need it too much for fear that it would be taken away. I still carry that fear, and when I come upon it, unguarded enough to allow it beyond my barriers, it weakens me. And I hate myself for that weakness.

That's how I was that night, unguarded. I allowed Ross's kindness to comfort me, to accept me. Because of that, he, too, found himself baring his wounds.

"I don't want to disappoint Lisa," he'd said. "I promised her that I'd take care of us. I promised myself, and her family. Everything that I've depended on all these years—my values, certain truths, the core of who I am—has evaporated right in front of me. Nothing's like I thought it would be. Nothing."

"Is it ever? I mean, really. All of this is an illusion, temporary images and ideas that we've conjured up to make life livable."

I saw him take a quick look at me from the corner of his eye. "You sound . . . bitter."

"I wouldn't say bitter. Maybe resigned is a better description. Resigned to the way things are. There is an irrefutable plan, you know." I laughed. "An unstoppable plan, and we are all just players. We can either go along for the ride and make the most of it, or live miserably as we constantly ask ourselves the unanswerable question: *Why?*"

Ross shook his head and chuckled. "Is that *why* you always live your life on the edge, at full speed—no holds barred?"

I turned to him, read the meaning beneath the question. "Yes," I answered simply.

His looked at me for a moment as if he were trying to see something that wasn't visible to the naked eye. "You're nothing like Lisa," he said, his tone filled with the sudden realization.

"No, I'm not."

Now, walking down the corridor of Karen's apartment building, I wonder if those words of confession between us will be mirrored in our eyes, in the turn of a head, the catch in a voice?

"Are you okay, Asha?" Vincent asks. "You've been preoccupied for hours and have hardly said a word."

I take his hand, both to reassure him and to regain my balance. "I'm fine." I peck him on the cheek, then brush away the lipstick smudge with the pad of my thumb. "Thanks for coming, Vince. I'm sure you had any number of hot dates lined up for tonight."

The corner of his mouth curves upward into a wicked grin. "My life isn't as fast and furious as you think." His grin widens. "You give me too much credit."

I nudge him in the side with my elbow. "I'm there in the studio taking those messages that come in for you, remember? And that's not counting the ones that come directly to your apartment. Don't try to act like an altar boy, Vincent. I know you—in the biblical sense." I wag a warning finger at him, which he wraps his hand around. I ring Karen's bell with my free one.

"And I miss that," he says all too intimately.

We both look at our hands simultaneously, at the erotic gesture.

"And I miss you—"

Vincent could still ignite that fire in me. I only wish I were the woman he really needs.

"Vince—"

"Hey, it's about time you two got here," Karen says, swinging the door open. Her smile widens when she sees us holding hands. "Hmm. What were you two talking about?"

"You're much too young to know," I reply before giving her a kiss and a hug.

"That's why no party is complete without you, Asha. You are too wild! Come on in." She hugs Vincent. "Looking edible as always, Vincent. When are you going to make her settle down? She'll be sorry if somebody else steals you." Karen hooks her arm through his.

"That's what I keep telling her, Karen. She won't listen to me."

Karen laughs. "Asha listens to her own drummer. Right, Asha?"

"All the time," I answer in the same up-tempo tone.

"Well, Vincent, you'll have to find a way to change the beat."

"That's my plan."

They both laugh.

"Everyone is in the living room," Karen announces. "Make yourselves comfortable."

Everyone. I steel myself for the night ahead and follow Karen inside.

EIGHTEEN

May I Be Excused?

ROSS

The doorbell chimes for the third time since me and Lisa have arrived. Karen, always the perfect hostess, hands Cliff the tray of snacks and hurries to the door. My heart begins to thud as the door swings open.

I hear her before I see her. There was a time when I would never have recognized Asha's voice. Now it rings in my head, sometimes waking me from my sleep. But maybe it's my conscience screaming at me for being such a weak fool.

The past two weeks have been a living hell. A hell that I created. Every time I look at Lisa, I want to make it all go away. I want to take back that day and start over. When I make love to her now, it's with a passion born of guilt. I feel as if I can pound it away, stroke it away, that Lisa's body will erase Asha's body from my mind, her taste from my lips, her touch on my skin. Nothing works. The brand is there. Burned on my chest: ADULTERER. Adulterer, someone I swore I'd never become.

I've heard so many men laughingly talk about the affairs they've had outside of marriage. They'd joke about how easy it is to cheat, how it's expected of them. "It adds variety, man," one of my former college buddies said one night over drinks at our local hangout. "Who wants to make it with the same woman night after night?"

"But how do you feel about her stepping out on you with another man?" I'd asked.

"Shit. I cut it short right then and there. My woman doesn't mess around on me."

Generally that was the consensus: Men do, women don't. Men are more readily excused for being bad boys, while women are condemned as whores, their names scrawled on the walls of men's bathrooms, the butt of rude jokes told at ball games.

Is that how I think of Asha now, a tramp, easy?

Here she is, as accessible as she's always been—there but not. That in itself is the allure. I barely want to look at her. If I do, I'm sure everyone will see in my eyes what I have done.

I wish I could blame it on her. I wish I could say she got me drunk and seduced me. That would be a lie. Women like Asha don't need traps to seduce a man. Their natural act of breathing is a potent seducer. The strange thing is, I don't think she really is aware of it. And if she is, she doesn't really care. It's simply who she is, someone with the innate ability to focus totally on you as if you were the only person in the world, if only for that small space of time. Her eyes hold you like magnets. She seems to reflect on every word you say. And sometimes that's all a man needs—to be listened to, made to feel that his opinions matter, that his feelings count, you know. Asha zeroed in on that need, and fed my hunger. And like a man starved, I ate it up.

It seems to have been forever, my entire lifetime since anyone truly listened to me—except for maybe Karen. Even Lisa listens only to what she wants to hear. But I mean, really heard and felt me. Until that night.

I suppose that night what I needed more than anything was simply to be listened to and made to feel worthwhile.

On the drive home to her apartment, I listened to her soft sobs, her words of self-recrimination, something so uncharacteristic for the Asha I thought I knew. I was profoundly touched by her openness with me, her revelations. I guess that made it easy for me to open myself up to her, as well. I've asked myself a million times what was it that crystallized between us and pushed our everyday defenses aside, allowing us to reveal those unseen corners of our souls? The time, the circumstances, our innermost selves laid bare? I found myself revealing things to Asha about my life that I'd never said to anyone, not even to Lisa—especially not to Lisa. I never wanted Lisa to see me as "less than." I didn't want to dim her opinion of me, make her see me as weak or incapable. Not my wife.

But that night with Asha, it was as if for the first time in my life I didn't have to be strong, be right, be responsible. I could be held, I could be heard without being judged. I won't lie. It felt good. It felt liberating, as if some enormous weight had been lifted from my chest and for a moment I could actually take a deep breath.

And it wasn't only me needing—wanting—something. Asha did, too. And I drank her need like a man lost in the desert and finding an oasis. It somehow replenished me. You see, with Mom gone, Karen on her own doing her thing, and the hidden single-mindedness that Lisa possesses and which she'd carefully kept shrouded in a guise of gentile femininity, all had combined to loosen my foundation—and then the job. Shit. I'd lost everything familiar, the centerpiece of who I was, and for a time Asha allowed me to feel that it was okay—as wrong as I knew it would be. For the moment, it was all right. Asha held me, and it was all right. . . .

"Ross, relax. It's a party. You're as stiff as a board." Lisa's voice drifts to me as if I'm coming out of a light sleep. I feel her hand on my thigh. I turn and force a smile. Fortunately, I don't have to respond. Lisa stands the second Asha crosses the threshold, her arms outstretched to embrace her friend.

I need a drink. Our eyes meet for a telling second before I head to the bar.

"It's so good to see you," I hear my wife say. "And, Vincent, what an incredible surprise. How long has it been?" Lisa asks, being the perfect co-hostess.

"Too long. Look at you. Married life is treating you great, I see."

Lisa laughs. "It's wonderful. You should get our mutual friend to try it."

"I've given up trying to convince Asha of anything."

Asha's voice grows stronger as she nears. "I refuse to be the center of conversation tonight," she says. "I'm sure there are other things and other people we can serve for appetizers." She laughs that smoky laugh of hers, and I almost join her. Only she could say something like that and make it sound like something enjoyable.

I know I can't stand here at the bar forever with my back turned to my sister's dinner guests.

"What's up, man?" Cliff sidles up beside me and reaches for the bottle of Scotch. "You're kinda low key tonight. Everything cool?"

"Yeah, sure." My drink has suddenly become very important—getting the measurements just right, one cube of ice, no splash, and that first swallow.

Cliff lowers his voice. "You, uh, tell Lisa yet?"

"Naw. I was hoping things would pan out for me first."

"It's been two weeks, Ross, almost three since the layoff. How long do you think you can keep something like that from her? She's bound to find out. It's best if it comes from you."

"I know that."

"Look, I did what you asked. I haven't said anything. You're my friend, but Lisa's my sister."

"And she's my wife." I hear the words hiss through my teeth. "I'll handle it."

Cliff gives me a hard stare, almost daring me to go back on my word. He nods his head once and returns to Lynn.

Fortified by a half glass of Scotch, I return to the gathering, feeling that with each step I'm leading myself to the slaughter. Something my mother always said, "What's done in the cloak of night will find its way to the light," begins to ring through my head like a nursery rhyme—over and over. I want to stand in the middle of the floor and shout it at the top of my lungs, expunge it from my being: "I cheated on my wife with her best friend! I have become what I abhor in men. I've done something I don't know how to fix, how to make it right. How can I make this guilt go away?" Why can't everyone hear me screaming?

"Hey, Ross. Good to see you, man." Vincent stands and extends his hand to me.

Absently I shake it. "You, too." If only I could pretend I don't see *her*, delay this moment just a little while longer. "Asha. Good to see you, too." By rote, I lean down and place a light kiss on her cheek. The scent of her and the memories rush through my head. I nearly spill my drink.

Her hand clasps around mine, both of us holding the glass now. "Almost got me," Asha says with laughter underscoring her voice.

"Yeah, sorry about that."

She holds my hand a moment longer, almost as if to soothe me. "How have you been?" Her gaze doesn't waver. Her question is basic, her intent clear.

"Good, and you?"

"Pretty good. One day at a time, that's my motto." She smiles, letting the sage advice settle around the corners of her mouth.

"I'll keep that in mind." I tip my glass to her and return to sit next to my wife.

"Feeling better?" Lisa asks.

"About what?" I feel the Scotch burn its way down my throat.

"About whatever it was that was bothering you earlier."

"Who said anything was bothering me?"

"No one had to. It was written all over your face. You looked like you were about to face a firing squad."

"Don't be ridiculous." The sound of my own laughter seems to ease the knots in my stomach. I slide my arm around my wife and pull her close. "I'm fine. Really."

She brushes her thumb across my bottom lip and then strokes that tiny space between my brows. "I love you," she whispers.

"I love you, too."

I feel her lips against mine, and I want to die.

"Okay, okay, break it up," Karen singsongs from across the room. "As our mother used to say, there's a time and place for everything."

The room erupts into good-natured laughter and Lisa reclines in my arms, giggling like a little girl.

"Listen to your little sister," Cliff chimes in. "Gonna give us old married veterans a bad name," he says, laughing.

Lynn taps him on the arm. "Old veterans! Well, if we're going to be old vets, I sure hope you take after your father! They still have the spark going after fifty years." She turns to Lisa. "What was that, their fourth honeymoon they just came back from a couple of weeks ago?"

"Something like that," Lisa says. "That's what I'm looking forward to, fifty years and counting with this man of mine."

I hug Lisa to me to assure her of something that I no longer know is attainable.

Asha gets up from one of the lounge chairs and moves toward the bar.

"Asha, I didn't get a chance to say hello when you came in," Cliff calls out as she moves the few feet away. "Haven't seen you since you were at the folks' house a couple of weeks back, but you were in and out of there so quick." He chuckles.

"I didn't know you'd stopped by, Asha," Lisa says as she reaches for the snack platter on the coffee table. She pops a taco dipped in salsa into her mouth.

The room suddenly feels as if all the air is being sucked out of it.

"Spur of the moment thing. I'd gone by to see my mother and needed absolution afterwards," she says as smoothly as if she'd rehearsed the lines, and punctuates it with a gentle, almost sad laugh. She crosses her legs and takes a sip of wine before turning and saying something only for Vincent's ears.

"I can understand that," Lisa says. She leans into me and lowers her voice. "You have no idea how Asha's mother can be sometimes."

But I did know. I knew how she made Asha feel. I knew the names she called her, and all the things she never said to her. Yes, I knew. I knew too much.

"I haven't had a chance to call my folks since they've been back," Lisa says. "Maybe we can stop by one evening after work next week, Ross. I could meet you at your office."

I feel Cliff's gaze sear my skull as a trickle of sweat forms along my hairline.

Lisa takes my hand. "This man works so hard," she says to the group. She snuggles closer. "He's determined to get our house before the end of the year."

The love and admiration in her eyes make me want to run away.

"Where are you two thinking of living?" Vincent asks.

"We'd love a brownstone in Harlem," Lisa answers for the both of us, although I've said more than once that if we spend that kind of money, I want more than four square feet of concrete out front and a patch of green out back. I guess she didn't hear me.

"Where would *you* like to live?" Asha asks, directing her question at me.

The room grows suddenly silent, and for an instant I hate what she is attempting to do, but at the same time I'm grateful for the opportunity she hands me—*my voice*. "I've seen some great homes in Westchester. Fabulous structure, plenty of space, nice neighborhoods, good schools."

"Sounds great." She turns to Lisa. "Maybe you should think about finally getting out of the city, Lisa. You could always commute."

Lisa laughs, an uncomfortable sound. "You're the world traveler, hon. Not me. I want to know I can get to where I'm going in twenty minutes or less." She scans the room for approval.

"If you're thinking about having a family, moving out of the city is definitely something to consider," Lynn offers in that understated way of hers. "I'm glad we're out of the day-to-day traffic. And it's not that far from civilization," she adds with a smile.

"I know some great real-estate brokers when you're ready," Brian offers, the first comment he's made during the evening.

"Well, I don't know about everyone else, but I'm starved," Karen announces as she comes in from the kitchen. "Dinner is buffet. So help yourselves."

More often than I would have liked, Asha and I bump elbows, our fingers touch, or our bodies brush against each other as we reach for one item or the next from the buffet table that my sister has elaborately set. The effort to avoid each other, avoid eye contact is beginning to wear on me, and I want the night to be over. When I dare to look at her, I wonder if she is in the least bit fazed by the evening. It doesn't seem so. And then I wonder if it meant anything to her at all, changed her in the ways that it changed me. When she looks at Lisa, does she feel the same depth of remorse that I feel? Does she hate herself as much as I do? How does she face herself in the mirror, move through her day without being tormented by what we've done? I want to ask her all those questions. I want answers.

The questions haunt me. The answers elude me. Each night when I lie next to my wife, I'm certain that she can smell my fear, feel my shame. Each morning when I rise, I think that maybe it was all a dream. But it's not.

"Great evening," Cliff says as he and Lynn head to the door and put on their coats. "We need to do this more often. And, Brian, it was great meeting you. We'll have to talk about some of those investments you mentioned."

"Anytime," Brian says.

"Thanks for coming," Karen says. "See you both soon?"

"Next time, my house," Lynn offers.

"Or ours," Lisa adds, sliding her arm around my waist.

I watch Vincent help Asha with her coat, and I wonder if he will wake up with her in the morning.

"Dinner was great, Karen . . . and Brian," she says with a smile. "Thanks for inviting us."

"You know you're always welcome. Don't be a stranger."

"I won't," Asha promises.

"Do you two need a lift?" Cliff asks me.

"Lift? We came in Ross's car," Lisa says.

"Oh, great. So you got it fixed."

Lisa looks at me, then at Cliff. The snake curls in my stomach.

"There's nothing wrong with Ross's car. Where did you get that idea?" She puts on her coat.

"When I came out of my folks' house the night that you were there, I saw your car still parked out front. Just figured you had car trouble and Asha drove you home."

"You were at my parents' house?"

"Yeah, you remember. I told you." *Not here. Not like this.*

Lisa frowns as if trying to search for the memory. "Maybe you did," she finally says, her tone confused and unconvinced. Her eyes search for Asha.

The sweat runs in a silent stream down my back. It seems as if time is standing still—waiting.

Lisa shrugs. "In any event, the car is working fine, brother dear. Thanks for the offer." She kisses his cheek, then Lynn's. "See you both soon." She takes my hand. "Asha, I'll call you during the week. Okay?"

"Sure."

Asha's gaze connects one last time with mine, the inevitable clear in her eyes.

NINETEEN

And So It Begins

LISA

A light snow dusts the ground as Ross drives us home from Karen's apartment. Tiny flakes of white sparkle like diamonds against the headlights.

On a night like this, there is nothing more romantic than watching nature unfold its splendid magic while you lie in the arms of the one who loves you.

I dare to steal a glance at Ross's stoic profile, hoping that in the strength of his jaw, the softness of his mouth, or the curve of his brow I will find something to slow the frightening beat of my heart. Find something that will settle the waves of nausea that have seized my stomach.

But all I see is Ross, the man I married, the one I love and have put my faith in. Please God, don't let it all be an illusion.

"I had a nice time tonight," he says, breaking the long stretch of silence between us. Immediately I examine his words, dissect them and look for hidden meanings.

"Yes, so did I. I'm glad we came. You know how much I love your sister. I have try to stay in touch with her more."

Ross reaches for the dial on the radio and turns it on. Luther Vandross's "A House Is Not a Home," fills the void between us.

"I couldn't really tell if you were enjoying yourself or not. You were pretty subdued most of the evening." I study his face in the shadowy interior of the car.

Ross's chuckle reaches for me in time with his hand that pats my thigh. "I was fine. Just taking everything in. You worry too much, babe."

"Do I?" I turn to stare out my window. "I'll try not to do that."

"Do what?"

"Worry."

"I'm not meant to be alone . . . turn this house into a home . . ."

Silence except for the radio.

I want to ask him all the unthinkable ugly questions that are racing through my mind. Why would he lie to me about being at my parents' home? Why did he leave his car behind? *Two weeks*. His and Asha's aloofness. *Two weeks*. A part of me wants to demand the truth. Another part of me is terrified of what those answers may reveal, and what will become of us as a result.

Impressions of the evening flash through my head: his body language, his tone, his silence. I watch him park the car, hold the door for me, walk before me, check that everything is secure in the apartment. I listen to the sound of his voice telling me he's going to take a shower and turn in. Simple, ordinary, innocuous things. Everyday innocent things. But suddenly they are not. Everything—word, action, reaction—is suspect.

Until the parting conversation with my brother at the door, I thought nothing of the uncharacteristic Ross who sat next to me playing the role of the attentive husband. But now . . . I dare not think these thoughts through to their conclusion. It's best that I wait, try to sleep tonight, and hopefully it will all seem ridiculous in the morning.

Maybe.

"Cliff called while you were asleep," Ross says.

I look up at him from above the rim of my morning coffee cup. "Hmmm." *He looks rested.*

"Said a few of the fellas are going over to the gym for a game of pickup this afternoon. I figured I'd get my game on."

He does some fancy Michael Jordan–looking move, fakes a jump shot, and smiles that million-dollar smile of his. And all I want at this precise moment is to walk into his arms, tell him that I love him more than anything in the world, that whatever is wrong we can fix together. I want to do that, say those words and hear him say them to me.

"Sounds like fun," I say instead. "Great day for it."

He comes around to where I'm sitting and crouches down in front of me. Nothing irregular shows in his expression. He reaches out with his index finger and brushes my bangs away from my forehead.

"Thank you," he whispers like a prayer.

"For what?"

"For being you, for loving me."

He kisses me so tenderly it's almost painful.

"I promise not to be too late. Maybe we can check out a movie or something."

"Sure . . ."

The front door closes behind him when he leaves. *Thank you*. Tears begin to fill my eyes. What is it? What is it you're thankful that I didn't ask *you*, Ross? What are you hiding?

I know what brought me here, but I can't seem to make my legs walk the few steps from my car to my parents' front door. Dad's car is not in the driveway, but Mom's car is parked in front of the house. At least we'll be alone.

Just do it, Lisa, I tell myself as I reach for the bell. *Nothing can be as bad as what you imagine.*

"Lisa!" My mother's arms wrap around me in that familiar embrace, and I wish I could simply stay there, protected. Her hug feels like home.

"I didn't know you were coming, sweetheart. What a wonderful surprise."

She slides her arm around my waist and ushers me inside.

"How are you, baby? It's freezing out there. I was just fixing some tea. Come into the kitchen."

"Fine. Just wanted to stop by." I shed my coat and hang it on the hook in the hallway, then follow her into the kitchen. "We haven't talked since you and dad came back." I watch her expression, which remains the same. Serene.

She pats my hand as I take a seat at the table. "We had a glorious time. The Bahamas is certainly the place to be this time of the year—get away from all this cold and snow." She wraps her arms around herself to emphasize her point. "I still can't believe your father and I have been married for fifty years." She slowly shakes her head in amazement and then focuses on me. "I hope you and Ross stay half as happy as your father and I."

"So do I, Mom."

"Ross is a good man, Lisa. And so thoughtful, too. He stopped by just before we left. Spent a lot of time with your father and your brother." She frowns in thought. "He did seem a bit distracted, though, as if he had a lot on his mind."

"Did . . . he say what it was?"

Her brows flick for an instant. "If he did, he may have mentioned something to your dad or Cliff. I figured it was man talk, so I didn't sit in." She looks at me and smiles. "It was certainly a day for surprises, though."

"What do you mean?"

"I'm sure Asha told you."

My breath stops moving through my lungs. I reach for the cup of tea my mom has placed on the table in front of me. I stop midway, knowing that if I pick it up, I'll rattle it all over the table. Instead I absently spin the cup in its saucer. My gaze alternates between my mother and the teacup.

"Asha's been so busy. . . . I've been busy. . . . What did she tell you?"

My mother slowly shakes her head, then lowers herself into her favorite seat near the backyard window. "I just don't understand that mother of hers. For the life of me, I don't understand Denise Woods one bit."

"What happened?"

"Asha came here. . . . I've never seen her in such a state, Lisa. It broke my heart." Pain is so clear in my mom's expression. "The things that woman said to her daughter I wouldn't repeat. I meant to call you that same night so that you could check on her, but I got so involved with packing for our trip the next morning, it totally slipped my mind."

"Did she seem okay when she left?"

My mother waves her hand in dismissal. "You know Asha. She puts on a good face, especially in front of the men, but she was a mess on the inside. I can tell you that. Worried me enough that I told her to let Ross drive her home."

Where was I? Right, the teacher's conference. "Did . . . she get a ride?"

"No. Not that I know of. Said she was fine. Ross left when she did, said he had to get home, too."

"Oh, I guess he wanted to beat me home." It was almost a question.

"That's what he said. He left here about five."

Ross didn't get home until nearly ten that night, said he was hanging out with some friends from work. He never said a word about coming here, about Asha, about anything. Oh, God. Oh, God.

"I'm surprised Asha hasn't said anything to you, especially with you two being so close. It didn't seem like something she would get over too quickly."

"Maybe she did mention something. . . ." My mind races in a million directions at once. "Asha's always been resilient. Maybe it didn't hit her as hard as you thought it did. She and her mother have been at odds for years."

"It's all camouflage, sweetheart."

"What is?"

"Asha's resiliency, her outward toughness. Under all those layers of protection—the jet-set lifestyle, gorgeous men, a glamorous career, and beauty all around her—is a very lonely, very hurt young woman looking for something—"

"Asha?"

"Yes, Asha." She tilts her head slightly to the right. "You don't know your friend as well as you think you do." Her brow arches.

"I know her well enough."

"Hmm. Well, as I've always told you, things are never as they seem. People, either." She takes a sip of her tea.

"I'm sure you're right. So after Ross and Asha left . . . she didn't call to say she'd gotten home or anything?"

"No. Not a word. And that's not like Asha. But"—she shrugs—"as I said, she was terribly upset, and then I got busy. Maybe she went home and went to bed."

My stomach lurches. I finally get down a sip of the lukewarm tea.

"I wish she would have told me," I say more to myself than to my mother as the insidious thoughts begin to bloom with life. Ross . . . Asha . . . Ross . . . No . . .

My mother walks to the refrigerator and takes out a box of pound cake—her favorite—and begins to cut a slice.

"What's really on your mind, sweetheart?"

The question shouldn't surprise me, even though it always does. Although I always felt somehow closer to my father, it was my mother who knew my every mood. She could determine from a casual look in my eyes if I was happy, hurt, confused, or lying. It's a skill that's almost frightening in its accuracy.

"Just concerned about Asha, that's all, and wondering why she didn't say anything to me." That much is true.

My mom releases one of those mother sighs, the gentle expulsion of air that is released with a dose of wisdom. "When two friends grow up as close as you and Asha have—like sisters—and one marries, the dynamics of that relationship, that sisterhood, change. It's inevitable. It's no longer the two of you, or a transient lover in the relationship. The husband has now made the duet a trio. The sound can no longer be the same."

"Why can't it? I haven't changed. What we've shared hasn't changed."

"That may well be. But the truth is, your relationship with Asha will never be what it once was. And there's a part of her that knows this. It's the part of her that didn't seek you out when she was troubled. It's that part of her that no longer sees you as only 'Lisa, my friend,' but 'Lisa, the wife.' And there's the part of her that resents that change."

"She has no reason to—"

"People feel the way they do about issues in their life for reasons no more complex than because it's simply the way they are."

I watch the lines in my mother's soft brown face shift with an array of emotions as she tries to convey her thoughts.

"The two of you love each other, always have, but beneath it all there was always that underlying jealousy of each other." Her eyes finally come to rest on my face.

"Jealous!" My head snaps back in surprise. "I was *never* jealous of Asha."

"Of course you were, and still are. Just as she is of you. And jealousy, if not tempered, is an ugly creature. It can turn you into someone you don't like. And it's deceptive. Sometimes jealousy appears in the guise of friendship that periodically gives poor advice, offers a cutting remark, or misses an important birthday. It can be subtle and unrecognizable."

A chill runs through me. I don't want to hear it. I won't acknowledge it and make it real. But in my heart I know it's true.

"So how are things with you and Ross?"

My mother, the master of changing the subject. "Great." I hear the feeble echo of my affirmation and hope my mother doesn't recognize the emptiness of it.

Does she know how desperately important it is for me not to fail again, not to run home with a shredded heart and my self-worth tucked beneath my arm? I want to be like her—my mom. I want to be the queen of my castle, keeping my family and my marriage intact. I want to look back fifty years from now and tell my children about *my* fourth honeymoon. How can I tell this woman, who to me embodies womanhood, a wife and mother, that I'm terrified? How can I tell her how incapable I feel when she is so capable and wise in all things?

I cannot.

Her voice drifts to me through the haze of thoughts. "That's good to hear. The first years are the toughest." She laughs lightly as I watch a memory take shape in her mind. "When your father and I first got married, I was determined to be a good wife." She shakes her head and chuckles lightly. "I was so determined that I used to iron that man's underwear. For the first six months we never ate leftovers. I was positive that the way to a man's heart was through a fresh, home-cooked meal every night. I washed all his shirts by hand and *then* sent them to the laundry!" Her tone suddenly loses its joviality. "And everything your daddy wanted, I wanted—or thought I did."

She looks away from me to some place that I cannot see. When she turns back, there is a heaviness that weighs down the lower lids of her eyes.

"Don't sacrifice who you are as a person of value, your future, your happiness for anyone. Not even for love. One day you'll wake up, and it will be too late."

She draws in a deep breath and then smiles. "I think your sister Tina is having a boy. You know you can tell the sex of a baby by how the mother is carrying."

I have to laugh. My mother is a woman of contradictions. One minute she espouses the wisdom of the elders, the next she's as certain of old wives' tales as she is about the time of day. And somewhere in between is the true Carmen Holden. Just as somewhere between the folds of her counsel is the truth that eludes me—for now.

TWENTY

Things Fall Apart

ROSS

The sound of the basketball pounding against the hardwood floor echoes through the fifty-year-old gym.

"Not as swift as you used to be, my man." I dash by Cliff, heading for a slam dunk. The winning basket is in my hand. *Two steps . . . up . . . and . . .*

"Not today, my brother."

The next thing I know I'm on the floor, looking up, and Cliff is tearing down court. *Up and in.*

All I can do is stare at the ceiling in disbelief. Just that quickly the game is over. I had it in my hand and blew it. My teammates were depending on me, and I screwed it up.

"How long you gonna camp out there, bro?"

Cliff is standing over me. His hand is stretched out to help me to my feet. I need more help than he can offer. It's more than the winning basket that was snatched out of my hands, it's my life. It's my marriage. And just like this game of basketball, I have no one to blame for the loss but me. Me for not seeing it coming. Me for not blocking, me for not protecting the prize. Shit! Tears. I can't start bawling. Not here.

"You all right, man? You hurt?" Cliff kneels beside me. I see the concern deepen the lines bracing his eyes.

"Yeah, yeah. I'm fine." I pull myself up. "Just shamed out of my shorts that I let an old man like you beat me."

Cliff chuckles loudly and pulls me to my feet. "Man, the biggest mistake anybody can make is to underestimate their opponent." He slaps me on the back. "Let's hit the shower, and I'll treat you to a beer. Everybody's going over to The Saloon."

"Yeah, I could use a beer."

"Everything cool at home? I didn't mean to put you on the spot the other night at Karen's house."

"Everything's fine. No problem. Just a little confusion, that's all."

I can feel Cliff's gaze try to probe under my words. "What was that all about, anyway? I know I saw your car out there."

Laughing, I drape the towel around my neck, hoping to buy some time. We head toward the shower. "Like I said, it was just some confusion. We got it straight."

"So that *was* your car?"

Wiping my face with the towel, I push open the door to the locker room. The heavy laughter, raw banter of male voices, and the familiar husky scent of the locker room greet us. Before I know it, I'm being bombarded with playful taunts about my game, or lack thereof. The male camaraderie pushes aside the questions and gives me some breathing room. Moments to recoup and recover. At least for the time being. I know at some point, I'm going to have to come up with something to tell Cliff. I know him. He can be as viciously relentless as a pit bull once he sinks his teeth into something. If it concerns his family, he won't let it go. I know he won't.

Now I wish I hadn't agreed to hang out with the fellas. But if I back out, Cliff will be sure to pick up on it. The last thing I need is him calling Lisa and quizzing her.

Is this what happens when you cheat: the guilt, the paranoia, the lies? How can people live like this—everyday—never knowing when the other shoe is going to fall? Never knowing when something you hadn't thought of will collapse your entire house of cards?

It's like a beautiful building that you construct brick by brick. On the outside, it looks great, but that one little crack, that fault line in the foundation begins to grow and spread until it's irreparable.

I don't want that to happen to me and Lisa. This isn't what I wanted for us. I can't lose my wife. Not over this. I can't.

The Saloon is crowded even for a Saturday afternoon. I guess it's because it also doubles as a restaurant that serves some of the best steaks in the city.

My hope is to chill, have a quick beer, and split. But now that the vacant seat next to me is in the process of being occupied by Cliff, I know that plan is out the window.

"I always did like this place," he says, looking around. "Just the right atmosphere. Especially after a hard game." He takes a long swallow from his bottle of beer, then turns to me. "Have you finally told Lisa about your unemployment status?"

Told her? How could I tell her the shame and humiliation I felt when I was called into the big boss's office?

"Have a seat, Davis," he'd said.

I sat down, sure that this was a conversation about the promotion I'd been working so hard to get.

He leaned forward and braced his elbows on the redwood desk. He steepled his fingers beneath his double chin. "There's no easy way to say this, Davis, but to get straight to the point. We're going to have to let you go."

The world had come to a screeching halt. I began to laugh at the absurdity of it all. "You're kidding me, right?"

"I'm sorry. I wish I were kidding. The project that you've been working on has been cancelled by the client. And with the downturn in the economy, our clients and our company has to scale back considerably. Maybe in six or eight months, things will begin to look up."

I didn't want to beg. I didn't want him to see the fear and anger that were raging inside me. But I couldn't help the question that reflexively spilled out of my mouth. "I just got married. We're planning on buying a house."

It took all my upbringing to keep me from leaping across the desk and strangling the patronizing look off his face.

"I totally understand your position, Davis. As I'm sure you do mine. You're welcome to finish out the week. Your severance is two months' salary and of course a letter of recommendation."

I was screwed. Royally. And for a little while, I'd been able to avoid truly confronting what happened. But here's Cliff in my face. I may have danced around it at Karen's house, but now that Cliff has me hemmed up, he won't let me off that easy. I should have known the question was coming.

"No. Not yet," I finally answer.

I hear his breath seethe in disappointment. "Man, what the hell is on your mind? What have you been telling her for damn-near three weeks when you go out every morning?"

"I'm not telling her anything." I try to keep my face emotionless.

"So, she just assumes you're going to work."

"Yeah."

"What if she calls? What if she decides to stop by the office? Shit, Ross, that's my sister you're bs-ing—making a fool of."

The cutting look I give him goes unnoticed.

"Where are you going everyday—the same place you went to when you left my folks' house a couple of weeks ago?" The note of suspicion strengthens his voice.

Slowly I turn to look at him. His entire body seems coiled, ready for anything. A trickle of sweat slides down between my shoulder blades.

"What's that supposed to mean?"

"Why don't you tell me?"

"I don't know what you're talking about."

He leans in close to me. "Don't you? What are you gonna tell Lisa when she gets around to asking you *that*?"

"The truth. What else would I tell her?"

"That's a good question, Ross. At one time, I wouldn't have questioned it, or you. But lately . . . I don't know who you are. The things you say are suspect, and my sister's too damned in love to look any deeper than what's right in front of her. On the other hand . . . *I'm* not in love with you."

His eyes bore into mine, but I refuse to look away.

"I don't know what you're hoping to accomplish with all this cloak-and-dagger bullshit. This ain't like you. So, yeah, my radar is on. You've always been a stand-up guy. I was the best man at your wedding. You gonna wait until you get married to change your stripes?"

I lower my voice to a hard whisper, squeezing the beer mug between my palms. "Do you have any idea what I'm dealing with? Any idea at all?"

"Do *you*? Do you have any *real* idea of what you've put into motion—the consequences of it?

Does he know? How could he know?

"You think it's easy for me to look Lisa in the face every day, knowing that I'm living a lie . . . that I can't take care of her like I promised? You know what that does to me as a man, every fuckin' day?"

"I know what it can *trick* men into doing—every day. And I pray to God that you're not one of them." He snatches his beer from the counter and walks off.

Fear and shame creep down my spine and cling to my shirt. My heart is pounding through my chest. Cliff all but accused me, accused me as if he could see into my soul. But maybe he could. Only a man would truly understand and recognize another man's frailties, the things that lure us, calling us into places we need not go. Another man can see the lie. Another man can sense the weakness.

I feel my stomach heave. Now it's only a matter of time. Time. Before everything I've lived and worked for falls apart—for one night. And there's nothing on this earth I can do to stop it.

TWENTY-ONE

One Night

ASHA

"Talk to me, Asha. Tell me what the hell is going on with you. You've been making mistakes, jumpy as a cat, and you haven't looked at me since the other night at Karen's."

If I keep my back to Vincent, remain in the shadows of the darkroom, I can move between the images of truth and fiction. I can create my own reality.

"Going on? You mean besides being so damned busy we're both working on a Sunday?" I laugh. The sound bounces back and slaps me for my insolence.

"Work is not what I'm talking about, and you know it."

"I don't know what you mean, then. And if it's not work, I'd rather not discuss it."

Vincent's hand suddenly grips my shoulder, turns me around against my will. His dark eyes are like needles piercing right through me. "You may be able to fool everyone else, but you could never fool me with the flip attitude and fast-mouthed answers. All that says is that you have something to hide. It always has. I'm the one who's seen you totally naked. Raw and at your lowest. So, what is it this time?"

"You think because we've awakened in the same space sharing sweat that you know me!" I try to pull away. "Trust me, you don't. If you really did, you'd run as far and as fast away from me as you could."

"Is that right?"

His voice lowers to the intimate level that always breaks down my walls. "Well if you're so tough and invincible, then why are you crying, Asha?"

Tenderness. I hate it. *Concern*. Can't handle it. Especially now.

"The chemicals are getting to me, that's all." Again, I try to pull away, but his fingers are like hot, molten steel burning into my shoulder blades.

"Since when? You've inhaled this stuff like air for years."

I dare to look at him for an instant. And in that moment of connection, he sees inside my soul. He always does.

He moves his body closer to mine, forcing a confrontation. "What happened with you and Ross Davis?" The air in the small room ceases to move. "I was there the other night, remember? You think I couldn't see how hard the two of you were trying to stay out of each other's way? There must be a reason."

"So what. Because . . . I wasn't in his face . . . that means something? He's Lisa's husband, for heaven's sake. And I was with you." Finally I tear away from his hold and find sanctuary on the opposite side of the developing sink.

The realization flows from him like a hot breeze blazing across the expanse of a burning desert. Disbelief mixes with truth in a hoarse whisper. "How could you?"

"Get out!"

"My leaving won't change anything."

We stare at each other, neither willing to back down. I just want him to leave. Go. Leave me alone with my guilt.

"In all the years I've known you, all the things I've know you to have done, I would never have believed this of you. This is beneath you. Some low-life shit."

His voice is so leaden, detached, and beaten down by the weight of my guilt. But most of all, the disappointment in his eyes tears through me.

I want to deny everything. Remove that knowing look in Vincent's eyes. Take that night back and start over. Refuse Ross's offer to drive me home. Not invite him to come upstairs. If only I'd gone home that night. Not sought out the solace and comfort of Lisa's mother. Had I not been so fucking needy . . .

"What do you think is going to happen when Lisa finds out?" His voice shifts from disbelief to accusation. "She will, you know. The wife always does. What then, Asha? Will you turn your back on her and tell her to get out, too?"

That nightmare lives with me, sleeping and awake. That phone call, that visit, that telling.

"Why, Asha? If you don't tell me anything else, tell me *why*?"

The sound of the glass I hurl against the wall can't drown out the only response I can summon. "I don't know! I don't know!"

"You do know!" His voice roars through me. "There's nothing you do without a reason. Nothing!"

All I want to do is run from the harsh accusations in Vincent's eyes. Run from the truth. Run from myself. But my feet are rooted to the floor, sealed in place, and the hideous truth comes tumbling out of my mouth.

"You want to know why? Because I *am* everything my mother says! I'm a whore, a slut, not worth anyone's time. Are you satisfied now? Is that what you wanted to hear?"

"Asha."

"Fuck you."

The sound of my name follows me out of the door. *Asha!* Up the stairs and out into the bitter cold night. *Asha!* Tears sting my eyes and quickly turn to frost on my cheeks. My throat burns from screaming. But I can't stop screaming, stop running away from it all.

Running even as Vincent's arms wrap around me, huddling me to the warmth of his body. Running even as he tells me the things my mother said were lies. Running even as he drapes a blanket around my shoulders and leads me home.

Vincent sits beside me on the couch.

"I didn't mean it. I swear to you I didn't mean it. I never wanted to hurt Lisa. Never."

The words bubble up from my belly where they've smoldered, erupting now like unchecked lava, mixing with my tears of shame and regret.

"What am I going to do, Vincent? She can't know." I clutch his arm, balling up the sleeve of his shirt in my fist. "She can't find out."

Now that the damning words have been spoken, a chilling fear grips my insides. Panic rises to the brink of hysteria as the scene overwhelms me.

The years between Lisa and me flash in my mind, one image after another, frame by frame. And in our background is my betrayal of a friendship of more than two decades. It's all crumbling before my eyes.

Gentle fingers stroke my cheek, push away my tears. "Tell me what happened."

"You can't help me."

"You need to talk to someone, Asha. I'm here to listen, not judge you."

"I can't."

"Try."

I look at him through tear-filled eyes. "So you can hate me, too?"

"I could never hate you. I want to understand. *You* need to understand. Maybe I can help."

"Nothing can help. Not even you, Vincent. Not this time. Talking won't fix it or make it go away."

That one night in my bedroom emerges like a creature from the deep, looming large and dangerous. I see Ross standing in front of me, so tentative and uncertain—unlike the Ross I've known. That night I needed so desperately to know that I was needed, and I blinded myself to the reality of what I was doing—pushed aside the consequences for that one moment of validation.

I don't ever remember feeling so incredibly vulnerable, so wanting.

For the first time in my life, my defenses had been beaten down, leaving me with nothing but my nakedness, the only thing I was sure of.

I didn't see Ross—Lisa's husband. All I saw was a man hurt and uncertain about every aspect of his own life. I saw myself in his eyes and truly understood. I saw a man who no longer believed in his self-worth and who had to be affirmed to survive.

When I touched his bare chest and felt the erratic beat of his heart, saw the instant of doubt hover in his eyes, I should have turned away. I should have buttoned his shirt and sent him home to his wife. I should have grabbed my robe to cover my aching flesh.

I didn't.

I shouldn't have stopped him when he uttered my name, needed to speak, maybe wanting to talk away what we both knew was happening . . .

"Asha—"

"No." I put my finger to Ross's lips. "Don't talk."

He took my hands and pressed his lips to my open palms, closed his eyes as if to block out my face before he kissed me.

He didn't want to see me.

Abruptly I push up from my fetal position on the couch. I've made my decision.

"There's no way in hell I plan to say anything to Lisa or anyone else about what happened—or didn't. I won't do that to her."

"What if she does find out? What if she confronts you?"

Pacing in front of Vincent, I run through all the possible scenarios.

"That will never happen. Lisa's not the suspicious type. She loves Ross. There's no reason for her to get something like that in her head about him. And she trusts me." Those last four words are like a stake through my heart. *God, what have I done?*

I fold my arms in front of me, trying to harness my doubts. "The thought would never occur to her. It just wouldn't."

TWENTY-TWO

The Beginning of the End

LISA

The conversation between my mother and me repeats in my head. *"You don't know her . . . jealousy . . . things and people are not what they seem . . ."* I try to concentrate on the snow-covered roads, on the beauty of the falling snow, praying that it will magically wash away the turmoil that has seized me. Focus on the inevitable storm that's building. Focus on the icy patches that are so deceptive. You can feel their slickness take your balance out from under you—in an instant. You see it, yet you can't see the fall coming, and all you have is the fear of what might be.

The irony. If I were to write an essay today on the tragedy of my marriage to Ross, I would describe it as an icy patch tempting me to challenge it, covered in a thin blanket of beautiful snow, invisible to the eye. Have I always been aware of its presence, but ignored the dangers—the slips and falls that awaited me? Aware and ignorant of its existence, willing it not to be there until I'm now flat on my back broken in little pieces? And all because a silly part of me believed that I could beat the odds. It would never happen to me, and Ross, we'd never become a statistic. A fool in love. That's a song, isn't it?

How many girl talks have we shared? How many articles have I read on all the reasons *why*? Why? But I didn't believe it could ever be me. Ever happen to me. And not like this. Not Asha and Ross. God, not Asha and Ross.

I want to drive around this mounting storm. Avoid the pain. But the worst of it is yet to come. Of that I'm certain. The dark cloud of my future looms in the distance—waiting to rain down upon me. All the indicators are present. But maybe, just maybe the forecast is wrong.

A threatening silence hovers over me restlessly—waiting. I don't want to go home.

How can I find the words to confront him with these mere suspicions? Dare I open that doorway of mistrust, allowing its insidiousness to take root in our home? Once I allow it entry, there is no evicting it.

Could my instincts be wrong, and I be seeing things that are not there? Could this sick sensation in the pit of my stomach and this ache in my heart be symptomatic of something else?

Instinct is a powerful emotion, yet it's often ruled by nothing more than a feeling, a reaction, a look, things said and unsaid, deeds unseen but done. Instinct is what caused the hairs on my arms to rise at Karen's house. It brought me to my mother's kitchen table, seeking answers. It made me question my husband's loving attention and devotion. It made me look into my friend's eyes, only to find no trace of the woman I once knew. It made me think words like *adultery, infidelity, cheating, betrayal*.

Instinct stands between what I believe to be true and what I hope is false. It is the gateway that separates my today from my future.

I can make it all go away. All that is required of me is to remain quiet and compliant. Let go of the questions that whisper among themselves in my head, and silence the nagging suspicions in my heart.

So simple, so easy. Things could go back to the way they were. The choice is mine. All I have to do is to close my eyes to the truth.

The light from my bedroom window twinkles like a beacon. Leading me home? Funny, that such an image should come to me. Light leads to safety, but often it warns of peril ahead. Which light is this?

Above my head, I can hear Ross moving about in our bedroom. Was it here that . . . *it* happened? Some hotel on the fringes of the city where they wouldn't be recognized? My head pounds with the questions, the images. Will he see the knowledge in my eyes? Will I be able to hide my desolation behind a veil of familiar greetings: a sweet kiss, a comforting hug, a loving pat on the thigh? Will I be able to withstand the answers to my questions?

This walk up the stairs takes my breath away as if I were climbing the face of Mt. Everest, ill prepared and without a team of climbers to break my fall.

The bedroom door is partially open. Ross is stretched out on the bed, eyes closed, listening to Miles's album *Kind of Blue*. The trumpet blown by the Prince of Darkness pierces the air with an achy tenderness, the clean, smooth bubble notes packed with emotion. Indecision holds me in place. I'm frightened of what I need to know to move my life forward. Maybe this is the one time when it would be better to hear a lie. Some slick, smooth words to cool the fears and suspicions. Still, I know that once I cross this threshold, nothing will ever be the same—one way or the other.

"Hey, babe. I didn't hear you come in."

He sounds the same, looks the same. There is no sign of betrayal. His open smile greets me, inviting me to join him. I can feel the tears burn my eyes, setting fire to my throat.

Decide.

"How was the game?" Halfway into the room, I want to cross the short distance between us and press my head against his heart. Instead I turn toward the closet, knowing that if I face him and look into his eyes, my resolve will weaken.

"Great. The usual stuff."

I feel him behind me, his arms sliding around my waist. "I think I'll take a shower. Did you eat?" I ask, moving out of his reach.

"Yeah, we all went over to The Saloon after the game. I could fix you something if you want."

"I'm fine . . . thanks."

"So . . . where've you been?"

"Where've I been?"

"Yeah."

The knot builds in my throat, cutting my words off at the pass. *Say it. Tell him. Watch him.* "At my mother's."

His hands withdraw from my waist. I feel the warmth of his nearness dissipate. "Really? She, uh, okay? You didn't say anything about going over there."

I hear him move away to the other side of the room. *To safety?*

"It was a last-minute decision."

"Oh. Hey, I'm gonna check out what's in the fridge. I'm a bit hungry." He chuckles. "Must have been all the talk about food." He chuckles again. *Nervous?*

"I didn't know we were talking about food." I turn to face him. "I thought we were talking about my visit to my mother's house." I pause to take that last breath. "And yours."

For an instant, his eyes register alarm, and the muscles in his cheeks twitch. The tension heightens a notch.

"Why didn't you tell me you were there?"

"Why?" His eyes dart around the room. "I didn't think I needed a reason to visit your folks. Do I? I thought I was part of the family. But if I'm wrong, let me know. I'll be sure not to go without your knowledge and permission."

He makes a move to leave the room, suddenly wearing the solemn demeanor of a victim. I should let him walk out, forget it, let it go. I could let him off the hook. But I can't.

"Don't walk out, Ross. I want to know what happened."

He spins toward me, his face dark and threatening, like an animal that's been cornered as he braces for attack. His body shows it all in his stance, coiled to defend.

"What are you talking about, Lisa?"

"What happened when you left my parents' house with Asha? You didn't come home. I know you didn't come home."

His voice doesn't falter. "Of course I did. You were here when I got in. What is this? More of your crazy notions—"

"Hours later. Hours after you left. Where were you, Ross?"

Then it happens. That split second of unspoken truth. The bitter truth. All he does is look away from me, work hard not to face me, and at that moment I can see straight into his soul, and a part of me dies right there on our bedroom floor. It is an admission of guilt, just as if he had spoken the words.

"Lisa, I . . ."

"My best friend, Ross?" I feel the room begin to spin. Through a haze I see him move cautiously toward me. "Don't. Don't you dare come near me."

"It's not what you think. God, so much was happening. So much was wrong. I didn't know how to tell you . . . everything. The things you wanted . . . what I'd promised . . . I—"

"So you fucked my friend! Is that what you're trying to tell me? You fucked my friend because life got in the way!"

"Lisa, please, please listen to me. I love you. You've got to know that. I love you so damned much."

"I don't want to hear it! I won't hear it. This is what you call loving me so damned much? I don't need that kind of love. I don't deserve that kind of love. Not from you. Not from anyone."

"Lisa—"

"Did she seduce you, Ross? Did she drug you? Is that what you're going to tell me? You didn't know what you were doing?" I hear hysterical laughter coming from some raw, ravaged place, and I realize that it's my own. "I would have believed it of Asha, but not you."

"It wasn't her fault. Don't blame her. It was me, my own shit. My own feelings of being inadequate. Not able to measure up to what you wanted. What you expected. Can you understand that?"

"So it's *my* fault?" My entire body is trembling with rage. "It's *my* fault that you slept with her? You want to turn this on me? You bastard! How dare you? I've given you everything. Planned for us, worked for us, sacrificed for us. For our future. And you blame this on me!"

"It's always been about what you want, Lisa. When have you ever thought about what *I* wanted, what *I* needed? When? From the very beginning, it's been all about you. Never about me or what I wanted."

I can't believe what I'm hearing, what I'm being accused of. This isn't my fault. It isn't.

For a few seconds, neither of us says anything. It's as if we are two boxers sizing each other up, looking for weaknesses, looking to win. He is looking for a way out. He wants things to be as they were. But never can be. Not ever again.

"I want you to leave my house, Ross." I surprise myself with the sudden calm that envelops me. My entire body seems to relax. The tone in my voice sounds as commonplace as if I'd asked him to take out the garbage. "Now."

"That says it all doesn't it, Lisa? *Your* house," he says in a near whisper. "*Your* everything."

"Now."

He looks at me one last time before moving to the dresser, the closet. I can't stay to watch him pack a few belongings. His hands tremble. I don't want to watch him walk out the door, don't want to ask him where he's going. I don't want to see the regret, remorse, and guilt on his face. I've made a choice, and now I have to live with the aftermath of that choice . . . *for better or for worse*.

The Masquerade Is Over

ROSS

I love my wife, Lisa. I think I fell in love with her the first moment I saw her in Cliff's office. She's everything I've ever wanted in a woman. She's beautiful, intelligent, a hard worker, a great lover. But something happened along the way, something that will haunt me for the rest of my life. The scary part is, sleeping with Asha seemed like the most natural thing in the world. It wasn't about the sex or boredom, or about revenge, it was about . . . I still don't know. That's what makes this thing so damned hard—makes it impossible to explain to my wife why I slept with her best friend.

I'm not the kind of man who runs around. I've always been a one-woman man. I believe in fidelity. That's why this . . . is just so incredible. Lisa won't talk to me. Her family hates me. But if I could just tell my side . . .

TWENTY-THREE

The Psalm of Regret

ROSS

My third drink of the night. Still feel that dull ache in my gut. Still see the look in Lisa's eyes. *That look.*

"Last call, buddy. We close in a half hour."

The back-and-forth motion of the white cloth wiping down the counter is making my stomach swirl.

"Another Scotch."

"Bad night?"

I reach for my refill and realize my hands are still shaking.

"You awright, man? Maybe you should call it quits for tonight."

"Quits!" I start to laugh. "Funny you should say that. My wife called it quits. Told me to get out of her house. Her house. Know what that does to a man?" *My . . . my tongue keep . . . getting in the way . . . trying to explain.* "See, I knew I was living in her house. Didn't want to, though. Nope. Never wanted to."

"Hey, you know how women are. Once she calms down, she'll be beggin' you to come back. They always do."

I shake my head, and the room shifts dangerously from left to right. "Naw . . . not . . . this time. I screwed up."

"We all do. Give it some time. She'll come around. Send her some flowers. Works like a charm."

The room shifts again. I reach for his shirt. "You don't understand . . . my wife hates me. She'll never forgive me. Never! I . . . don't know what I'm gonna do. Lost everything. My job . . . my wife . . ."

"Take it easy, bud. You need some coffee."

The Scotch glass is taken from my grasp, and I suddenly feel as if my last anchor has been cut.

"Drink this."

The aroma of fresh coffee floats under my nose, and in the haze I wonder how long ago he knew I needed it.

"You'll feel better."

"Think so? Coffee will make it all better?" The laughter begins again, and I don't know if I can stop it this time.

"You want me to call somebody? Friend, brother, your pops?"

In a moment of clarity, I realize there is no one to call. No one. Mom and Dad are gone. I can't call Cliff. And I don't want Karen to see me like this, know why I'm like this. Not her brother. Her big brother.

I have no one. Not a fuckin' soul besides a bartender whose name I know only because of a tag pinned to his white shirt. KENNY. Well, Kenny can't help me, either. I'm beyond help. In fact, what I did was low, really low, so low that I don't deserve help.

"You want me to call somebody, cause you're in no shape to drive, especially on a night like this."

The pitch-black brew shoots a jolt of clarity through me as it crashes to my belly.

"What'sinthisstuff?"

"Say what?"

If only I could untangle my tongue from my teeth, maybe he would understand me. "Forget it." I'm too mind weary to repeat what I've already forgotten.

"Got some place to stay tonight?" Kenny asks.

That sobers me up pretty quick. I try to focus on his face and slowly the two of them merge into one. Is he trying to hit on me? Do I look that desperate? The ugly truth is I'm going to have to spend tonight in a hotel, and maybe the night after that and the one after that. Shit!

"There's a pretty good hotel about three blocks down on West Twelfth. Clean, rates are good."

I look at Kenny through new eyes. Just a decent guy trying to look out for me. It's so easy to stick labels on people, make them out to be something they're not, based on what we think we see or know. One simple act. Not knowing all the reasons why.

Lisa's probably thinking all kinds of things about me now. Everything I've ever been, the man I always tried to be is now erased as if he never existed. I've become another statistic, my marriage another tragedy to be discussed over lunch. But I haven't changed. "I made a mistake."

"Huh? Say something?"

"I said . . . I made a mistake. And now I won't be worth a damn to anybody."

"Listen, man. I don't wanna get all in your business, but whatever you've done, just face up to it. Deal with the consequences like a man. Then move on. If whoever it is can't forgive you or forget, then the only person you can worry about is you."

I'd heard it all before, even spouted the same sage advice. Never thought it would apply to me.

"Want more coffee?"

"No. Thanks. How much do I owe you?"

Kenny smiles like a benevolent priest. "It's on the house: the drinks, the coffee, and the advice."

I don't deserve to be treated with any kindness. Not after what I'd done. Kenny is probably the only person in my world right now to whom my actions wouldn't matter. A virtual stranger. How screwed up is that?

Pushing up from the chair, the harsh reality of the rest of my life rushes up from my gut, threatening to spill all over the freshly wiped counter. All I've known, all I've been to myself and for others is over. Done. Finished. I can't go back. But how can I move forward?

Maybe I'll take Kenny's advice and wait a few days. Wait it out. Then I'll try to talk to Lisa. I'll get her to forgive me. Right now she's hurt and disappointed. But underneath it all, she's got to know how much I love her. She's got to know that what happened between me and Asha had nothing to do with love, nothing to do with how I feel about her.

We can work this out. Lisa is not an unforgiving woman. Whatever we have to do to make this work, I'm willing to do. Even if it means moving away from everyone and everything and starting over. Just the two of us.

I'll make it work.

TWENTY-FOUR

Look at Me

ASHA

A ringing doorbell? I don't have the will to get up, to do anything. Since Vincent left, all I can do is lie here on my bed. Lie here and pray that when I open my eyes, everything will be back to the way it was.

That damned bell again!

Go away, Vincent! I know it's you wanting to pour more salt on the wounds you opened. I can't handle that look in your eye or the censure and disappointment in your voice.

More insistent. More demanding. Commanding me to answer. Do not ask for whom the bell tolls; it tolls for thee. . . . Maybe if I bury my head beneath these pillows, I can block out the ringing, stop its plea for me to answer for what I've done.

"Pretending it didn't happen won't make it go away." Shut up, Vincent. *"No matter how far you run, or where you hide, your conscience will be right there with you."* Shut up, damn you!

You're supposed to be my friend, Vincent! I trusted you with my ugly secret, and you made me feel shame, regret, disgust for myself—all the things I'd been trying to deny these past weeks. But you wouldn't let me deny them. You kept pushing that mirror up to my face and forcing me to stare at my reflection—at who I really am. And you know what the worst part is? The reflection was empty.

So I won't listen anymore, Vincent. I won't allow you to stay in my head whispering to me, telling me to go to Lisa before she comes to me. I'll stop you from whispering. You won't do this to me. What more do you want from me beyond my confession? Should I sit in a warm bath and slit my wrists like the ancient Romans? Will that satisfy you—make you get out of my head—stop the ringing? I'll say my piece, slam the door in your face, and maybe you'll finally go away.

"Lisa . . ."

"May I come in?"

"Wh—what are you doing out in this weather?"

"Are you going to make me stand in it?"

"No, oh, of course not. I'm sorry. I was lying down. My head is still foggy."

"Alone?"

"What kind of question is that?"

"It wouldn't be the first time I've come over unannounced and interrupted you. I want to be sure this isn't one of them."

I've never seen this Lisa before. Never seen this chill in her eyes, the resoluteness of her mouth, the determination of her step walking past me as if *I* don't exist. Watching the stiffness of her back and the way she turns slowly to face me, I realize that *she knows*.

"Can . . . I get you anything?"

"There's nothing you can get me, Asha, nothing you can say or do for me."

It hurts so bad to look at her, to see the pain swimming in her eyes and know that I am the cause. The hate is reflected in the tears she seems to refuse to shed. *Just say it, say what you've come to say. Get it out and over with. I can't stand the waiting.*

She sits down on the couch, unbuttons her coat, and tosses her purse to the side as if she plans to stay awhile. Maybe, just maybe—

"Why did you fuck my husband?"

The question is asked so calmly, so matter-of-fact, so uncharacteristic, as if she's asking directions. For a moment, I can't speak. "Lisa . . . it's not what you think—"

"You've sat at my table. You were welcomed into my home. I loved you like a sister for as long as I've known you—from that first day on the stoop. I trusted you! Trusted you with every ounce of my being, and you betrayed me. Not just a friendship. Not just a sister, but the vows said before God. You stood by my side when I spoke them. How could you? Do you value yourself so little that nothing is beneath you? My *husband*, Asha?

"Don't you look away! Don't you dare look away. I want you to see what you've done. See me. I want you to remember this every day that you breathe."

"Lisa . . . I . . . I never wanted to hurt you."

"Never wanted to hurt me!" Her voice cracks like a whip across my flesh. "How long, Asha? How long have you been after my husband? Did you plan this?"

"Of course not. How could you think that? I never planned any of this. It happened. It was a terrible mistake."

Afraid to move, I watch her as she paces the floor. She stops and spins toward me. Her expression marred with unleashed fury.

"A mistake! Knocking over an ashtray, breaking a glass, stepping on someone's foot are mistakes. You knew what you were doing. You always do. Was it here in your bedroom? Is that where it happened? Was it?"

Suddenly she storms off toward my bedroom and swings the door open, almost as if she expects to find Ross there.

I can't move as I watch this nightmare come to life. "Lisa, don't do this—"

She stalks toward me and stops within inches of my face. "Don't do what? Tell you what a bitch you are? What a selfish, soulless bitch you are? For all of your proselytizing about being carefree and unattached to anyone or anything, you've always wanted what *I* had." She pokes a finger hard at her chest. "You wished my mother was your mother, my father your father, my life your life, and now my husband. Was it jealousy, is that what it was about?"

Something inside me snaps, all the things my mother has said, the loneliness, the fears that I kept hidden behind bravado and glitter rush to the surface. And suddenly I want to hurt her the way I've been hurting for years when I watched her receive all the things I never could.

I whirl away, cross the room, and then toss my head back and laugh. "Jealous! Why in the hell would I be jealous of you, Lisa? You call what you have a life? Your entire world consists of Brooklyn, Manhattan, and Queens. Your love life sucks, always did. You're the one who was always jealous of me and my life. You don't have anything I want."

"Apparently I did," she says with a steely quiet that chills me to the bone. "I always did. And now you've proved it."

"Maybe if you'd been taking care of your husband at home, he wouldn't have needed to turn to me." I hurl that barb at her as my only defense. "Maybe if it wasn't always all about what Lisa wants, what Lisa had to have, none of this would've happened. I didn't come on to Ross. If it hadn't been me, it would have eventually been someone else. Maybe if you would've let him be a man—"

I feel frozen as I watch her stalk back toward me, certain that a blow is coming. Instead her words are more punishing than any physical force. "Don't turn this on me," she says, enunciating every word. "*You* did this. *You* made a choice." Her light eyes are mere slits beneath her lids. "Now live with it. Live with that moment when your choice changed everything forever."

She steps closer, so close that I can see her cheeks tremble, and she stares at me as if she's never seen me before.

"What kind of woman are you? *Who* are you? I feel sorry for you, Asha, because you have no idea what you've done. Maybe one day you will. And when you do, maybe you'll finally become a human being." She grabs her purse from the couch and brushes past me. "My mother was right. I don't know you." She's heading for the door.

The enormity of what I've done crashes against me in a tidal wave of reality. "Lisa, please. I didn't mean what I said. Don't leave. Let me—"

"Don't touch me."

"Please just listen to me, let me explain. I'm so sorry, Lisa. I didn't mean any of what I said." A blast of cold air rushes in as she opens the door and hurries out. "Come back! Pleeease! I'm sorry. Lisa! I have no one. Do you hear me? I have no one but *you*. No one!" I run out behind her to the top of the outside stairs. My thin robe flaps in the icy wind.

My voice reverberates in my ears, down the stairs, and out into the street, trying to catch her, stop her car from pulling away from the curb. My cries echo through the stillness of the night, between the diamondlike flakes that cover me in a veil of icy white purity.

So I sit here on the steps huddled in my robe, the terror of being truly alone more biting than the bitter wind. In my mind's eye, an image forms, the photograph is snapped, captured forever—a woman lost and alone, frozen in time with nothing but darkness in her background.

TWENTY-FIVE

You Can't Go Home

ROSS

The silence is sure to drive me mad. A killing silence. Lisa won't answer my calls. The locks have been changed on the condo. The message? There's nothing that can be done now to salvage our marriage; that there's no room for talking. I keep waiting for a thaw, but it's been two weeks. I was sure by now she would have had time to think, to realize that we can work this out between us.

I know it's crazy sitting out here in the car, watching the building. But I need to see her—if only for a minute—face-to-face. If I could see her, I could talk to her, make her understand that it was all a terrible mistake and that I still love her.

I'm not sure where to turn, who I can go to. The worst part is, the only one who could possibly understand what I'm going through is Asha. I've been tempted to call her to see if she's all right. But I know I cannot open that door again for any reason.

When I finally went home last weekend to try to talk to Lisa, all my bags were packed and waiting. Even now, I can't believe what's happened to my life, to us, in a matter of weeks. All from one foolish act.

I hardly recognized Lisa when I came through the door. There was a coldness about her that I'd never seen before. A distance that I couldn't cross. She barely looked at me. When she did, it was as if she were looking right through me. No doubt when she looked at me, she saw all her crushed hopes and dreams. Pain, betrayal, and disappointment in human form.

"I'm sure I packed everything that belongs to you," she'd said, and lit a cigarette, something I'd never seen her do. She blew a cloud of smoke in my direction. "If I missed anything, you can contact my lawyer." She pointed to a small white business card on the coffee table with the tip of her cigarette.

"A lawyer, Lisa?" I asked in disbelief. "Why can't *we* talk about this? There has to be some way we can work this out. Just hear me out. Whatever you want, I'll do it if it will make things right."

She looked at me with such disdain that my stomach rolled. "I'll tell you like I told your playmate: There's nothing you can do for me." The bitter tone of her words stunned me more than what she said.

I kneeled in front of her. "Lisa, please don't turn away. I love you. I made a terrible, terrible mistake. I can't take it back. I wish I could. I would do anything to take that look out of your eyes. Baby, I never wanted to hurt you."

"You did, Ross, more than you'll ever know. Now, please leave."

"Lisa." I could feel the desperation building in my chest. I was losing her, and I didn't know how to stop it from happening. "Listen, let me stay tonight. We can talk. There's so much I need to tell you, so much I should have told you."

"You're joking, right?" The corners of her mouth turned up in a sarcastic grin. "There's nothing you can do to stop this feeling I have in my stomach day in and day out. Nothing."

"Tell me you don't love me, Lisa." I place my hands on her thighs. "Tell me what we've had, what we've been to each other, was meaningless. Tell me and I'll leave. I'll leave your life and never bother you again."

It was not an ultimatum, but a desperate plea to her reason, to the memories of happier times. It was a last-chance move to lift her away from her feelings, which were still raw and aching. I thought it was working. For one brief instant as I held my breath, there in the depths of her eyes, a flicker of the old Lisa, the loving Lisa, surfaced and softened the hard line of her mouth. Then she disappeared again.

"Get out, Ross," she said in a quiet, even tone. "Leave. Now."

I've never felt that kind of defeat, that total sense of futility. I didn't feel it when my father refused to see me off when I went to college, or when he died before we had a chance to make peace. I didn't feel it when I opened my heart to Michelle and she crushed it, changing the man I had once been. Neither did I feel so defeated and insignificant when my supervisor told me that he was sorry but they would have to let me go. But at that moment, kneeling in front of my wife, I felt beaten as surely as if I'd been whipped to my knees. And it was at that moment that I truly understood the depth of loss and how much I loved my wife—and how much I had given up.

My body felt like lead as I pulled myself to a standing position. I glanced at the white business card on the table and picked it up.

"If it's what you want." I turned away and started putting my four suitcases out in the hallway. When I looked back, Lisa was standing in the doorway with that same warm and vulnerable look she had the first day we met. It was obvious she was battling inside with the possibility of talking things out. I realized then that none of this was easy for her, either. I took a tentative step toward her, but then her expression changed into that mask of cold indifference, and she quietly shut the door.

So here I am, sitting outside of her building like some kind of fool, hoping that I'll catch a glimpse of her. Hoping that she'll offer us a chance to rebuild what we once had.

Funny, but as much as I tell her we need to talk this out, as much as I beg her to let me explain, the reality is, I have no idea what I could possibly say. I've asked myself a million times how did it happen, why did it happen, and why Asha? I've yet to come up with a reason that satisfies even me.

Yes, I felt lost and afraid. Yes, I felt less than the man I knew myself to be. I felt unneeded by everyone around me: my sister, my employer, and my wife. And that night, for the first time in far too long, I was made to feel that I mattered, that what I was saying was being understood.

That night I talked to Asha, really talked about things I'd never said out loud. I told her about my childhood, my parents, Michelle, losing my job, feeling distanced from my sister and her new life, and being controlled by the wants of my wife. And not once, not once did I feel as if I were being judged. As if I was being looked at as "less than."

"Maybe if it was just one thing, you know," I'd said to her. "But I'm not feeling this way all of a sudden. It's been building, growing over the years."

"Who we are at any given time is an accumulation of our experiences," she'd said to me. Her response was like wisdom from the elders—certain, clear, and full of truth.

"Have you ever felt valueless?" I asked. I really needed to know.

She smiled, almost laughed. "More often than I would like," she'd confessed. "I suppose you and I are more alike than different. We both move through life with the wonderful façade in place, but none of what everyone sees on the outside reaches below the surface."

She began telling me of her various affairs, the thrill of the moment and the emptiness afterward. She told me how lonely she's always felt, how much she's wanted to know the feeling of love and to be loved in return.

"It's a very lonely place to be," she'd said. "And it doesn't help when you can't relax and let the mask ever fall. That you must always be on, always in character, for all the world to see. Who would ever believe that *the* Asha Woods is afraid to face the morning, is terrified of being alone, of giving in to her emotions because she knows that if she dares, it will all be taken from her? So I live in and create a momentary world. Here and gone in the blink of an eye, the snap of a camera lens."

"But those images are preserved," I'd mildly challenged.

"Yes, those that I want to keep."

Was it then, that moment, that I turned the corner from "impossible" to "yes"? Was it then that my foolish male ego wanted to succeed where others had failed—become that one indelible imprint on the heart and mind of this haunted and elusive woman—immortalized in her mind's eye? An achievement I'd been unable to secure in any area of my life. For some irrational reason, I needed to believe that sleeping with Asha Woods could somehow validate me.

How can I ever explain that to Lisa—say those words? I glance up at the darkened window, one last time, knowing the answer, and finally drive away.

TWENTY-SIX

Lay My Burden Down

LISA

How long have I been laying here in bed, staring up at the ceiling, counting the grooves in the molding? It feels like eternity.

I can barely get through my classes these days. My every waking hour is filled with images of Ross and Asha, making it impossible to concentrate. It's like a recurring nightmare that even haunts me in the daylight. All the torturous questions plague me: Did he kiss her the way he's kissed me? Did he caress her breasts as lovingly as he's caressed mine? Did she cry out his name when his body filled hers? And afterwards, did they realize what they'd done? Did they care? Did they plan to keep it a secret and see each other again and again?

The questions and visions torment me with the precision of a sadist. I looked at myself in the mirror this morning and didn't recognize my own reflection. The dark circles like half-moons under my eyes, the tight drawn skin across my cheeks, and the way my clothes fit as if they should be a size smaller, as if they all belong to someone else—the new me.

Now I sleepwalk through my days. Hang on by my fingernails waiting for the weekend so that I can sink into sleep to keep from crying. I know I can't go on like this. I know I can't continue to avoid answering my phone, or telling my family what's happened to my marriage. I must regain control of my life, or I'll lose it totally.

So today I've made a decision. I'm going to shower, get dressed, eat breakfast, and visit my parents. I can't keep up this charade anymore, and the longer I put it off, the more it hurts me. And I'm tired of hurting. I'm tired of being tired.

"Is Dad at home?" I ask my mother as I step across the threshold of my childhood home, even though I'd already spotted his car in the driveway.

"He's out back." I feel her eyes take me in. I see the questions forming on her lips. She moves closer to inspect the ravages of what the past few weeks have done to me. "You look awful. You've lost weight, and you look like you haven't slept in days."

I hear the escalating concern in her voice and turn to face her, willing myself not to break down. "I want to talk to both of you. Can you get Dad for me?"

"Lisa, you're scaring me. What is it?"

"Mom, please. I can only do this once."

She stares at me one last time, draws in a breath, then leaves in search of my father.

While left alone in the comfort of the room in which my family has shared so many good times, I wish that I could turn the clock back to those carefree days when the future looked bright and promising. How often have I sat opposite my father as he told me all the things he wished for me, listened to my mother tell me that the world was mine and nothing would make her happier than to see me settled and happy in my career and in my life? How proud they were of me.

How can I tell them that all those dreams and wishful hopes were nothing more than that? How can I face the disappointment that I know will be in their eyes, the sympathy in their voices?

"Lisa?" My father is always fearless, invincible. But for the first time in my life, I hear a note of panic in his voice, uncertainty.

My own distress magnifies in response. I try to smile as I turn to face him and my mother. Their concern is mirrored in almost identical gazes and in this telling moment I fully comprehend my loss. I will never stand hand-in-hand with Ross, feeling what he feels, our love so secure from years of knowing each other that our thoughts are conveyed without words. I will never have what is here in front of me, a partnership that will stand strong whatever life may bring. And that realization saddens me in a way that nothing else in these terrible days has.

My father moves toward me, but my mother gently takes his hand, instinctively knowing that I need space, some breathing room.

"I . . . guess Mom told you that I wanted to speak to both of you . . . together." I swallow over the dryness of my throat. "Uh, I don't know of any way to say this, but to just say it. Ross and I have separated. I've contacted a lawyer."

"What?" my father booms incredulously.

I know how much Ross means to him, how he looks at him as a second son. I know my news will devastate him, and a part of me doesn't want to hurt him with my revelations. But . . .

"Lisa, my God. What on earth happened?" My mother slowly lowers herself into the armchair as if she's suddenly experienced a physical pain.

"It's been barely a year, for god's sake. Whatever it is, you need to sit down and work it out with him," my father says as if I'm the one at fault.

I shake my head, hoping the words will follow. "Not this time, Dad."

"I want to know what happened," he demands, and begins to pace.

"Please sit down, Dad."

He whirls toward me, pointing a finger. "Did he hurt you, Lisa? Because if he did, I swear—"

"Louis, please," my mom interjects. "Let her tell us what happened."

Funny, but now the mirrored images are no longer true reflections.

One is a face of pain-filled concern; the other, a mixture of rage and disappointment.

"Ross . . . Ross . . . had an affair."

"I don't believe it! Not Ross. Where on earth are you getting such foolishness in your head?" my dad blusters in disbelief. Not his Ross. The chosen one.

"From him . . . and from Asha."

Silence fills every crevice of the room.

"That . . . how . . . no, Lisa, baby. Not Asha," my mother cries, covering her face in her hands.

"When?" is all my father asks, rising from his seat,

"The night that he and Asha were here together."

I watch that night replay in my mother's eyes and then my father's before they turn to each other in acknowledgment.

"Where is he? I'll kill him, I swear I will." My father's thunderous voice seems to bounce off the walls. His nostrils flare as he sucks in oxygen.

"Louis! Calm down."

"Calm down!" He spins toward my mother. "Did you hear what our daughter just told us, Carmen? That son of a bitch slept with her . . . best friend." He sounds as if he's choking on those last two words. "That same girl who we practically raised like a daughter!"

I'd never seen my father cry. Never. But there are tears in his eyes, and my heart breaks again and again. How I hate Ross and Asha for what they've done to me and now to the two people who loved them like their own.

"Are you sure, sweetheart?" my mother gently asks.

All I can do is nod.

She comes and sits beside me, wraps her arm around my shoulder. "You'll be all right, baby. You will," she whispers, the same way she used to when I was a little girl and was afraid of sleeping in the dark. "Where is Ross?"

"I . . . told him he had to leave about two weeks ago."

"Two weeks? You've been carrying this around with you—alone—for two weeks? Lisa, you could have come to us—to me."

"I couldn't. I . . . wanted to, but I couldn't. It's taken all I have just to get up in the morning."

"Where is he?" my father demands, repeating my mother's question.

"I don't know."

"I'll find him." His words are precise and chilling.

"And then what, Louis? What are you going to do when you find him? Beat him to death? What will that solve?"

"I'll feel better, and he'll know that we aren't sitting back and taking this lightly. He needs to be taught a lesson." My father heads toward the door. My mother and I run after him.

"Louis!"

"Dad, please." I grab his arm, and he tosses my hand away like it is an annoying fly.

"I won't sit still and let him hurt you this way. Humiliate you." His face muscles tremble with rage. "I'd be less than a man, less than your father if I did."

The sound of the slamming door jolts us both with its finality.

"I'm calling your brother. Cliff is the only one who can talk some sense into him when he's like this—totally irrational."

I grab my mother's hand, my eyes pleading with her. "Please, don't tell Cliff. I don't want him to know. Not yet."

"Lisa, would you rather have your father find Ross and wind up in jail—because that's what's going to happen—or tell your brother? Cliff loves the ground you walk on. He'll be there for you. He won't judge you."

I feel as if someone has stuck a pin in me and let out all the air. I nod my head in reluctant agreement as I helplessly watch her walk into the kitchen to call my brother. All I can hear is her muffled voice, punctuated, I think, by intermittent sobs. Finally she returns.

Her eyes are red, but her face is calm, resolute almost. She forces a weak smile.

The hole in the dam that I'd been holding back by sheer force of will finally bursts. "Oh, God. Oh, God. I didn't want this. I didn't want this to happen. What if Dad finds Ross?" The terrifying scenario plays in my head. "Why, Mom? Why did he do this to me? I love him."

"I know you do, sweetheart. And whether you believe this or not, Ross loves you, too."

I feel the warmth of my mother's protective embrace wrap around me, and I sink slowly into the sanctuary of her arms. "You don't do this to someone you love," I sob against her breasts. "You don't. And not with my best friend. Not Asha, Mom. Not Asha."

"Come and sit down, sweetheart." She guides me to the sofa and sits beside me. "I know this will sound like a cliché, but you will be all right. No matter how things turn out. But you need some time to think things through. You stay here tonight, stay here as long as you need to. Take some time off from work if necessary. But you need to think about how much your marriage is worth to you. You need to think about how much you love your husband and if that love can survive what happened. And you need to think about if you can forgive him. Really forgive him. Not just for his sake, but mostly for yours."

"For mine?" I swipe the tears from my face and focus on my mother.

"Yes, yours. Betrayal is a powerful, ugly, and devastating thing. It erodes everything that we once believed to be true. But what's worse is that it often changes the betrayed far more than the betrayer. It hardens your heart, Lisa. It makes you suspicious, questioning, and often unable to let anyone get close to you because of that underlying fear of being deceived again. And it's all because a part of you can't let go, can't forgive what was done to you, and it lessens the quality of your life."

"I don't know if I can ever forgive him, Mom. How can I? Ross isn't some boyfriend. He's my husband. He pledged his love and fidelity to *me*. Me. It meant nothing to him. I meant nothing to him."

"I don't believe that, Lisa."

"How can you say that after what he's done?"

"Infidelity happens for as many reasons as there are people. You'd be surprised at how little it has to do with lack of love for the one they're married to. It's about urges and sensation and even fear."

I want to believe her. I want to accept her wisdom. I want to be able to get up, dust myself off, and make this marriage work. But I can't. Maybe I don't have what it takes to forgive—some genetic flaw. Because all I can see in my mind is Asha's naked body locked with my husband's. And each time that I do, the pain battles with the fury, like a hurricane that has finally found land and destroys everything in its path.

Slowly I shake my head. "I can't do it."

"You don't know what you're capable of until you try. Have you spoken to him?"

"I . . . confronted him."

"It's not the same thing, Lisa. You need to talk to him and listen to what he has to say. This happened for a reason."

"What are you saying—that it was my fault, that I'm the reason why he went to her? I did everything in my power to make him a good wife, take the burden off him, give us a comfortable place to live, arranged everything, saw to all his needs—"

"Do you hear yourself, sweetheart? Do you *really* hear what you're saying? Where does Ross fit into the grand plan? What role did he play in your marriage?"

"So you *are* blaming me." I spring up from the couch. "I thought you were on my side."

"I am, darling. You know that. But I want you to take some time and think this through. Don't be rash. Marriage isn't something to be taken lightly or thrown away."

"Tell it to Ross, Mom. I'm not the one who went outside of our marriage. It was him!"

"Lisa, you need to listen to me. Really listen to what I'm saying to you. Yes, what Ross did was wrong, reprehensible. *And* Asha. But things are often not what they seem."

I start to laugh, a kind of hysterical laughter that suddenly explodes out of control. "How would you know? You and Dad have had the perfect marriage. He never ran out on you. You never had to go through what I'm going through. You—"

"Your father went through it with me."

She says the words so softly, so suddenly I'm certain I've heard wrong. I step closer, look into her eyes, and her gaze slides away—and I know. Slowly I lower myself onto the couch.

"Ma? Wh-what are you saying to me?" Before she speaks I almost know the answer, but I want her to say something else, make me wrong. Anything but that.

"We were married for about four years," she begins in that same hollow voice. "Cliff was three, Sandra barely two. I was working at the school all day, picking them up from the sitter, and then coming home to my second job as housewife. I'd put on about twenty pounds—and I was never thin to begin with. I was feeling old at twenty-six. Your father and I rarely had time for each other. He was so busy working he hardly noticed me, unless I came to him with a problem. I was lonely, so very lonely—in a house full of people, I was alone. When I tried to talk to your father about it, he would brush off my concerns, tell me things would ease up when the kids got a little bigger—give me a peck on the cheek, turn over, and go to sleep. And I would lie there at night and cry into my pillow so that he wouldn't hear me."

"Oh, Mom . . ."

"I guess I was looking for something I wasn't getting at home—someone to listen to me."

She sighs deeply and the melancholy sound pushes open the door to the past.

"I met him at the supermarket." She laughs a sad laugh. "He'd asked me what was the best detergent to get out stains—of all things. Not your routine come-on line. I recommended something. I don't even remember what. Then he noticed the baby food, and boxes of Pampers . . ."

My mother paints the scene so clearly that I imagine myself in it.

"So you have little ones at home, I see."

"Yes, two."

"You don't look old enough to have two children."

"I feel it."

"Can't be that bad, can it?"

"At times it can be quite overwhelming."

"I bet you work, too."

"I teach third grade."

"Really. So do I. Well, not third grade, but sixth. I had third graders a couple of years ago. They can be a handful." He laughed, and I noticed the wonderful smile he had.

"That they can be."

"My name is Gil. Gil Scott."

I laughed. "Like the singer-musician?"

"If only," he joked. "And your name is?"

"Carmen Holden."

"Pretty name for a pretty lady."

Blushing, I said, "Thank you."

"I didn't mean to embarrass you. My friends say I'm too forward sometimes."

"It's okay, really." It had been so long since Louis told me I was pretty, I drank it up, like a woman dying of thirst.

"Are you finished with your shopping?" he asked.

"Almost. Just need to pick up something for dinner. What about you?"

He pointed to his cart, which was loaded with steaks, ribs, two heads of lettuce, a box of tomatoes, and about eight bottles of barbecue sauce. I know he must have seen the expression on my face.

"I love to barbecue," he offered by way of explanation. "Winter or summer. Nothing like it."

"So you cook?"

"Clean and do my own laundry." He chuckled. "That's one thing my mama always stressed. 'Boy,' she used to say, 'never think that just cause you're with a woman she's there to be your maid. You make sure you can do for yourself, no matter what. You be her partner, not another dependent.' "

My mother turns and looks at me for the first time since she began this unthinkable confession.

"At the time I thought, 'I've never seen Louis so much as pick up a broom, or ask if I needed help around the house, or with Cliff and Sandra.'

We both took it for granted that maintaining the house and the kids were my responsibilities."

"So this is your explanation for what you did to Dad?" I ask, accusation blasting through in my voice. But she keeps talking as if she doesn't hear me, as if she needs to get it all out, to absolve herself in some way.

"We walked together to the checkout counter, talking the entire way about our teaching experiences, where we went to school, and our opinions on the New York City school system. And I realized as we walked to my car that this was the first real adult conversation I'd had in longer than I could remember. I actually had someone asking my opinion, my advice. And it felt damned good. I never expected to see him again, but I did."

"Why?"

"It wasn't anything planned, at least not on my part. But I was coming out on my lunch break a few days later and he was waiting for me in front of the school . . ."

She takes me back to that day with her.

"Gil? What on earth are you doing here?" I knew he worked quite a distance away in the junior high school.

"I decided to take a mental health day, and I thought of you."

I looked around to see who might have heard him.

"Well, that's very nice, but . . ."

"I thought I could entice you to a quick lunch."

"I was planning on grabbing a sandwich at the deli and eating in the teacher's lounge."

"Now how unappealing is that? Let me treat you to a real lunch."

"I . . ."

"Come on. Just this once."

"I thought about how nice it would be to be treated like I mattered—if only for a little while . . ."

She continues: "'All right,' I agreed.

"Lunch was wonderful. We talked and laughed for the full hour. It went by much too fast. Gil was fun, intelligent, worldly. And he *listened*. I went back to work feeling renewed almost, and secretly hoped that we would see each other again. At home, I became more discontented, more withdrawn. Your father didn't seem to notice, and if he did, he never said a word. Gil became my sounding board, and one afternoon, instead of lunch . . . we . . . went to his apartment."

I can't look at her. *My mother*. The woman who I've held up to the highest of ideals, the one I aspired to become one day. She had flaws. She made mistakes. She wasn't perfect. How naïve I had been, never seeing my mother or my father as fallible human beings, thinking them icons that could do no wrong.

"Did . . . did Dad ever find out?"

She nods her head, and my heart breaks all over again, my love for my father rising like sap from a tree.

"Oh, Mom. How?"

She pushes herself out of her seat and stands. "I had to tell him."

"Because you felt guilty?"

"No."

I watch her throat work up and down. "I had to tell him . . . because I was pregnant."

The room begins to spin and my stomach rolls dangerously. *Pregnant. Pregnant. Cliff. Sandra. Me?*

"Mom," I whimper. "Please, please don't tell me that Dad . . . isn't . . ."

"I didn't know for sure until you were born, Lisa, and blood tests were performed. For nine months, I didn't know if I was carrying your father's child or Gil's. It was a hell like none other."

"What about Dad?" Tears roll unchecked down my cheeks, my own sorrows forgotten.

"That's when I finally knew the kind of man I'd married. He was devastated when I told him what I'd done. I can't begin to imagine the level of pain I caused him. I'd never seen your father shed a tear, but he did that night. And knowing all that I'd done, he stood by me. During those very stress-filled and trying months we talked, really talked for the first time in our marriage. And he listened to me. It was almost as if what I'd done had forced us to take a look at our marriage, at ourselves, and come to terms as to both our roles in what happened.

"I was just as much at fault as your father. I should have insisted that we work out our differences. I should have spoken up for myself and not retreated, allowing someone else the opportunity to cross that very thin line."

"And he . . . forgave you?" I ask incredulously.

"Over time. Yes. He did. And when you were born . . . well, we both realized that you were our second chance, our diamond in the rough. That's why your father adores you so, more than his other children. You are our validation that love can conquer. It can heal, and it can help you to forgive. And I pledged that I would spend the rest of my life making up to your father for what I'd done."

It explains so much, my mother's doting on my father at times, which we often took for weakness. It's really her way of saying over and again, "I love you, and I'm sorry."

"Do . . . Sandra and Cliff know?" I ask between my sobs.

"No. Your father and I promised never to bring it up again. And we never broke that promise—until now."

"Why, Mom? Why tell me this now?"

"You needed to know. As difficult as it was for me to tell you, you needed to hear it. You needed to understand that if your father could find a way to forgive me, the opportunity is there for you to forgive Ross and find a way to rebuild your marriage, make it stronger. But it depends on the two of you, if your marriage is worth it, and how much you both want it."

"I don't know. . . ."

"No one is perfect. Human beings make mistakes. And things don't happen without reason, Lisa. You need to look deep inside yourself at all the reasons why and be honest about your role, as hard as that might be for you to do. Ross didn't sleep with Asha because he stopped loving you or because Asha had been working on seducing him. That would be too simple, too sordid. It's more than that. You owe it to yourself and to Ross . . . and to Asha to find out why—no matter what you finally decide to do."

The sound of keys turning in the lock draws our attention to the door and then to each other. And by silent agreement, the passing of that particular torch will go no further.

Cliff walks in first, followed by my dad, who still looks furious but is contained. Heaven only knows what Cliff said to him or where he finally found him.

Cliff walks directly to me and kneels in front of me. He takes my chin in his palm, forcing me to look at him. "Are you okay?"

"I will be."

He nods, looks at my mom, then back to me. "You know you can talk to me if you need to and if you never decide to say a word about it, I'll understand. Whatever decision you settle on, I'm behind you one hundred percent. Got it?"

"Thanks, Cliff."

He rises, kisses my mom's cheek. "You need to go talk to Dad," he says in a hushed voice. "He's really shook up. I don't know what he would have done if he'd actually found Ross. Lucky thing the cell phone was in the car or I'd still be out there combing the streets."

"I don't even want to think about it. Thanks, honey."

Cliff heaves a deep sigh. "I gotta get back home. Told Lynn that Dad's car got a flat and I had to help him."

I clasp Cliff's hand. "Please don't say anything to Lynn. I can't handle anyone else knowing."

"You got it." He kisses me tenderly on the forehead. "Get some rest. Call me if you need me."

"I will."

"Dad, you go upstairs and take a pill or something and relax before you burst a vessel. Lisa will be fine, and I don't want to have to see your face on the front page of the news. I'll call tomorrow."

My mother walks Cliff to the door and locks it behind him. My father looks at her for a long moment before she walks into his arms and presses her head against his chest.

I almost feel like a voyeur watching the intimate display of love flow between them. As unobtrusively as possible, I ease out and upstairs to my old room to think. To decide if what Ross and I have is salvageable, and if I have what it takes to forgive.

TWENTY-SEVEN

No Easy Place to Be

ASHA

In another eight hours, I'll be gone. Gone from here. Gone from everyone's life. Who will miss me? No one, probably. How sad is that? Getting this new photo assignment in Mexico is the perfect excuse to leave. It will appear that I'm simply going away, not running away. This is what I need. I need to gain some perspective, see my life through untainted lenses.

The truth is I'm afraid. I'm afraid of walking through these familiar streets and possibly running into Lisa, and not being able to hug her or grab a cup of coffee together. Or worse, seeing her and have her turn her back on me. I don't know if I could handle that. What is sadder still is that there is no one to share my feelings with. Lisa is the only friend I've ever had. As much as I've quietly dismissed her, secretly laughed at what I perceived to be her weaknesses, her naïveté, it was me who was weak, me who believed that my life was *the* life. Being Lisa's friend made me feel better about myself. I could go through life unaffected by it, laughing my way through it, laughing at those who had been slowed by it. But it was *me* who was not truly living, *me* who was missing out on the things that were important. Fear will do that to you. I've been afraid all my life. Now I want to shout to the world and share my epiphany: "I'm just like you. I'm not different. I'm not better. I'm just an ordinary woman." But there is no one to hear me, no one who will care. I did that. I made things this way. Sadly, it is the only real thing I've ever done.

So I'll pack my bags, let Vincent handle the business, and I'll disappear, maybe start over somewhere else where no one knows me. Give myself time to forget what I've done and give everyone a chance to forget me.

Vincent surprised me by offering to take me to the airport. We haven't spoken since that evening he confronted me. I can't blame him, really. What's left to say?

To be truthful, I wish he would've asked me not to go. I wish he would've said, "This is the coward's way out, Asha. You've never been a coward." But he didn't. When I told him I was taking this assignment for an indefinite period of time, all he said was, "If it's what you want." No more, no less.

Well, let's get it over with, then. Put me on a plane and send me on my way. Put me out of my misery.

The doorbell?

I'm not expecting anyone, and it's much too early for Vincent to arrive. But maybe he's decided to visit with me for a while for old times' sake. For a moment, I almost feel happy until I open the door and see Cliff on the other side.

"Hello, Asha."

"Cliff? Is something wrong?"

I pull the door open and he steps in.

"That's what I came to talk to you about." He looks around at the row of suitcases and then turns to me. "Going somewhere?"

"Mexico. I have an assignment."

"Convenient. I'm glad I didn't wait any longer."

"What is it, Cliff?"

He slides his hands into his pockets the way lecturers sometimes do before launching into their presentations. "My intention was to stay out of it, let Lisa and Ross work it out themselves."

"What are you talking about?" I ask, stalling for time.

"Ignorance doesn't become you, Asha. I know. Okay? So we can forget about playing games with each other."

So, another showdown. "Fine. Since you know all the answers, say whatever you have to say, Cliff." I fold my arms partly in defiance, partly as a futile attempt at protection.

"Why? Help me to understand why you did this to her."

"Me? Why is it only me, Cliff? What about Ross? Am I to be the only one to wear the scarlet letter on my chest? Isn't it always easier to blame it all on the woman because we accept that behavior from men? They even have names for women like me. What about Ross? Why don't you pound on his door demanding answers? Why me?"

"You know why *you*, Asha, because barring everything else, it takes a certain kind of woman to do what you did. Lisa wasn't some faceless wife that you'd probably never see; she was your friend."

I turn away from him, away from the truth and the question I know I can't answer. *Why?*

"I watched you grow up, Asha. I watched Lisa trail behind you for years like a loving pet, hoping that from time to time you would remember she was there and give her a kindly pat on the head. She looked up to you for some reason I still can't fathom. She loved you. We all did. But you don't know what that is, do you, Asha? You think kindness, trust, and love are qualities beneath you, unworthy of you."

"Are you finished, Cliff? Are you going to tell me what an awful human being I am, how I've destroyed lives, ruined a marriage, a friendship, a family? Don't bother. I already know."

"Do you? In your perfect-picture world where everything is as you see it, do you actually understand what you've done? You know what I see,

Asha? I see a beautiful, intelligent, talented woman who at the core is totally empty. A woman who moves through life, taking and taking, hoping to fill that dark hole inside—incapable of giving anything in return, especially herself."

"You don't know me, Cliff. You don't know anything about me or what my life is really about."

"I've met women like you, Asha. Shells."

He heads for the door, then stops, and I want to push him out. Get him out of my house with his proclamations and damnations.

"I'm glad you're going away. I hope you stay away and out of Lisa's life forever. Out of all of our lives. She's a good woman. She would have done anything for you. I think she loved you more than her own sisters. The saddest part is not you sleeping with my sister's husband, but how what you've done will change her from the woman she once was. You've taken away her innocence, her freedom to believe that all good things are possible. Something no one else has ever been able to do, and that's because she truly loved you. She'll never get that innocence back. That's the greatest crime of all."

At the door, he stops and looks at me one last time. I refuse to let him see me break.

"When you go to bed at night, ask yourself was it worth it."

He starts down the steps, and I see another doorway to the life I once knew closing in my face, and I want to stop it, I want to stick my foot out to keep it from shutting.

"I tried to talk to her!" I yell at his back. "I tried to tell her that I was sorry, that I didn't mean to hurt her." He won't stop. He won't listen. "I didn't mean it, Cliff. Why won't anyone believe me? I'm not what you say I am! I do have a soul. I'm not empty inside. I'm not, damnit. Do you hear me?"

The car engine drowns out my screams as Cliff pulls away.

I'm not even sure why I'm here, at my mother's house, of all places. The last time she and I were in the same space it was a disaster, one that altered the course of my life, Lisa's life, and Ross's life. I suppose I'm still looking for answers. Trying to unravel the mystery of her power over me. I need to understand that, and then maybe I can finally be free to live.

It's a shame to actually admit, but my mother is all I have left. When I look at my life, the full measure of it, I realize how right Cliff was. For all I have, I have nothing at all.

She opens the door, and oddly there is a look of acceptance on her face, as if she'd known all along that I would come. But how could she know? Silently I follow her into the kitchen. Flashes of that afternoon snap in front of me.

"I won't stay long. I just wanted to say good-bye."

"That's not why you're here. You could have said good-bye on the phone." She sits down at the table. "Why did you come?"

"Like I said, I came to say good-bye. That's all," I say with as little emotion as I can summon.

She stares at me for a long time until I'm forced to look away. She sighs deeply before she speaks. "I realize over the years you and I haven't had the perfect version of a mother–daughter relationship, but I know you, Asha. Probably better than you know yourself."

"Do you? Do you really, Mother? Then tell me who the hell I am." I desperately need to know. And this woman before me is the only one with the answers. The one person who's always despised me.

"Why don't we start by you telling me the real reason for your impromptu visit? You look like crap, so it must be serious. You wouldn't go to the laundry mat without having every hair in place."

I turn away. The words are on my lips, but I can't seem to say them. Yet there is a part of me that believes my behavior is what my mother would expect of me. Nothing I say will come as a shock. She's always known. Hasn't she continually reminded me of how worthless I am?

I whirl toward her and pelt her with the stones of my guilt. "I slept with Ross. I've ruined their marriage. I've destroyed the only friendship I've ever had. I've turned my business over to Vincent, and I'm running away! Satisfied? Isn't that what you wanted to hear? Isn't this what you expected of me all along?"

She lowers her head and covers her face with her hands as if even she is ashamed. "Oh, Asha." Slowly she shakes her head and then looks up at me. And if I didn't know my mother better, I would swear that there was real pain in her eyes. "All your life you've wanted what Lisa had: sisters and brothers, a father, a family, stability—a real mother—and now her husband."

Slowly she looks up and focuses on me, perhaps seeing me for the very first time and realizing what she had created. Her voice comes to me disembodied and weighed down with sadness. "How do we first begin to covet, Asha? We covet what we see every day," she says quietly. "I used to watch you all those years, drinking in what the Holden family had to offer. I saw Carmen take you under her wing, talk to you the way I couldn't. I saw you spend your holidays at their kitchen table, become a part of the pictures in their family album. And I resented it. I resented them, and I resented you. You were all I had. But what was worse, I saw the hunger in your eyes. The burning desire to have more and more."

"Why . . . if you knew . . . why didn't you do something? . . . Why wouldn't you be my mother?"

"The more they gave, the more you needed, and I could no longer compete." Her eyes beg me to understand. "So I tried to put the fire out by being hard on you, trying to make you see that you didn't belong in that picture. And all it did was drive you further away. After a while it was easier to ignore it all." She looks me straight in the eye. "It was inevitable. The path was set when you were twelve years old."

"I don't believe that!" I slam my hand on the table. "I didn't plan it. I didn't want it to happen." Pain builds in my chest. "I was unhappy, and confused, hurt by the horrible things *you'd* said to me that day." Tears fill my eyes, but I refuse to cry. "He . . . he . . . needed someone to talk to. Lisa wasn't listening. She couldn't give him what he needed. . . ."

"And you could. Finally you could. You could have something Lisa had and make it better. Outdo her. Prove to yourself and maybe even Ross that you were just as good as Lisa, better even."

"That's not true." I fling this at her, taking my last stand.

"Of course it is. You'd already acquired every other aspect of her life, and for the first time in years, Lisa had something that you didn't. A husband."

The statement stings like a slap. "You're crazy. I'm not going to listen to any more of this bull." My mind begins to swirl, her words taking on life. *Is it true?*

"I should have stopped it years ago. But I was too wrapped up in my own anger and bitterness. And you paid for it. I'm so sorry, Asha. I'm sorry for everything, for not being what you needed. But in the end, the only one who can be accountable for your actions is *you*. You made a choice, based on years of conditioning. You'll have to find a way to break free of it if you're ever going to be the Asha you can be—a whole person."

Realization as sure as the rising sun settles within me. *This* is the power my mother has. *Knowledge*. She knows me. Knows my soul. Knows my weaknesses and my darkest desires. Knows me in a way that only a mother can. She sees the part of me that I keep hidden from the world.

The tears blur my vision, but I feel as if I can finally see for the first time in my life. Tentatively, I reach across the table for my mother's hand. She looks into my eyes before taking my hand in hers. At least for now the unanswerable why has been answered.

"I'm so sorry," I confess, and press my face against our joined hands.

I try calling Lisa's house before Vincent arrives. There are things I need to say to her so that she will know what happened is not her fault. And that maybe with me gone and out of their lives, she and Ross can have a chance at rebuilding what they had.

All I'm getting is her answering machine, over and over again. Maybe a message is best.

"Lisa, this is Asha. I know how much you must hate me now. But not more than I hate myself. I can never explain to you how sorry I am about what happened. I'm going away for a while, try to sort everything out, sort myself out, try to make some sense of it all. I hope that one day you'll find a way to forgive me, at least a little, but most of all to forgive Ross. He's a good man, Lisa. Well, anyway, Vincent is here to take me to the airport. I'll miss you. I'll miss us. Be well, Lisa."

TWENTY-EIGHT

If We Try

LISA

. . . *Be well, Lisa."*

Asha's voice drifts to me from my machine. Had I come home moments earlier, would I have picked up the phone, listened to what she had to say? I'm not sure. I reach for the PLAY button, thinking that maybe there is something hidden in the folds of her words that will explain *why*. Instead, I press ERASE. I suppose now I will never know. Yet a part of me firmly believes that there is no real answer, at least not one that will change my reality. The solution is within me.

For weeks, I needed someone to talk to—a friend. And I realized how narrow my world was. Asha *was* that friend, the one I would have turned to in crisis, in happiness. I no longer can. I thought of my sisters, Sandra and Tina. But Sandra would have offered "I told you so," and Tina would have crumpled into disillusioned tears.

And so I find myself having to learn for the first time to rely on my own instincts, right or wrong. You know, in an odd way, it feels good.

I realize, too, that the only way I can move on is to set things right between Ross and me, whatever that means. I won't go through my days with lingering questions about my marriage or with the guilt that there may have been something I could have done differently. We are all accountable.

My forever begins today. I'm ready to make that first step.

"Hi, Karen. It's Lisa." I brace the phone between my cheek and shoulder.

"Lisa, I don't know what to say." She pauses. "Are you all right?" I hear her anxiety and wish that I could ease it, but I can't.

"I think I will be. I've been trying to find Ross—"

"He's here. He's been staying with me." She lowers her voice. "He's . . . he's different, Lisa. He's not the same man he was. It's as if the life has been sucked from him."

I want to feel bad for him, but I don't, not really. "I think all of us are different, Karen. There's no other way to be. Would it be all right if I stopped by?"

"Sure. I know he wants to talk to you. I have some errands to run, so you two will have some privacy."

"Thanks. I'd appreciate that, Karen. I'll stop by in about an hour?"

"I hope you two can find a way to work this out, Lisa. Ross really loves you, and so do I. No matter what happens . . . I hope you and I can stay friends."

"Thanks. I'll be there soon."

My first thought when I see Ross is that he looks older, maybe wiser somehow, certainly different. And I wonder if he's changed as much as I have.

"Hello, Ross."

"I'm glad you came, Lisa. I'd pretty much given up . . ."

"Why, Ross?" I walk farther into the room. "Help me to understand what went wrong."

He turns away, and I watch his proud shoulders sag. Slowly he shakes his head. "It's so many things, and almost nothing at all."

I sit down on the couch and take out a brand-new pack of cigarettes from my purse. Ross looks at me curiously but doesn't comment on them. "To be truthful, it started with the plans for the wedding. . . ."

I listen this time, really listen without interrupting him with my anger. He tells me how he never felt a part of things, that he felt pushed along, swept up in my vision of what I believed our life should be.

"I wasn't used to it. For so long it was me that everyone depended on, turned to for answers and support. And then all of a sudden, it was like my existence didn't matter."

I want to stop him right there and tell him how incredibly wrong he is, but I won't. I promised myself that I would listen this time. My mother's wisdom rings in my head: "As hard as it may be, you need to see your role in it."

". . . Then I lost my job, and I didn't know how to tell you. I didn't know how to tell you that my promises to you were put on hold. I couldn't tell you that I was not the man and provider that I made myself out to be. How could I when you had such high hopes and so many plans? Every day that the charade went on, I lost a part of myself, my manhood. It got harder and harder to find my way back."

What was my role? I wanted to be like my mother, I conclude. I wanted to provide the perfect nest, the sanctuary. I wanted to remove any worry and stress from Ross's life. I wanted to do what I thought my mother did, and for *those* reasons. Now I realize that Mom's agenda was for different reasons, my father's acceptance was for different reasons.

How deluded we all were. Each of us was operating out of our own vision of the world, not allowing ourselves to see it for what it really was.

". . . What happened with . . . me and Asha had nothing to do with you. . . . It had to do with me needing to validate myself as a man, reclaim some part of myself that I'd lost. It was stupid and thoughtless. I never wanted to hurt you, Lisa. Please believe that."

So simple, I realize. The answer was always there, right in front of us all along. Me, Ross, Asha, all each of us ever wanted was to be accepted and valued. I needed to prove to myself, my family and to the world that I was lovable, that I could live up to expectations. Ross needed to affirm his manhood, redeem himself in his father's eyes, and Asha . . . I may never know all the reasons, but she, too, was searching for affirmation. The problem was, we were all looking in the wrong places—everywhere but inside ourselves.

"I needed to hear that, Ross. I mean really hear what you were saying."

"Do you believe I love you, Lisa?"

Love has the power to heal, to forgive.

"I didn't, because I didn't believe that anyone could hurt someone they loved so completely. But I've come to understand that love has only as much power as we give it, Ross. I allowed it to make me blind to everything but my own desires. You allowed it to erode the core of who you were. And Asha walked right over it because she never understood what it was. I wish I could blame her for all this. But Asha is no trashy novel mistress, or the sultry femme fatale who lurks in bars ready to seduce some unsuspecting man, or the cutthroat friend ready to steal your man as soon as you turn your back. She's just an ordinary woman, flesh and blood with dreams and goals like anyone else. The thing that sets her apart from any other woman who may have done this is that she was my best friend, Ross. She wasn't just a woman in a bar or the office secretary. She was my best friend."

I reach out and stroke his cheek. For a moment, my lids flutter closed, and I remember how good it once was, how wonderful it could have been.

"I love you, too," I say. "And my love for you will make me stronger."

He clasps my hand tenderly against his cheek, and I watch his eyes fill. For a moment, I almost relent, but I understand that I will not be as strong as my father, able to look Ross in the eye each and every day for the rest of my life, *knowing*. And I realize that I could not live with the knowledge that although I will forgive, I won't forget. Will it show in my eyes when he comes in late from work or when he doesn't want to make love? Will I sometimes shrink from his touch, refuse to go to places that the three of us have gone to together? Will my actions or my unspoken words force him to make it up to me day after day for the rest of our lives? I don't want to live like that, and neither should he.

"I just want to say . . . that we all had a role in this. Myself included. In our wildest dreams, none of us would have envisioned this day. But it happened, Ross, and we have to find a way to deal with it."

"We can do it together, Lisa. Whatever you want, I'll do. I can make this up to you."

"That's not possible. What happened with you and Asha was more than a one-night stand. It was a violation of everything we held sacred, of friendship and trust. I don't know what could ever make that right."

I watch the ache in his expression, and that old Lisa wants to make the hurt go away. But I don't believe I can.

"Good-bye, Ross."

"I'm sorry."

"I know. So am I."

TWENTY-NINE

And So it Goes

ROSS

"What happened? Did you two work it out?" Karen asks, ever hopeful.

"We talked." I slowly turn the beer can between my hands. Karen sits opposite me on the love seat.

"And? . . ."

"And Lisa is going to move on with her life, and I have to move on with mine."

"Oh, no, Ross. I'm so sorry."

She reaches for my hand, and the tenderness in her touch nearly breaks me down. I had such high hopes for Lisa and me. I wanted to set an example for my sister. I wanted to be a good husband and provider. I wanted the family that I'd always dreamed of. And now . . . I've failed at everything.

"What are you going to do?"

"I have a job offer in Baltimore. The pay is good, and moving away will give me a fresh start."

"But maybe if you stay—give Lisa some time, maybe she'll change her mind," she says, grasping at straws.

"Maybe she will; maybe she won't. But I can't keep my life on hold on a maybe. I don't think even she expects me to do that."

"What about Asha? Have you spoken with her at all?"

"No. I wouldn't know what to say, Karen. I really wouldn't. It's best that Asha and I stay away from each other."

"Do you . . . Did you have feelings for Asha? I mean . . . I don't understand how . . . You two were never that way with each other. Were you?"

My sister's expression is so full of hurt and disappointment. Her voice is filled with the sadness of a disillusioned child. I know how deeply she cares for Lisa and how much she admires Asha's bounce and vibrancy—at least she did. I hate that I am the cause of tarnishing a part of my sister's life that she held dear. To her, Lisa was the stable older sister and Asha the fun-loving best friend. Now all the dynamics have changed. They'll never be what they once were, all because of one unplanned, irrevocable act.

"It was never that way with me and Asha. Never. I swear to you. That's why this . . ." I won't break down. I won't. "You know, sometimes at night when I can't sleep, I just keep running it in my head, over and over. How could I have been so foolish, so weak? I think of all the what-ifs. What if I hadn't been at Lisa's parents' house that night? What if I hadn't insisted on driving Asha home? What if I'd just taken my car and dropped her off at her door? The questions dance around until they almost make me crazy. A part of me believes that there's a plan to life. But how could this be it, sis? How could this be the plan for me and Lisa?"

"I know this will sound empty and clichéd but too often bad things happen to good people, Ross. You're a good man. Don't doubt that. I know you. I know your heart. You made a mistake. But that doesn't change the core of who you are."

"Doesn't it? I'm not the man I was, Karen. And as long as I keep deluding myself into believing that, I'll never be able to move past this. I'll be trapped in what could have been. That's not what I want."

"People make mistakes Ross, worse mistakes than this. And that's all it is, a mistake. It doesn't make you any less of a man or any less of a human being. This is not who you are. Just like who you are isn't only an architect, a brother, a friend, a son. It's the sum total of you as a person."

"Thanks for the pep talk." I try to smile. "And you're probably right. I just can't see the forest for the trees at the moment."

"You will. And maybe Lisa will change her mind. Maybe she won't. But no matter what happens, don't you dare let yourself down. I watched you struggle through our childhood. You put yourself through college. You came home and took care of me and Mom and put your own life on hold for us. Those are the qualities that I admire: your strength, your selflessness. And none of that can be negated by one mistake."

"I wish Lisa felt that way."

"Do you want me to talk to her? Maybe she'll listen to me."

"No. I don't want Lisa worn down into being with me. She has to want this. And I don't think she does."

"She's still hurting, Ross. I think—"

"Listen, I know you mean well. But . . . I can't talk about this anymore. At least not right now."

"Sure." She pauses and then pats my hand. "Are you hungry?"

"Naw. I think I'll go out for a drive. Don't wait up, okay? I don't know when I'll be back."

"Ross, I don't really think you should—"

"I'll be fine. And I'll be back." I kiss her cheek, pick up my car keys from the hall table, and head out into the night—seeking what, I'm not sure.

You never know in this life who your friends will be. Who would have thought that one of my dearest friends would be Kenny the bartender? He greets me like someone who is really glad to see me. That feels good, better than the Scotch burning down my throat.

"So, how'd it go buddy? Get the old lady to reconsider?"

"Naw, man. As far as she's concerned, we're through."

"Sorry to hear that. It'll be rough for a while, but you'll get over it."

"Yeah, that's what I keep telling myself."

"So whaddaya gonna do?"

I take a long sip of the liquid fire. "Hmmm. Got a job offer out of town. Figure I'd take it and start over."

"What if she changes her mind after you're gone?"

"I don't know."

He begins to wipe down the counter in front of me and refills my glass without asking.

"Hey, I uh, hope you don't mind me asking but—and you don't have to tell me if you don't want to—but what happened? You seem like a decent guy, hardworking. I seen you in here with your friends. Don't seem like the type to fool around. I don't get it."

I look up at him, and I know the moment I confess, the image he has of me will immediately change. And as sad as it is to admit, I need his friendship if only for the time being.

"Hey, who knows? Things just started falling apart. All the little things started adding up until we couldn't deal with it anymore."

He looks at me curiously, as if he really doesn't believe the bullshit lie I just told him. "That's a damn shame. But maybe there's something better out there for you."

"Yeah. Maybe. What about you? You married? Kids?"

"Divorced. I have two daughters. Great kids."

"They live with their mother?"

"Naw, they live with me."

Checking out this guy in front of me, I don't see him in the Mr. Mom role. But things aren't always as they seem. "You? Get outta here. How old are they?

"Eleven and fifteen."

"Wow. How do you manage with the hours you keep?"

"We worked out a system. I'm home days to get them ready for school, see them when they get home and have dinner ready. And when I leave for work, I have a woman come and stay with them until I come home."

"Older or younger?" I ask, half joking.

"Older woman. She lives down the hall. Retired. The girls love her."

"So let me ask you something: Why aren't they with their mother?"

The corner of his mouth curves up. "Since we're only tellin' half-truths tonight, I'll just say I won the court case for full custody." He watches for my reaction.

"What are you saying?"

"I'm saying that the lame story you gave me about little things adding up is crap. It takes more than that to end a marriage. Believe me I know. I been there." He shrugs. "So you tell a little, I'll tell a little, and we'll call it square. Refill?"

All I can do is lower my head and chuckle. Folks always say bartenders are the best therapists, that they hear and see a million life stories a week.

I twirl the glass slowly around on the table, thinking whether I should say anything to him. At any other time in my life, Cliff would be the one I'd turn to. He was always good for solid advice, or maybe none at all if that's what was needed. I'll miss that, and the Sunday afternoon basketball games with the fellas. How could I face Cliff? There's always Karen, who would love me no matter what, but there are just certain things I can't explain to her—man things. I suppose the draw to bartenders and even cabdrivers is that they are virtually anonymous. If you don't want to, you never have to see or speak to them again. I do need to talk. No, what I need is someone to listen. Someone who doesn't have a stake in the outcome, you know. Someone who will hear me out, maybe offer some advice, and then move on with their life. Someone like Kenny.

I take a long swallow of my drink. It goes straight to my head. "What would you say if I told you I stepped out on my wife?" I wait for the look of recrimination, but it doesn't come.

"Figured that's what it was when you said you'd 'made a mistake,' the last time you were in here. Some chick at work?"

"No. Her best friend."

"Hmmm."

I can't believe he doesn't react. At most, there was a slight twitch beneath his left eye. He starts wiping down the counter again, walks away to serve another customer, and then comes back.

"Quid pro quo. You tell me something, I tell you something. What happened to you, happened to me."

"You? But I thought you said you won custody—"

"I did. She wound up really in love with the guy, and she eventually married him—wanted to start a *new* family, she said."

"She? But I thought—"

"You figured like most folks figure, it must be the man." He shakes his head. "Not true."

"The guy was somebody you knew?"

"I'd seen him around. He came in here all the time with some other guys from his office, I guess. Your turn."

"Hey, to be truthful I'm still asking myself why. It was never like that between me and this woman. She's pretty, intelligent, well traveled, but I'd never thought of her as someone I would . . . anyway . . . What's so weird is that when I think about it, she reminds me of this woman I knew back in college, Michelle."

"Maybe it was an attraction you weren't aware of."

"Naw. When Michelle left me—"

"She left you?"

"Yeah. It wasn't about another woman, if that's what you're thinking. It was her. She wanted out. She wanted a bigger and brighter life without me. Told me on the night I asked her to marry me."

"Wow. That's tough. But you said something about—hang on a minute, let me get them their drinks."

While Kenny fixes the drinks, I have a minute to really think about what I'm saying. Michelle? Asha? Does Asha remind me of that time? Even now thoughts of Michelle still hurt. What she did was bad enough, but it was how she did it—with no thought for my feelings. I guess it was and still is hard to swallow, that the woman I thought I loved, was totally self-absorbed. After all these years, I'm not sure if I've gotten over her. Was I drawn to Asha because of those memories or in response to them? The thing that remains paramount in my mind about Michelle is that I wanted to hurt her. I wanted her to feel as much pain as I did. Shit, what could be more hurtful than ruining someone's life, taking away the things that are most precious to them? That's what I've done to Asha.

"Sorry about that. Business." He chuckles. "You were saying something about this woman you were with reminding you of Michelle."

"Yeah. She does in a way. They both have that same kind of energy and daring." I shake my head. "Maybe in the back of my head that was part of it. But the simple truth is I was feeling like crap, and she found all the ways to make me feel better. And I don't just mean physically. That was really the least of it. It was just listening and understanding. Not expecting anything from me, just accepting me for who I was. While I was with her, I felt good about myself for the first time in a long while."

"Where is she, still around?"

"I don't know. We haven't spoken."

"You got yourself in one helluva mess."

"What would you do?" I ask, suddenly seeing Kenny as full of wisdom.

"I'll be truthful with you, pal, I know how I felt when it happened to me. There's no way to explain how deep that hurts. And as much as I loved my wife, I knew I could never go back to her even if things didn't work out with her and that guy. I'd never be able to trust her. Everything that we'd based our marriage on had been ruined."

"Do you think my wife will change her mind?"

"Hard to say. But even if she does, I don't think it will ever be the same."

I stare into the half-empty glass, knowing how right he is. As much as I may want it, as much as I may promise to make things right between us, it can't be the way it was. I reach into my pocket and pull out my money. "Thanks." I push away from the bar and stand, not feeling as rocky as I'd expected.

"Hey, man, take it easy, all right?"

"Yeah."

"Good luck with the new gig. Whenever you're in town, drop in, drinks on me."

"I'll do that."

I head toward the door.

"Hey, what's your name?"

"Ross."

"Kenny."

I smile. "I know."

In the End Is a Beginning

MEXICO

THIRTY

In My Room

ASHA

Life is different here—slower, easier. It's been almost three years, and I'm still getting used to the pace. From my room, I can step out onto the veranda and even through the hazy mornings see the entire city spread out before me. Picturesque. In my background now are warm hues of burnt oranges, golds, and vibrant reds. Even the ruins are magically beautiful. For the first time in my life, everything is clear and focused. Vincent and I speak often. He keeps me updated on Lisa, whom he runs into from time to time, and Ross, who he says is still in Baltimore somewhere. Business is going well, and he even confessed that he's found someone he thinks he can really be happy with. And I'm glad for him, really glad. There would have been a time when I would have the pangs of jealousy, would have taunted and teased him about his choice. Not now, and I know I am changing.

As I walk along the ancient streets of the city cataloging the people, the vendors, and myriad shops, it is with new eyes and a fresh inner lens. Before I would search for the darkness that lurked behind my subject, juxtaposing beauty with life's harsh realities. I suppose where I was during that time in my life was a place that held too many dark corners and unanswered questions. I superimposed my vision onto the world, forcing them to see it as I did.

Since I arrived here, I've traveled to the Caribbean, South America, Nigeria, and Australia. But I keep returning here, drawn by a force that I can't describe. Many nights I lie awake and wonder why I keep coming back to this place. It is more than the pulsing nights or the lazy afternoons or the people who are so full of energy and life. It is here that I finally discovered who Asha Woods really is.

It was a few months after my arrival. The project I'd been sent here to do was almost finished except for developing a few rolls of film. I'd decided to take one of the tours to the Ancient city of Teotihuacán, one of the most frequently visited of Mexico's archaeological sites. The Aztecs believed it to be a holy place, and it was the Aztecs who gave the city its meaning, "The place where men become gods." It was there that I met Juan Rivera . . .

As usual, I had my cameras, always ready to capture a moment. I'd been to Mexico before, but it was always a rushed visit. I'd never had time to really see any of the sights. Immediately I was captivated by the sense of history and spirituality that permeated the ruins, and the Pyramid of the Sun—the third largest pyramid in the world, took my breath away. Many of the artifacts gave a glimpse into lives of the people thousands of years ago. For a moment I thought of Ross and how much he would enjoy the architecture of the structures. I could almost hear him explain how every stone was laid. The idea that something as simple as sharing a conversation with someone who would appreciate my thoughts was an impossibility, reminded me once again why I'd left the States. I pushed Ross and the past out of my head and moved on.

I was photographing one of the incredibly well-preserved murals and an exquisite piece of intricate clay pottery when an inquiring voice drifted from behind me.

"They say that the women spent hours, sometimes days perfecting each and every piece of pottery and jewelry."

I turned toward the voice and was immediately taken in by the dark, penetrating eyes that seemed able to look right through me. He immediately reminded me of a bronze Zorro—exciting, dangerous, and lethally charming.

"You must be American," he said.

"Yes. I am." I slung my bag securely over my shoulder.

"My name is Juan. I come here to study. I've been here hundreds of times, and there's always something new to discover."

"You must be a big fan."

"An archeologist. And you?"

"A photographer. I'm here on assignment. Well, not here actually. My assignment is over. I had some time and decided to visit. I'd heard so much about it."

"Is there something I can help you with?"

"Just looking around. Thank you for the offer."

He smiled.

I thought he would leave me then, but he didn't. Instead he walked casually beside me as I moved from space to space, room to room, explaining some of the rituals that took place as far back as the first century A.D.

"Aren't there other needy tourist that could use your help?" I asked him after about five minutes.

"I'm sure, but I would rather be in your company." He smiled again, displaying even, white teeth against his swarthy complexion. "Would you prefer to be left alone?"

In the few months that I'd been in Mexico, I'd kept pretty much to myself. Staying solo. I did my work during the day and developed the film at night. Sometimes I would walk the streets after sunset and listen to the guitar music coming from the many restaurants and outdoor cafés. When I would return to my room, I would write in my journal, a practice I'd started since I'd arrived. I would document my days and my thoughts, put my emotions on paper. Many times I would surprise myself with my revelations about my parents, my childhood, my numerous love affairs. I found that the more I wrote the better I began to feel, as if I were purging my soul. In my journal, I could confess things I could never say to another person: my fears, my doubts, and my feelings of insecurity. The pages could not judge me. I looked forward to those times when I could pour out my heart. And each day that I let go of another demon, I felt stronger. I'd grown accustomed to being alone, finally with myself. But at that moment, solitude wasn't what I wanted.

"No, I don't think I would like to be alone," I confessed. "Tell me more about what happened here."

Juan began to tell me of the ancient city of Teotihucán. "By 150 B.C. it was the largest settlement. While other settlements diminished, Teotihucán thrived and became a religious and economic center."

"Then what happened? How did everything . . ."

"Become a ruin?" He laughed lightly. "In A.D. 650 a fire swept through the city, destroying many communities. For some unknown reason, there was a swift decline and no reconstruction."

"It's still incredible how well so many things are preserved."

"Scientists are still trying to determine how the ruins were constructed without our tools and equipment."

"The same problem they have with the pyramids in Egypt," I said, laughing.

"Some things can't be explained."

I turned to look at him. His tone had lost its light note. It was almost as if he saw inside me, knew my heart, and directed his comment at me.

"I know. But we always want to dig out the answers, find solutions, give explanations for everything in our lives."

"What questions are you here seeking answers to?" he asked, his dark eyes holding me in place.

"What makes you think that I'm seeking anything?"

"Today is not the first time that I've seen you. I've watched you in town, roaming in and out of the shops, taking pictures, taking notes, but always alone."

I should have been frightened, but I wasn't. "I didn't know I was that interesting."

"I believe there is a great deal you don't know about yourself."

"And you do?"

"Self-discovery is a lifelong process. And once we accept the fact that there may be things we will never know, that is when we find contentment."

"Do you really believe that?"

"It is what I have come to accept as true."

"How?"

"Are you done here?" he asked instead of answering.

I looked around, thought about the number of photos I'd taken. "Yes. I think so."

"Would you like to accompany me into town?"

"All right."

What made me go with him I still don't understand. But if I'd asked myself, "Why are you doing this?" I may not have gone, and my life may have never changed.

That day was the first of many that I shared with Juan. We toured all of Mexico, drank tequila, danced until the sun rose, and we learned about each other. It was the first time in my life that I had a relationship that wasn't physical. And it was okay. We were friends. I told him about my childhood, my parents' breakup and what that did to me. I told him about my friendship with Lisa, and I told him about Ross.

Never once did he cast judgment or treat me differently. Instead he told me about his life in Mexico, his studies in the States, the loss of his wife during childbirth.

"Life is never easy, Asha," he said to me one evening, as we sat in the courtyard. "It is filled with pitfalls and temptations. But it is the choices we make that determine our path. For me, I could wallow in my sorrow, bemoan my mistakes. But if I did, if I continually questioned, why, why me, I would be trapped in the past forever. Life is about living, learning, and accepting."

"But if we don't understand the reasons why, how can we avoid making the same mistakes over and over in our lives?" I asked.

"Life is not a mistake. It is a series of events in which we are the participants. The results of our actions, our choices, and our attitudes are the lessons, not the questions. What we do about it, how we decide to live are the answers. It's all very simple." He raised his glass in a toast and brought it to his lips.

"If I were to accept that, then I would have to accept the idea that what happened with my parents, with my lovers, with Lisa and me . . . with Ross was a series of events, one leading to the other."

"And when the pitfalls and temptations were placed in front of all of the participants each one made a choice, with good and bad results—*life*. Each of us has an effect on those we come in contact with. And each of us operates in our own reality—what is real for us. Every day our reality collides with others', bringing all the events to one place, one outcome. How you decide to accept each of those results as part of your life will determine how you live. That is the answer, no more no less."

I thought about that conversation one night as I was entering my day's events in my journal. And suddenly everything became so clear. Each step we take brings us to another juncture in our life, the people we meet, the jobs we take, the decisions we make. And all of that is not haphazard, but a life path with countless numbers of possibilities converging at one point in time. What we decide to do is based on our own reality, the cumulative effect of our past. *Life*. That is the only answer. *To choose life*.

One afternoon Juan came by my apartment as I was packing en route to St. Croix.

"Leaving again?" He stepped over the suitcases and took a seat in his favorite wicker chair near the window.

"I have an assignment. Two weeks in St. Croix. Remember I told you."

"Hmmm. And then what?"

I shrugged. "I hadn't really thought about it. Maybe I'll stay there for a while."

"What about home?"

I turned away. "Still not ready to go back. Not yet. Maybe one day."

He chuckled. "My gypsy. Always on the move. One day you will have to plant roots, find a home for Asha in this world."

"One day, I suppose." I looked him in the eye. "Maybe my life plan is to roam the earth, take it as it comes, accept the inevitable," I challenged.

"Perhaps."

I'd expected him to say something wise and enlightening, and was sadly disappointed. I'd come to rely on him to guide me through my days, open my mind. But perhaps he'd given all he could, I'd concluded. The rest would be up to me.

Languidly, as was Juan's way, he rose from the chair and stretched like a lazy cat. "When are you leaving?"

"In the morning."

"Then you have time."

"For what?"

"Get dressed, there's someplace I've been meaning to show you."

In that first month or so that I'd spent with Juan, I'd learned that it was pointless to ask where we were going. Each of our outings was like one of his excavations, the purpose was to surprise and uncover. Part of the surprise for Juan was seeing my expression when we arrived.

"Where are we going?" I asked anyway, as I climbed into his jeep, expecting his standard response: "You'll see."

Instead he surprised me by answering. Maybe Juan was changing, as well. "To a place where understanding first began for me. The Museo Frida Kahlo."

I'd read about the famous surrealist artist Frida Kahlo and her equally famous husband, Diego Rivera. I'd studied some of their work and even owned a few pieces. But walking into the Casa Azul that they'd shared was like taking a precious page out of history.

As Juan and I strolled through the house that was now a museum, he told me the story again of Frida and Diego, the two most unlikely people to find each other and fall in love.

"It was instant attraction for Frida," he began. "But most could not understand how this very tiny woman could be attracted to such a gargantuan of a man. But Frida loved Diego to obsession. The one thing she couldn't give him was a child."

"Because of an accident she'd had."

"Yes. She faced a lifelong battle against pain. But she endured operation after operation because of that love for Diego, who although he loved her, was a womanizer. Unexplainable to most."

"Her work is filled with pain. . . ."

"Yes, and love. Her life is sprawled on the canvas, just as yours is captured on film. She had a fierce spirit and lived life to the fullest. Frida was fire and passion. It shows in the vibrant colors that she used. You can see it in the way she lived, the bright yellow floors, the orange pottery and blue walls. Color everywhere, bold and daring. She could have decided to question her pitfalls, her disabilities, her husband's infidelity, and her initial unacceptability into the art world. But she didn't."

"No, she chose to challenge it. Not be subdued by circumstances," I replied, recalling the stories I'd read.

"She decided what effect she was going to have on the world and on the people who came into her life. And she fulfilled that choice." He turned to me and tilted my chin up to meet his gaze. "So can you."

Now, nearly three years later I find myself returning time and again to Casa Azul, thinking of Frida and Diego. Somehow it refreshes and revitalizes me. I tell Juan how often I visit, and he only shakes his head and smiles that easy smile of his, then invariably asks when I've spoken to my mother.

"You only have one," he reminds me over a breakfast of refried beans and steak.

"I know, Juan. I spoke to her last night." I look across at him. "I've invited her to visit me. She said yes."

Slowly he looks up from his meal. The corner of his mouth inches up, his thin mustache cocked at an angle. I grab my camera and snap. Captured forever. The perfect unforgettable look of hope and expectation, like that first day on the steps of Lisa's house. I think I will put them side-by-side, what was and what could be. Life. I want to live it.

BALTIMORE, MD

WASHINGTON, D.C.

THIRTY-ONE

The Best of Men Are but Men at Best

ROSS

"Hey, man, good to see you." I give Kenny the current one-fisted hug, right in the middle of the Reagan Airport arrival terminal. "Glad you could make it down."

"Hey, I've been promising for years. Figured I'd finally take you up on your offer."

"Yeah, three years and counting. But who's counting? Let me get one of those bags. How did you manage to get away with the kids at home?"

"Kids! Ha, those are two grown women, if you ask them. They were more than happy to get their old man out of the house so they can blast their music and run up my phone bill," he says, laughing. "And I still have Claire, the lady in my building to check on them. They're fourteen and eighteen now."

"Wow. Time is really flying."

"Yeah, don't I know it." He slaps me on the back. "You're looking good, Ross. How's life treating ya?"

We head out of the airport to the parking lot.

"I have to admit, it was hard at first making the adjustment from married to separated to divorced, but I'm dealing."

"Good, good. Anyone special?" he asks with a gleam in his blue eyes.

I turn and give him a half-look. "As a matter of fact, I'm slowly moving in that direction. We'll talk about it at the house. I have a place not too far from the Capitol."

On the drive over to my townhouse, Kenny and I play catch up. Over the years since I'd been gone, we kept in touch at least every few months or so. It was great to know that I had someone to talk with when I needed to and that I could be there for him, as well. Although Cliff and I had been close, and there were still times that I missed his friendship, there was a different vibe between me and Kenny. There was a part of me that always believed I must measure up to Cliff's expectations of what I should be as a coworker, a friend, and a husband to his sister. It's not like that with Kenny. We both share our battle scars, and it's all good. It's amazing to realize how and why people come into your life. I never would have thought that one of the turning points in my life would have been meeting an anonymous bartender. Go figure.

"So tell me about this mystery lady," Kenny asks after we get settled. "But first point me to your bar so I can whip us up some drinks for old times' sake."

"Straight ahead. Everything a seasoned bartender could want is under the cabinet."

"Great. Okay, so let's hear it. You know I have to listen while I work," he says, and chuckles.

"Yeah, all right. Anyway, her name is Chris. Christine. We met about three months ago. She was temping at the office."

"Secretary?"

"No. An architect."

"Hmmm. I'm impressed. Is she any good?"

"Good enough to get hired full-time."

He raises a brow. "An office romance?"

"Naw. She turned them down, said she'd rather continue to freelance. She teaches, too, which is what she really loves."

"Nice, nice. Don't stop there. What's she like?" He brings over my drink. "Cheers, buddy."

"Back at ya. Hmmm. What's she like? She's different from Lisa. Different from most women I've met. She's independent, but in a totally feminine kind of way. I never feel overwhelmed by her wants."

"Well, you definitely seem more relaxed."

"I am. I really am. Maybe for the first time in my life. I was aching so bad inside, beating myself up about what happened, and feeling sorry for myself that I couldn't think straight. Couldn't see the forest for the trees. Since I've been out here I've had a lot of time to think, take stock of my life, you know."

"Hey, we all need that. I been there. I know. Sometimes we get so tangled up in the day to day we forget what's important."

"Yeah, exactly. For the first few months I was on remote control, man, just going through the motions. When my divorce papers arrived, I guess it finally hit me that it was really over. That was a blow, but it was also a wake-up call."

"Want me to refresh that for you?" he asks.

"Oh, it's gonna be one of those nights, huh?" I hand him my glass.

"Hey that's when the good stories come pouring out."

"Anyway, I wasn't dating, wasn't looking, just working and trying to forget. I guess I needed time to get myself together."

"Went through the same thing after my divorce. Didn't know my ass from my elbow most days. But I had to pull myself together for my girls."

"At least you had them." I wonder if things would have been different if Lisa and I had children. Would they have held us together, or would we still have wound up in the same place? I'm not sure if I could have walked away and left my children behind. But that's a question I don't have to answer. "So that's pretty much how it was for the first couple of years. Work and home. I bankrolled some money, bought this town house, and figured that's the way it would be."

"Until you met Chris."

"Yeah." I know I probably have this real stupid look on my face, but every time I think about Chris I feel good inside, like coming home to a warm house from the bitter cold. "She'd probably been working at the office about a month or so, but we never really said much to each other besides hello. Then one day out of the blue, she asked me out to dinner."

"Not lunch?" he asks, chuckling again.

"No, dinner. Believe me when you meet her, you'll see she's a straight shooter, doesn't waste time with a lot of preamble and games." I lean forward, recalling that afternoon. . . .

"Are you busy after work?"

I looked up from my computer screen and Christine (I didn't even know her last name) was standing over me.

"Excuse me?"

She smiled. "I said, are you busy after work?"

"Uh, no, not really. Why, is there some kind of meeting that I don't know about?"

"No, but if you'd agree, I'd like to have dinner with you. My treat."

"Dinner?" I asked, frowning. I figured this had to be some kind of weird joke. I didn't even know this woman. I took a quick look around the office trying to spot the setup.

"Yes, you do eat dinner, don't you?"

"Of course, but—"

"Well, you think about it and let me know. How's that?"

"Uh, sure. I'll let you know."

"Great. By the way, your designs in the lobby are simply wonderful. See you later."

I sat there for a few minutes, totally stunned. I glanced around the office to see if I saw any snickers, a sure sign that someone had put her up to it. But the ten or so employees were all busy working. I kept replaying the conversation in my head, trying to find some holes. But I couldn't. Maybe she was on the level. But why me?

"I can't wait to meet this one. She sounds like a real winner."

I laugh. "That she is. Anyway . . ."

It was getting close to quitting time, and I'd been debating all day what I was going to say to this woman. The truth of it was, I was scared. It had been more than two years since I'd been out with a woman and longer than that since I'd been with someone other than Lisa. I wasn't even sure how to handle myself anymore. I stole a look around the office and noticed that Chris was packing up to leave. She glanced in my direction, smiled briefly, and headed for the door.

Now, I had two choices: sit there and let an opportunity pass, or take a chance. I decided to take a chance.

"Hey, Chris." I caught up with her at the elevator. She turned toward me.

Her expression was inquisitive as if she couldn't imagine what I could possibly want. "Hi," she said.

"Listen, uh, about dinner—"

She put her hand on my arm. "I didn't mean to put you on the spot like that." She lowered her head a moment and then raised her eyes to mine. "My dad always said I was too forward and would scare any decent man away."

I smiled. "Your dad may just be right. I know you scared me . . . but for other reasons."

"Do you want to tell me about them over dinner?"

"Yeah, you know I think I do."

"Ready?"

"Let me close up shop. I'll meet you out front?"

"I'll be there."

Kenny laughs out loud. "Life with this one must be a blast."

"You have no idea, man. Every day is a revelation with Chris. She knows who she is, what she wants, and she's made me find out who I am, and not by pushing, but just from being there, from listening, from making life a constant adventure. One night out of the clear blue, she calls me up about midnight and asks me if I want to go down to the harbor and fish."

"Fish?"

"Yeah, at midnight, with work the next day. But I figured, what the hell. I went. So we get there . . ."

"Do you like to fish?" Chris asked as we sat on the dock. She handed me a fishing pole.

"Can't really say I do. Never been before." I expected her to be shocked the way Lisa was when I told her I couldn't swim, disappointed at the least. But she wasn't. Or if she was, she never showed it.

"It's relaxing. It forces you to calm your body and your mind. I try to fish as often as I can. Here, let me show you how to toss the line. It's all in the wrist."

We sat like that until the sun came up, shoulder to shoulder, speaking in whispers. She told me about the first time her dad had taken her fishing and how after she'd gotten over the "yuckiness" of it, she began to enjoy it, but mostly she enjoyed the quiet time with her dad.

"My dad said, 'just because you're a girl, don't think that you shouldn't get your hands dirty, take chances. Don't use being a woman as an excuse for not accomplishing things in life.' I miss him," she admitted. "What about your dad?" she turned to me and asked.

"Passed."

"I'm sorry."

"It was a long time ago."

"What was he like?"

"Just a dad," I said, wanting to avoid that touchy subject.

"Tell me about him."

"Why?"

"It will help me to understand you better."

I shook my head. "I don't think so. My father and I were nothing alike."

"Tell me anyway," she said, "I like to hear your voice."

I heaved a sigh, tried to think of the short version, but when I began to talk I found that I was telling her things I'd never said out loud: How much I'd wanted my father's love and respect. How I'd wanted to be my own man, but he'd wanted me to be the man he thought I should be. How hurt I was when he wasn't there to see me off to college, the harshness of his discipline when I was a kid.

"When he died, I left school and came home to take care of my mother and my sister, then my sister after my mom passed."

"Sounds to me as if you're more like your father than you realize. He was a man of principle and responsibility. You may not have liked how he exhibited those qualities, but you have them, too. Maybe you've been trying to replace him all these years."

"Naw. I never wanted to be like him."

"'Okay,' was all she said, and left it alone. But I began thinking about it after that night. More about what she *didn't* say. And I realized that she was right. I'd spent most of my life trying to be what I thought was expected of me. I did it with my family; I did it in my marriage. Kept my own wants and feelings to myself until it got harder and harder to explain them to anyone. But she gave me the space to work that out on my own."

"She sounds like a helluva woman, man."

"Yeah, she's easy with me, understands my shortcomings and lets me see hers, see that she makes mistakes and that I can, too. I can't help but open up to her, I want her to know who I am. And at the same time I'm learning. I've never had this before. With Lisa as much as I loved her, and always will, I fell into the same old habits I'd lived with all my life. Sacrificing myself for someone else until I didn't know who I was. Chris gives me the room to be whole, without recriminations."

"Did you tell her about . . . what happened?"

"Yeah, I finally did. I had to. If there's any hope of us making it, I knew I had to be up front with her."

"Risky move. What did she say?"

"She said, 'Sometimes in life as much as you love someone if there are needs unfulfilled, things left unsaid, emotions not expressed, it opens the doorway for someone to step in or step out, intentionally or not. I believe you truly loved your wife. And I believe that you made an unconscious choice built upon the holes that were in your life. Once those holes are filled, you'll never have reason to decide to walk through that same door again.' "

"Maybe she's the one, Ross."

"Yeah, she might be. But you know what, man, I'm still learning every day. I'm going to take my time, make sure that I'm all the man I need to be for me first and for her. I want to be sure this time, even if it takes a while. And if Chris is willing to wait, then so be it. If not, I'll still be a better man for it, for having had her in my life. But this time it will be my choice, my decision about my life. It's the only way it can work."

As I sip my drink, content in the company of my friend, I wonder what life has in store for me. I've learned some hard lessons and hurt many people along the way. But I know that whatever path I choose for the future, it will be the one in which I am a part of the grand design—consequences and all.

Kenny raises his glass. "It's all about choices, ain't it, man."

I touch my glass to his. "Yeah, to choices."

NEW YORK

THIRTY-TWO

To Everything There Is a Season

LISA

"I'm glad you waited, Lisa," Sandra says to me in the chapel dressing room. "You needed time to heal and put the past behind you."

I look at my sister in the mirror. In the four years since my divorce from Ross, Sandra and I have grown close, actually becoming friends for the first time in our lives. I always thought of her as judgmental and bitter, never understanding how she could allow a failed marriage to turn her against the world. I didn't understand until it happened to me. She was just as frightened as I was. Hurt and disappointment can do that to a person. Make them afraid of living, turn them inside themselves, cutting themselves off from the world.

After the dust had settled, I went through the phases of mourning. I was shocked, hurt, angry, sad, and then resentful. But instead of letting the resentment go, I held on to it like a lifeline, fueling it every day with all the fury I could gather. I stayed away from family gatherings, turned down dinner invitations from colleagues at work. I spent most of my free time alone at home hating Asha for "doing this to me." I thought I'd reconciled it all when Ross and I last spoke. But I hadn't, not really. When I'd walk around my empty condo, looked at my wedding gown in its case in my closet, or flipped through the photo album of our honeymoon, all the pain would resurface. And I clung to it. I clung to it because a part of me believed that was all I had left to hold on to.

While I was going through my wounded period, shutting myself down and staying full of self-pity, it was Sandra who made me realize that the only person I was hurting was myself.

I was doing what I'd gotten into the habit of doing in the months since our separation; sitting in the dark and watching old black-and-white movies. That's when Sandra turned up at my door.

"What are you doing here? Is something wrong with Mom or Dad?"

"No. They're fine. I came to see about you."

"I'm fine, too."

"Can I come in, Lisa?"

Reluctantly I stepped aside. "Sure." I plopped down on the couch and lit a cigarette.

"Why are you sitting in the dark?"

"Because I want to."

"Well, I'm older than you, and I can't see." She began turning on the lights in the living room.

"Satisfied?" I asked.

"No, not yet." She took a seat opposite me, and I did everything I could not to look at her.

"Listen, sis, I know we haven't been close over the years," she said to me, "but I've been where you are."

"I really don't feel like talking, Sandra. But I appreciate your concern."

"Then don't talk, just listen to me for a minute."

I crossed my legs and blew a cloud of smoke into the air.

"I've watched you meticulously put your life together since you were a little girl, like you always knew you had to have a plan. Everything had to be in order for as long as I can remember. When Tina and I used to toss our clothes and toys everywhere, you were the one who always picked up and put everything in its proper place. Even when you could barely reach the top drawer."

As much as I didn't want to, the memories brought a smile to my face.

"And you took that meticulousness with you out into the world, looking for perfection and order."

"So what's wrong with that? What's so wrong about wanting things to be right, Sandra?"

"Nothing, if you can accept the fact that everyone is not as perfect as you, that they make mistakes, screw up, that life gets out of order."

"I already figured that one out."

"Have you?"

"Yeah. Look, I'm really tired. Okay?"

"Tired of what, sitting alone in the dark, being alone in the world, shutting yourself off from the people who love you?"

"Everyone has their own life to live, and I have mine. It's as simple as that."

"And this is how you intend to live it? You're not hurting Ross or Asha. The only one you're hurting is you."

I sprang up from the chair and glared at her. "I don't want to talk about . . . them."

"You made a decision to let him go, Lisa," Sandra continued, unmoved by me. "You made the decision to walk away from your marriage. You need to reconcile with that. You need to accept the fact that it's over."

"I know it's over!" I fell my body trembling with pent-up rage.

"Do you? Or are you still living in that romantic world of yours where everything turns out wonderful?"

"Go home, Sandra—"

"Resentment is like an untended wound. It festers and grows until it affects every area of your mind and body. The only way to get rid of it is get to its core, clean it out bit by bit until it finally heals. You've got to try, Lisa." Her voice suddenly softened as she reached for me. "Please."

"How? How, Sandi? It just hurts so damned bad."

"I know, honey. I know."

She came to me and wrapped her arms around me, and I cried like I hadn't cried since I first found out what had happened. I cried for all the lonely nights, for the time lost, for the disappointment, for the pain, for what could have been.

"The best revenge against a broken heart is to live again," she said against my hair. "The funny thing is I'm here trying to give you advice, and it's you that I've learned from."

I wiped my eyes and eased back. "Me? What do you mean? I have it all wrong. All wrong."

"I've been trying to stay out of your way these past few months. I figured, Lisa was always able to handle everything. She'll handle this, too. So I tried to ignore what was happening with you. Brushed off the things Mom and Dad were saying about how much you'd changed, how worried they were about you. But you know, the more I tried to ignore it, the more it ate at me. Right in front of my eyes you were turning into me. And I know how unhappy and miserable I've been. What a bitch I've been. I don't want that for you, Lisa.

"I know things can never be the same, but maybe they at least can be different, maybe even better. I'm tired of living the way I've been living. And I was hoping . . . that maybe . . . you and I could work on this healing thing together. Find a way to forgive ourselves, forgive *them* so *we* can move on, open our lives up to possibility again."

That was the beginning of one of the most rewarding friendships I've ever had—with *my big sister*, who was there all the time. She knows me like no one else, just like I know her, warts and all. There's no room in our relationship for pretense or one-upmanship. It's real. And I love it.

One of our first sister projects was the great purge. We got to go to each other's apartment and toss out or store away anything that we thought was counterproductive to our healing process. By the time we finished, we had boxes full of sentimental cards, photos, theater and airline ticket stubs, first date outfits and first night lingerie, our wedding rings and gowns.

"Guess we're making room for opportunity," I said, fingering a photo of me, Ross, and Asha at an office picnic, before Sandra sealed it in the box.

"One day when we're really better, all healed, then we can open the boxes, maybe even toss the stuff for good if we want," she said as we took them to her basement.

"Yeah, maybe we will."

Sandra and I spend a lot of time together now and share plenty of babysitting duty for our sister Tina, who is on her third baby. But one of our favorite pastimes is Saturday brunch, followed by a rigorous round of shopping to replace all the things we've quarantined out of our lives.

It was during one of our outings that I met Justin. I noticed him right away.

"If you're going to stare at him, you should at least go over and say hello," Sandra said over her glass of white wine.

"I will not."

"Why?"

"Because . . . well . . . because."

"Good answer," she teased. Then all of a sudden she got up, marched over to his table, and said something to him I couldn't hear. He turned to look at me and smiled, the prettiest smile I'd ever seen. But I was mortified and swore over my chicken salad sandwich that I was going to kill my sister. It got worse. He came over, Sandra disappeared, and I had nowhere to run.

"I'm Justin." He chuckled. "And you're Lisa."

I could barely speak over the knot in my throat. "Um, yes I am. You have to excuse my sister, she's a little crazy."

"Mind if I sit down?"

I scanned over the heads of the restaurant crowd and didn't spot Sandra anywhere. "Sure."

He pulled out a seat and all of a sudden he wasn't so bold anymore, but nervous, shy almost. "I don't usually do this kind of thing—walk up on a woman in a restaurant. But I have to admit, that was one of the most refreshing introductions I've had in a long time. I couldn't walk away."

"You and me both."

He smiled and stuck out his hand. "Justin Harris."

"Lisa Davis. I mean Holden."

His brow arched in question.

"Divorced. Still getting used to it."

"Sorry. That can be tough. Kids?"

"No."

"Hmmm. I guess that's good and bad."

"What do you mean?"

"Well it would be hard on them to see their parents break up, but at least you would have them to keep you going. On the other hand, with all the issues I'm sure you've had to deal with, that's not one of them. You know what I mean?"

I nodded. "What about you, married with children?"

"No. Don't stay in one place long enough to settle down. I don't know many women who could handle their husband's being away so much."

"I suppose it would depend on the type of relationship you have."

"True. It would definitely take a lot of trust."

"So what do you do exactly?" I asked, steering away from issues of trust.

"Pilot for Delta. I have the East Coast–West Coast route. I'm in California at least three days a week."

"It must be exhausting."

"It can be. But once a month I get to go to Hawaii, and every three months, I'm off for two weeks and can fly pretty much wherever I want for free."

"Nice perks."

"Yeah, I've been everywhere." He chuckled. "Almost everywhere. I love it. New places, new people. The world is quite an incredible place. What do you do?"

"I'm a writing professor. Pretty dull compared to you."

"It's all in what you make it."

We talked for what seemed only minutes, but when I looked up the sun was setting.

"Wow, it's five o'clock."

"Where in the world is my sister?"

"I'll tell you a little secret."

"What?"

"She told me she was going to leave us alone. She said she was sure we had plenty to talk about, and that we were perfect for each other. I think she was right. What do you think?"

"I . . . she . . ."

"I'd like to see you again."

"You would?"

"Yeah, I would. Maybe go on a real date."

"Justin, I don't think I'm ready to get involved in a relationship. I'm still trying to get over my divorce—"

"Then how about if we simply start out as two friends who seem to have a lot in common, who enjoy each other's company and can share a meal or a movie every now and then?"

"Friends, that's it?"

"Absolutely. Or until we both decide that we want something more."

That was three years ago. A year after my divorce from Ross. And my life has never been the same. We were friends, both physical and emotional. Whenever he could during those early years he would send for me to meet him in Hawaii, San Francisco—I've even been to Paris and London. And it's absolutely wonderful. Because of Justin I learned to open myself up to the world, step out in it and claim it, enjoy it for what it is. I took my blinders off, the ones that kept me looking in only one direction with one purpose. And because I was finally able to see beyond my own needs and wants, I was able to finally forgive so that I could be the woman that was waiting in the wings. And each day that I spend with Justin I realize that the possibilities are as endless as the heavens.

Sometimes I wonder if I'd stayed with Ross or if the affair hadn't happened, would I be the person I've become. Who knows. Everything happens for a reason.

"Are you ready, sweetie? I think they're playing your song," Sandra says as she adjusts my short veil.

I turn to her, and I hope she sees the love I have for her reflected in my eyes. She gave me my life back, and for that I will be forever thankful.

"Yes, this time I'm ready. Really ready."

As we walk toward the entrance of the church and I see my husband-to-be waiting for me, I turn to Sandra. "You know that box of stuff you have of mine in your basement?"

"Yes?"

"I don't need it anymore."

Epilogue

All Good Things

ASHA

It's my mother's sixty-fifth birthday, and the first time I've been back in the States in nearly five years. I wouldn't have come back for any other reason, other than my promise to be here to celebrate it with her. I'm enjoying my life in Mexico and my time with Juan. I still travel, but not as much. I guess you could say I've finally put down roots.

Kennedy Airport is just as hectic as I remember, and to be truthful I can't wait to get back on a plane and go home.

Heading through the crowd toward the exit, I feel my heart begin to race. At first I'm not sure, but as she gets closer I know it's her. *Lisa.*

In an instant waves of memories wash over me. The pangs of loss beat in time with my heart. She doesn't see me, and I think maybe it's best. Perhaps I can just keep walking. But I know I can't. Not anymore.

"Lisa!" I wave my hand above the crowd, and I see her turn in search of the voice.

When she finally spots me, a multitude of expressions cross her face: surprise, regret, remembrance, and acceptance. Tentatively, I move past the bodies to where she's stopped in the aisle.

"Hi," I manage.

"Asha . . . It's . . . been so long. How are you?"

"Good. Great actually. And you?"

"Fine." She rubs her swollen belly and smiles. "June," she murmurs.

"Congratulations."

She nods, and for an instant we're caught in that awkward moment of silent uncertainty.

"Coming home?" she finally asks.

"For a while. It's my mom's birthday."

"Great. Give her my regards." She looks at me curiously. "You look happy, Asha."

"So do you."

"I am."

"Where are you headed?"

"I came to meet Justin . . . my husband. His flight just came in."

"Oh, well, I won't keep you."

"Sure. Um, how long will you be in town?"

"About a week."

"Maybe we could get together for a movie or something," she says in that formal way of hers that I remember so well, and I wonder what we would possibly say to each other.

"Sure, sounds great." I reach into my purse, pull out one of my business cards, and jot my mom's phone number on the back. She did the same. "It's really good to see you, Lisa. Good luck with the baby."

"Thanks." She pushes the card into her purse. "I'll call you."

I nod my head and tuck her card in my pocket. "I better get going. Take care, okay."

"You, too, Asha."

I step into the moving mass of people, but I look back one more time. The laughter and the tears, the times we shared rush up and fill my eyes. For several moments, Lisa simply stands there as the crowd moves around her, and I wonder if she is thinking the same things that I am. Gently she rubs her swollen belly and takes my card from her purse. She looks at it for a moment and then rips it in half before dropping the pieces on the floor and walking away.

In that one act, I realize the true consequences of our choices, the price that is ultimately paid and the losses we must live with. But more important, I realize that Lisa is not the romantic little girl that I'd always envisioned, but the embodiment of what a real woman is: strong, independent, and true to herself. An ordinary woman. The woman she'd always been, but that I'd been unable to see. The woman I hope to one day become.

I watch her until she disappears into the crowd before I turn to leave. At the exit I pull out the business card she gave me, committing the numbers to memory. Maybe one of these days I might get the nerve to call her—just to see how she's doing—and maybe, just maybe, explain.

ABOUT THE AUTHOR

DONNA HILL began her writing career in 1987. Now she has seventeen published novels to her credit and her short stories are included in ten anthologies. Three of her novels have been adapted for television. She has been featured in *Essence*, the New York *Daily News, USA Today, Today's Black Woman,* and *Black Enterprise*, among many others. She has appeared on numerous radio and television stations across the country and her work has appeared on several bestseller lists. She has received several awards for her body of work as well as commendations for her community service. She continues to work full-time as a public relations associate for the Queens Borough Public Library system and organizes author-centered events and workshops through her co-owned editorial and promotions company, Imagenouveau Literary Services. Donna lives in Brooklyn with her family.

An Ordinary Woman is Donna's second fiction release from St. Martin's Press. You may contact Donna via her Web site at http://www.donnahill.com. Or e-mail her at writerdoh@aol.com. Donna is represented by the Steele-Perkins Literary Agency.